Mustang Sally

☆ ☆ ☆ ☆ ☆ ☆ ☆ ☆ ☆ ☆ ☆ ☆ ☆ ☆ ☆ ☆ ☆ ☆ ☆

ALSO BY EDWARD ALLEN

Straight Through the Night

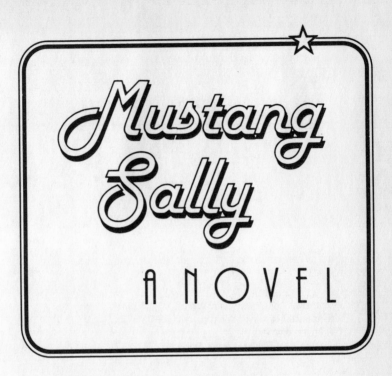

Mustang Sally

A NOVEL

Edward Allen

W. W. NORTON & COMPANY
New York   London

The text of this book is composed in 10½/13½ Amasis Light.
Composition and manufacturing by the Haddon Craftsmen, Inc.
Book design by Charlotte Staub.

Library of Congress Cataloging-in-Publication Data
Allen, Edward, 1948–
    Mustang Sally : a novel / by Edward Allen.
        p.   cm.
      I. Title.
    PS3551.L39225M87   1992
    813'.54—dc20   92–6911

ISBN 0–393–31156–2

W.W. Norton & Company, Inc., 500 Fifth Avenue, New York, N.Y. 10110
W.W. Norton & Company Ltd., 10 Coptic Street, London WC1A 1PU

2 3 4 5 6 7 8 9 0

To Barbara

Mustang Sally

☆ ☆ ☆ ☆ ☆ ☆ ☆ ☆ ☆ ☆ ☆ ☆ ☆ ☆ ☆ ☆ ☆ ☆ ☆

Chapter 1

Christmas in Las Vegas is nearly invisible, as if someone had draped a few strings of lights over the entrance to an amusement park. In the waiting lounges of McCarran Airport, the faces of the slot machines twinkle as brightly as ever, with so many different colors of light going on and off behind the plastic surfaces that most people don't notice the electrified ropes of greenery festooned over the arrival gates.

A young girl in a University of Missouri sweatshirt who had the seat in front of me on the flight has met her boyfriend at the gate (they have started letting people go out to the gates again and turned off those endless recordings about reporting suspicious packages); and now they are standing very still in each other's arms, swaying almost imperceptibly, the way kids used to slow-dance at unchaperoned parties, to songs like "Sleepwalk" and "Misty." Through most of the St. Louis leg of my trip, a small handful of her blond hair lay shining across her seatback, just above my tray table.

One of the things that I still love about my teaching job—besides the hours and the calendar and not being able to get fired unless I do something really stupid—one of the things that keeps me from walking away from tenure and becoming a traveling salesman for a frozen food company is the way some college girls look, on those mornings when it is not raining and they choose to show up. I like how unstudious they are, with their Greek letters stenciled on their gray sweatshirts in the same shade of open-mouthed pink as their lipstick, and how their hair is all puffed out behind where it has been gathered together by a vertical banana clip.

Here and there along the gray walls, an artificial spruce tree, its branches wound with a few strings of pinpoint bulbs, has been fitted neatly into a sort of recessed nook, where it won't get knocked over by some homebound passenger dashing to the gate from his last losing run at the dollar slots and the dollar poker machines. The airport slot machines stand clustered into several miniature casinos, franchised by the Barbary Coast, each with its own cashiers and change attendants, in the round spaces from which multiple departure gates branch off at the end of each long concourse.

I'm in a hurry for no sensible reason besides the fact of where I am, as I move through the long corridors, along their stretches of moving floor above which the recorded voices of Don Rickles and Liza Minnelli plead with us to stand to the right and let people get through, but all the people traveling in couples stand side by side, blocking the chute like jammed cows.

Nowhere in this airport is there a sign of Krishnas hustling for money, or Scientologists with their white shirts and sunglasses confronting people in the hall, or gentle New Age devotees, at their tables full of pamphlets about the Goddess Gaia. The management of McCarran Airport are mostly members of the Mormon Church, and as such they have little sympathy with mindless religious cults.

Suspended from the ceiling above the railed-off area where we all wait for our bags to come riding around on the segmented meanders of the claim line, several four-sided Diamond-Vision arrays of colored bulbs have been programmed to show Frank Sinatra's face hanging in the sky over the Caesars Palace marquee, two nights only: the twenty-fifth and the twenty-sixth, tickets still available—and then the bulbs dissolve into a random froth of color, like a television tuned to a blank station, which becomes, as the cartoon view pulls back from it, champagne foaming in a narrow glass.

My favorite time of the trip is always the moment when it hasn't started yet, when I settle back in my rental car, after the shuttle jitney has let me off at the Holiday Payless office and I've filled out all the forms, initialed all the spaces where I decline the insurance I'm already covered for at home—when I can't yet see the lights of Las Vegas Boulevard, when I have adjusted the mirrors and the seat on the Pontiac Sunbird that comes with my three-night midweek economy package from Alice in Vacationland, tucked the rental agreement into the empty glove compartment, and tuned the radio to KNPR, which is the best classical music station in America, or at least much better than the classical station that I listen to back at Amherst University of Indiana. Like most classical stations, KNPR has been assigned a poor place on the FM band, in a low-frequency electronic ghetto full of intermittent static, like popcorn popping in a microwave.

And I love the moment when I have just pulled out of the rental yard, out onto Paradise Road, the Sunbird's cold motor racing for a moment until the automatic transmission shifts with a soft clunk.

This is the kind of night when it feels good to be divorced, in a city that my ex-wife refused to set foot in. I can still see the planes coming in from the east, lined up with their lights on, like a conjunction of planets. Everything sits out there in front of me, unspoiled, like a new deck of cards, like fresh pins in a bowling alley, though I don't bowl anymore.

☆ ☆ ☆

My ears are still thick with that underwater fullness from the plane's long descent into the Las Vegas area. At the rental desk I had no idea whether my voice was too loud or too soft, until the girl told me to please speak up. On the Sunbird's radio, the Tokyo String Quartet is muffled, its clean, papery dissonance seeming to come from far away.

It is hard to remember that I was just in the office this afternoon, marking the last of my final grade sheets, to be turned in to the after-hours depository slot beside the registrar's office. As usual I posted a grade list, without the names, in observance of the Indiana state law about privacy, grades keyed to the last four digits of each student's social security number. So many A's and B-pluses—anyone reading the list will know either that I have a classful of geniuses or that I'm too tired to struggle with giving them the grades they deserve.

With only three nights here on my package deal, I'm already in a hurry. I've already begun to make a schedule, just like at work: try to catch one of the stage shows tonight if I can get checked into my room at the Westward Ho in time, try a few shoots at a crap table, a couple of hands of blackjack—nothing serious, just enough to get back into the feel of playing at real tables instead of on the Macintosh shareware programs that I've been practicing with at the office every day when I should have been grading papers.

Then tomorrow, I actually have an errand, of sorts. Last week, when I said I was coming out here, Frank Iverson, the technical writing specialist in our department, asked me if I could look in on his daughter Sally, who had just transferred out to the University of Nevada, Las Vegas. He said he was getting worried about her, that her letters to him sounded vague; she wasn't returning his phone calls to her answering machine, and she hadn't even acknowledged his last letter, which included a round-trip plane ticket home for Christmas.

What makes this easy is that I have an ideal pretext for going to see her. Just a few weeks ago, Sally had sent me her term paper from a summer-session Intermediate Composition class that she took from me just before she transferred out. She didn't get it in at the end of the summer term, so I gave her an incomplete. Then in November, just before the deadline when her incomplete would have rolled over into an administrative F, she mailed me the term paper.

It was pretty bad; she was obviously just writing down the first thought that came into her head. But she is so cute that it would violate some of my long-standing policies to give her anything less than a C-minus. Plus, sometimes I have to grade people based on what they're *capable* of doing; and I'm confident that Sally was quite capable of writing a coherent paper, had she ever felt obliged to do so.

I suppose I could say that her previous paper had approached some kind of coherency. It was her "process" paper, describing the process called the "Broad Street Barf," in which a person on her twenty-first birthday visits each of the twenty-odd bars in town for one drink. The paper consisted of a series of paragraphs, each quite similar to the one before it, detailing the process of drinking a beer.

It will be fun to see her again, especially not being in class and not having to worry about saying intelligent things for a whole hour. Mornings in Drury Hall, she always had this wonderful crooked mischief-making kind of a smile, and I know she'll smile when she sees me, and she'll be flattered to find out that I read past the first page of her paper.

Plus, I can put her father's mind at ease. Frank's a nice guy, and a good racquetball partner, but he tends to dramatize everything. If the television says the temperature today is above average—it's Greenhouse Doomsday time. If Sally doesn't answer his letters for a week and a half—it means she's on the slow boat to the Bahrain slave market. Frank watches Ted Turner's Crisis News Network for so many hours every night that last spring he turned down an invitation from the American Rhetorical Standards Association to give a paper in Los Angeles because he was convinced that he would be gunned down on the freeways.

If I weren't friends with her father, I'd ask Sally to go out to dinner with me. But no doubt she has some Nissan ZX boyfriend, sporting a queue of hair down the back of his neck, some stud with wraparound sunglasses to guide her through the rigors of her junior year.

That's a word I can't use at school anymore; we have to call a junior a "third-year student," a senior a "fourth-year student," and so on, because the faculty senate, in a meeting that I skipped, condemned as sexist and derogatory the traditional terms.

☆ ☆ ☆

If I were a real gambler, all I would be thinking about now would be pulling out of the Holiday Payless rental yard and getting to the tables as quickly as possible. A real gambler never sees the lights, never knows or cares if it's night or day.

But for a low-roller like me, the tables are just a background. Ever since I got divorced, I've been coming out here to lose a few hundred dollars at the end of every semester. Each time I make fewer mistakes; now that I've been practicing on the Macintosh I really feel I have a handle on basic strategy.

But it's not just the games; it's the whole town, something I can feel in the back of my jaw every time I see a picture of the Strip on television, the way the town bathes itself in light, the way you can just walk into it and get lost and nobody will come chasing you with papers to grade. And then after one of these trips, when I go home again, to my office and the house on Verossika Lane, everything goes better for a few weeks. I stride from class to office to parking lot, my briefcase swinging briskly at my side, and I feel perked up and cleaned out, like a man who has just had a session of kidney dialysis.

One of my ongoing problems with teaching is that I like the dumb kids better than I like the English majors. I like the slouching marginal center guards, their thick eyelids not drowsing, exactly, but drifting, from window to blackboard to the Dennoyer-Gebbert pull-down map of Europe in the Middle Ages, their faces floating within a classroom dream of the ultimate flying slam-jam. Who am I to ask them to pay attention?

I prefer the kids who don't want to be there, the kids the other English teachers hate, the kids who sneak beer cans into a basketball game, jumping up and down with their faces painted half-and-half in the gray and orange Amherst of Indiana colors. And I've always been fond of the sorority girls, who show up on their own schedule, and who barely tolerate the hated English composition requirement. I like them despite their relentless comma splices, despite their remarkably brief discussions of Rush Week in fulfillment of my demand for a process paper.

In conference, they listen patiently to whatever I have to say about their empty papers. "What do you *want?*" they say, and I always have to explain, in my little office, while trying to concentrate on something other than the way their hair smells, and how softly their lip gloss shines in the cold fluorescent light, that what I want is not really the issue; the issue is how that paper can find its own thesis and so become interesting in its own right, and so on and so on, like the sample papers that I have shown them in *Writing with a Purpose.*

15 ☆

But maybe that's a lie; I don't even know; I just know that it sounds sensible to say that, and it puts the ball back in their court, so to speak. I suppose the only reason they tolerate me at all, and recommend me to all their friends (so that every semester the class fills up and there's always someone still *begging* to get in), is that I'm such an easy grader. I learned long ago that it's too much work to give a low grade; the lower a grade you give, the more you have to explain.

But even with grade inflation, things can get tense sometimes, like the time Kim Shepherd blew up in front of class because I gave her a B-minus instead of an A, when she really deserved a C-minus.

"This is a *bullshit* class!" she yelled as she stormed out of the room. I don't blame her. She was right. A bullshit class, with a bullshit professor, in a bullshit university that doesn't even know what state it's supposed to be in, so that everywhere I go I have to explain that we're not in Massachusetts and I've never been to Emily Dickinson's house. But oh their hair is pretty this year the way they wear it in a long banana clip; and the voices ring like metal off the hard ground outside my office windows when it gets cold. The girls who hate English are so good to look at; I look at them; they look out the window. When I try to warm the class up with a "freewriting" exercise such as Donald Murray recommends in his books on teaching technique, they just stare at the ceiling, or perhaps they write letters to their friends about what an asshole I am.

The good students I can do without: the English majors with their dull hair rustling above brown fatigue jackets. But I have to admit that they work hard, they revise their papers, they make my job easy with essays I can brush off with a generic A. And they always have plenty to say about things: pro and con whether the government should confiscate Exxon's assets, pro and con about raising the Indiana drinking age, pro and con whether it's better to grow up in a house where both parents work, and all such topics, topics, topics.

This is a vacation without topics. My briefcase sleeps in the darkness of my office in Drury Hall; the fall semester grade sheets, more inflated then ever, have been slipped through the registrar's night depository slot. On these Vegas trips, the university dissolves. The dry vegetarian hair of English majors disappears, along with their nylon book bags with political buttons all over them.

All I have to worry about now is luck. When I fly out here on these little two- or three-night packages, I like to think of myself as the Hero with a Thousand Dollars, as the perfect low-roller, the world's most cautious wanderer from five-dollar blackjack table to two-dollar crap table. I usually lose, but every so often I have a good night. I say "have a good night" because I believe that it is very bad luck to use the expression which is the opposite of "lose"—that is, the W word—speculatively.

It is wonderful to think how open-ended my luck is at this point of the trip, with a full packet of traveler's checks, and the night laid out in front of me like a big toy. I have reactivated all my favorite superstitions, and of course I am wearing my lucky herringbone jacket, with one of the nonfunctional cuff buttons gone.

I don't really believe in any of this stuff, of course, but what I do believe is that on a Vegas trip, everything affects everything else. See a penny, pick it up, change the world—walk in the front door of the Riviera one second later, one second earlier, and the world is transformed. You will get to the crap table you wanted to get to a few seconds later than you would have. Out of the corner of his eye, the shooter will see you take your place along the railing, and the gravity you have added to the gravity of all the other planetary crapshooters will pull the shot off-line, perhaps only by an angstrom (which word I know because I sometimes have lunch with people from the mathematics department), and he will make the point he was shooting for, or he will "seven out" and lose. A man who would have left the table this throw will stay, a man playing the "Don't" who would have stayed will give up and try blackjack, and the blackjack table he sits down at will be forever changed. A Chinese man will leave that blackjack table, and go cruising between the rows of roulette wheels and crap tables, and settle at whatever table he would not otherwise have ended up at. See a penny, pick it up. Or don't. Either way, the world is fragile, the line between one big result and another big result thinner than a membrane.

That's why a computer model of the weather can never succeed: the principle of Sensitivity of Initial Conditions—also known as the Butterfly Factor—which states that no matter how accurately the largest array of interconnected Cray 6000 computers can calculate the atmospheric conditions, one butterfly in Galesburg, Illinois will flap his wings one more time than predicted, disturbing enough air molecules so that over the next five days the progressive variation thus begun will exponentiate hourly—and so at last the rain finally does come, or does not come, and the soybean prices will go up, or down, along with the Massey-Ferguson sales figures, along with a young tractor salesman's commissions, and thus he will, or will not, have the money to marry the girl next door, thus the baby who is destined to blow up the world, or the baby who will persuade the man who would have otherwise blown up the world to give up politics and become a commercial artist, will be conceived, or will not be conceived.

So in time, because of that penny, every game at every table will be changed utterly. A man will say, "I can't get arrested in this place—I'm going downtown." And thus, the Strip is changed by his leaving it; and when he gets downtown, Binion's is changed, thus the Pioneer changed, and the change radiates out, onto the bright sidewalks of Fremont Street, in the faces in the windows of the jets taking off tomorrow, in the bank account of a man who will or will not open up or close down his car dealership.

One of the things that I most strongly believe, even though I know it's not true, is that I must never again allow myself to visit a state without touching my feet to the ground of that state. That is why I no longer fly out of Cincinnati. The Funjet Holidays package flight from Cincinnati stops at O'Hare to pick up Chicago passengers, and the passengers originating in Cincinnati are not allowed to get off the plane. So you end up spending time in Illinois without touching the ground of Illinois. I have never failed to get hurt under such conditions.

I would rather drive the two hours and get the flight from Indianapolis and change planes in St. Louis, and walk through the terminal between flights, and if any fundraisers from Krishna or Lyndon LaRouche or the Church of Scientology come up to me, I will tell them to get fucked, which in itself is good luck, I think; and then I will walk outside and touch my professorial wing tips to the pavement of Missouri, which puts me in the perfect low-roller configuration.

It's nonsense, of course, but I need the discipline. The questions are important. Should a low-roller wear a hat? If so, tilted which way? If I take a swing to the east and touch my shoes to the southwest corner of Ohio on the way to the Indianapolis airport, by the side of the exit ramp, wiping the crust of salt off the headlights as a pretext for stopping without looking suspicious—then all the day I'll have good luck, and if I don't, at least I can stand at the crap table with a clear head, knowing the trip is everything it had a chance to be, and it's not my fault that I'm losing, any more than it would be to my credit if I were "failing to lose." As I have said, I do not use the W word speculatively. Because it's too important, and everything is up in the air, along with cards and dice and butterflies—the future, convulsed, behind a screen, not having happened yet.

On a billboard overlooking Paradise Road, the eyes of a show-girl sparkle in their painted fringes, beneath a tiara of costume diamonds whose upper cascades have been built onto a special extension reaching above the main part of the billboard, advertising a show called "Fanfare," at the Bally Grand. From out of the darkness of the valley floor, the hotels rise in a soft light, like tropical shells.

Something seems different about the light here in winter, sharp and cold, the prevailing winds tending to blow the exhaust over into the next valley, something more open in the long view up Paradise Road to the huge squareness of the Hilton with its red letters on top, to the darkened flying saucer shape of what used to be the Landmark before it went out of business, now just a few strobe lights winking on top to warn airplanes.

My head buzzes. It's ten o'clock here, but for me, still on Indiana time, it's one in the morning. I wanted to drive all the way up the Strip from the Tropicana to the Westward Ho, which is at the north end of the Strip between the Stardust and the Circus Circus, but to save time I go up Paradise Road instead, racing from stoplight to stoplight, the Sunbird's engine winding out with a high hum, not shifting until I take my foot off the gas.

Just looking at the big shapes of the Flamingo Hilton and the Holiday Inn and the Imperial Palace and the Sands going by, one block over, on my left, I can almost hear the casino sound, an ocean of bells and buzzers. I can't wait to let that sound wash all over me, to let it rinse away the musty smell that collects in my office when it's too cold outside to open the window. Sometimes on winter mornings the non-English-major girls wear these patch-work jackets of various-colored rabbit pelts, and when they walk past my desk I want to reach out and touch the fur, in obedience to the same instinct that Lenny had in Steinbeck's *Of Mice and Men*.

That's a book I wish I still dared to use in class. It hasn't been banned yet, but the chairman of the department has asked us all to use our best judgement in avoiding confrontation with the evangelicals (or as most of the people on the faculty call them, the "gellicles," no relation to T. S. Eliot's cats), such as the group who staged a "pray-in" at the Greensburg High School library because *The Catcher in the Rye* was on the shelves. It has since been removed, along with the principal.

I haven't yet stopped teaching D. H. Lawrence's "The Rocking Horse Winner," but I'm sure that eventually some student is going to notice all the sexual imagery in that story, and I'm not going to be able to say a word about it, except to announce that the discussion is over, and to come up at the last minute with an alternate assignment.

I do think I could teach Steinbeck, though, because I know what Lenny must have felt like. Every time something soft comes near me, like a cat or a dog or a fur coat, like the hair of that girl on the plane, draped over her seatback, I want to reach out and touch it.

Fur, of course, is the new thing that people in English departments are supposed to hate; several offices along my corridor carry on their doors a poster of a woman hiding her face behind the sleeve of her fur coat, because she is ashamed to wear fur.

You always know when you're in the halls of an English department: on almost every office door the occupant's opinions announce themselves, via cartoons showing foxes wearing dead humans around their necks, or lurid color photos of a sad-faced rhesus monkey with an electrode drilled in his head to make him into a manic depressive.

Myself, I like fur, and I like the women who wear fur. I would especially like to see the beautiful Elvira, Mistress of the Dark, decked out in fur, her pale limbs and breasts wrapped in the softness of a black sable bikini. Imagine Elvira as Jane of the Jungle, and "Price Is Right" Bob Barker as an aging Tarzan, with leopard skins draped over his liver-spotted shoulders. Oh, some-day I will run down the list of all the things I am in favor of and all the things I am against, and maybe I can have my own litle de-partment faction, and my own little enemies, and I will nail the Packard Schmidt Manifesto on my office door.

In the meantime, I've managed to stay on civil terms with everybody, a serviceable fourth for bridge or tennis, and I stay thankful for all the vacation time we get in this business, and all the upcoming flights I can mark on my office calendar with a little drawing of a jet taking off, so that as I walk down the corridors of Drury Hall, past whatever angry posters shout about whatever angry issue from whatever angry doors and corkboards, I can begin to smell the thin kerosene jet-fuel fumes beneath the chalk-and-floorwax academic smell, can hear the high jet whine as a promised undertone to all my conferences, all my B-plus paper-grading marathons.

I don't remember if Sally Iverson had one of those rabbit-fur coats or not, but she deserves one. She's so cute that I'd like to buy her one if I get lucky. I mean lucky at the tables. I've actually read her paper twice, and I'm going to read it a third time, be-cause I'd like to be able to find something good to say about it when I give it back to her.

☆ ☆ ☆

It's cool outside, almost cool enough for a fur coat. I wish I could wear a fur coat myself, but an American gentleman may not, which is a pity. In a fur coat in any city but Moscow I would look ridiculous, like a giant Neil Sedaka waving to the cameras from a Golden Oldies float in the Macy's Thanksgiving Day Pa-rade, like an inflated Doc Severinsen, half bald, my mustache drooping, flown in with my trumpet to a New England Patriots game to render an embarrassingly jazzed-up version of "The Star Spangled Banner."

Last Christmas I tried to give my wife, Cath, a fur coat, and she hated me for it. She hated me anyway by that time. It was really just a last-chance gift, because I had nothing to lose. It was a beautiful parka-length coyote jacket, offered on special by American Express. We had already discussed the fact that she didn't approve in principle, and she was unmovable on that point; but I thought maybe that once she opened the box and beheld the gleam of gray fur, smelled the tanned and camphorated cleanness of it, wrapped it around herself and felt the ancient animal warmth around her shoulders—that perhaps she might be persuaded to let herself lighten up on those moral standards that had convinced her, beyond any possibility of instruction, that such animals as coyotes and rabbits and raccoons all teetered, as precariously as the California condor, at the brink of extinction.

But I could not even get her to try the jacket on. The warmth drained out of her face, frozen around a mouth that I had watched grow harder and harder over the three years of our marriage; and her tiny translucent chin whiskers, which I had begged her to have electrolyzed away, glinted in the lights of what we both already knew would be our last Christmas tree. It was the least painful divorce in history. Thank God we didn't have any kids, which was the only thing we ever really agreed about.

Cath's new husband seems to be a kind man, and living in Colorado makes up for not being an interesting man. He has some elaborate linguistic theories that he uses to write his historical narrative poems in the voices of people like Pablo Neruda's first wife; plus, he has this crazy habit of inflecting every sentence as if it's a question: "I just got back from *Managua?*" Poor Cath, I wonder how she's holding up out there, in her new job at Planned Parenthood, answering the bomb threats.

☆ ☆ ☆

The Westward Ho is one of the smaller casinos, but it advertises itself as the World's Largest Motel, with row after row of two-story room blocks ranged out behind the casino building like a series of military barracks. At the front of the casino, which is nested between Slots'a Fun and McDonald's, an array of curious structures serves as a trademark: a group of domed canopies like big mushrooms, or umbrellas, or fountains, with trails of light falling from the top of each like water from a lawn sprinkler.

I pull off the strip, park the car in the "Check-in Only" parking area, push open the heavy glass door—and step into another one of my favorite moments. This is the first time on the trip when I get to hear the casino sound, like a thousand cash registers and a thousand video games all jumbled together into a sort of musical surf of bells and wheels and coins dropping into metal pans.

Instantly my fatigue lifts. Light moves everywhere. The "Quartermania" sign glows in pink neon cursive above one of the elevated change booths. The blackjack tables are ranged in two long rows, with a space between for the pit bosses to walk around with their clipboards.

There is a particular smell that a casino has, not clean, yet not dirty either: deodorized, its basic component being cigarette smoke, but with the ashtray stink filtered out of it, the tobacco smell mixed up with a hundred other substances—cocktails, carpet deodorant, sweat, perfume, halitosis, but everything processed and blended and softened into something very general, something warm and round and lived-in. It is an odor that exists nowhere else, and it is the same in every casino, the air of the posh Caesars Palace scarcely distinguishable from the cheapest quarter-crap-table joint on Fremont Street in the downtown section of the city.

I walk up to the Show Reservations desk and buy a ticket for that "Fanfare" show, which starts in twenty minutes, which means that I don't even have time to put my suitcase in my room. I just move the car from the Registration Only area into a regular parking place and walk back out to the Strip, where I flag down a Whittlesea cab and tell the driver, "Bally's."

I still can't fully register that I'm here at last, even though I've been thinking about it for weeks. It's strange to think how all the times I'm not here, these lights flash just as frantically for everybody else.

All over the strip I can hear the boom-boom of stereos, from little purple Nissan pickup trucks lowered close to the ground with their open beds somehow tilted up against the back of the cab as if they have been crushed between two trucks, the superpowerful bass speakers tuned to one bass drum note, bunnng-bunnnng. All over the strip, everybody is tuned to the same radio station, the same precise epileptic grunt of crack music.

It's wonderful to think how far away my real life is, how only a few hours ago I was in a different climate, clumping around, in wet shoes, in my big olive drab overcoat, which I've left folded on the backseat of the Sunbird.

Already Drury Hall was empty, and the bicycle yard outside my window stood silent, with no more voices to echo off its brick surfaces, a few patches of snow tucked into the corners of the low retaining walls where on warm days students would sit with their books and their cigarettes. As I walked down the stairwell on the way to turn my A's and B-pluses in to the registrar's slot, I saw that the janitors had not yet stripped the fliers from the cork bulletin boards as they do at the end of every semester, the walls still busy with a jumble of posters obscuring other posters: the International Students Thursday coffee hour, a typed news report of a former student detained by "Zionist forces," the weekly meeting of the Campus Crusade for Christ, of the Koran Study Group, of the Young Socialist Alliance, of the College Republicans (daubed, as usual, with felt-tip swastikas), of Students for Korean Unity, of the Latin American Liberation League, of the Palestine Solidarity Committee.

All semester we have walked up and down the stairs as if through a zoo from which caged animals roared slogans at us;

and we never really paid much attention to them, except perhaps to glance for a moment at a photocopied ad for a 1982 Volkswagen Rabbit, complete with grainy photograph and a row of vertical telephone numbers across the bottom, scissored apart like a fringe, none torn off.

We pass the Mirage Hotel just as the volcano is going off. In the middle of a floodlit jungle of palms and waterfalls, fire belches out from under the water, great eructations of propane so hot I can feel the radiant heat of it through the taxi window. The sidewalks are crowded with people staring into the flames.

It's hard now to imagine how quiet the town of Amherst, Indiana, has become, with the students gone, loudspeakers hooked up all over downtown, so that during business hours, such as they are, the voice of Perry Como rings through the empty streets, "God Rest Ye Merry, Gentlemen"; at night the student bars nearly empty, where they used to wait in line for hours in the cold, now only a few townies, or students with plane reservations for tomorrow, huddled over the stools at the counter, at a bar that the rest of the time you can't get anywhere near.

During school I like to drive along High Street, along the edge of the campus, when the dorms are all lit up from within their tall rectangular windows; and I can imagine the marvelous disorder of the lives inside, imagine the thunder of stereo noise, of rap and metal and new wave, that fills the air inside those brick walls every night until the resident assistant comes around to enforce Quiet Hour; imagine the kids, in groups of three, at night, marching up the hill to town, for beer, beer, beer, which the administration this year has banned from anywhere on campus property, even from faculty receptions.

A dry campus. I like the academic life, but some things just don't work. College without beer. It's wrong, grotesque. Like college without football. College without anything dangerous or crazy, without anything to look back on and say How did we ever survive? Imagine Brigham Young on a Saturday night, just over in the adjacent desert state, the dorms ringing with the bright hilarity of 7-Up parties long into the wee hours of eleven-thirty, even a few "darns" and "hecks" now bursting from their loosened mouths.

Oh, my town, Vegas, my new plaything, merciless and soft. Sometime when I get drunk I am going to bend over, with my ass toward Mecca, and kiss the shampooed carpeting of my motel room, because this has been a difficult year. I got divorced. I lost more friends than I gained. I gained more weight than I lost. I spent more money than I earned. I don't trust my cleaning lady. The girls in class are getting prettier and prettier. They don't seem to fall in love with their teachers the way they used to. Maybe they never did. And even if they did, you can't get away with anything anymore; I would lose my job. And the weather—as long as I'm complaining, I might as well complain about the terrible weather that my students cannot cope with. Nobody in my classes even seems to own an umbrella. Poor kids. I've had whole days rained out. I walk down the halls on a day when I have had to cancel class, and my shoes squeak, and I wish they didn't, because I'm afraid somebody will hear me going past and come out and strike up a conversation and I'll end up saying something even dumber than the dumb joke that got me in trouble two years ago, and I'll find myself in the middle of a feud. A man has to watch every pronoun. The comparison-and-contrast papers are getting stupider: McDonald's versus Burger King. Libraries versus bookstores. High school versus college. And so many humorous essays about where the lost socks go. They just get lost, folks.

Chapter 2

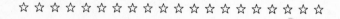

Keno is the worst game in Las Vegas, but it's the only gambling game you can play while eating. In the Riviera buffet, where I have come from across the street with Sally's term paper and my Funjet Holidays half-price breakfast coupon, the long-legged keno girls hurry back and forth in black tennis-dress outfits trimmed in white and red, an almost military eroticism, like a cross between an old-fashioned movie usher's uniform and a Frederick's of Hollywood teddy.

Keno goes on twenty-four hours a day in most casinos, but to me, the red geometry of the keno board on every wall in every direction you look is a distinctly daytime sight, here in the windowless light of the buffet, on a day when I have woken up in a motel with no homework, and the telephone saying, "Good morning. This is your wake-up call. Thank you for staying at the West-ward Ho," and me saying, "You're welcome," the way I always do, because I believe that it is good luck to be polite, even when I am talking to a machine.

The girls bustle from table to table, back and forth between breakfast fatsos and the ticket-registering station; guys in white chef hats hurry back and forth between the kitchen door and the sneeze-guarded buffet table, carrying steam trays full of blueberry muffins and sausage links and kippers and scrambled eggs with bacon chips mixed in. Somewhere at the other end of the casino, swarms of Ping-Pong balls numbered one through eighty are whirling around in the air of a clear plastic globe; and when the betting has closed, twenty balls will be pulled by vacuum out of the chamber, their numbers recorded and lit up one by one on boards all over the hotel. The point of the game is to check off however many boxes you want to on your card with a black keno crayon, give the card to the runner along with your bet, and see how many of your numbers match with the numbers that come up on the board. On every table in the buffet room there is a booklet showing what the payoffs are, depending on how many numbers you've checked and how many of them have come in. It looks easy, but it's really a mathematical illusion. Your chances of hitting fifteen out of fifteen and winning fifty thousand dollars are about the same as your chances of winning the Florida sucker pot that families on welfare keep selling their cars for.

Between filling out the keno cards and rereading Sally's paper so I'll have something to say when I look her up, I have quite a bit of paperwork for breakfast. So I just fill out two cards, a straight six-spot and a straight seven-spot (although there are dozens of complicated ways to play, such as way-tickets and combination tickets and all kinds of strategies which I have never figured out). A thin-lipped girl with short black hair takes my cards and my two dollars and hurries to the next table, while I get down to some serious work on the paper with my red pen. The assignment was to come up with a personal theory about some aspect of reality, and to use as many specific examples as possible to show how that theory operates in real life.

THINGS HAPPEN IN PAIRS OF THREES

Term Paper
Sally Iverson
Proffesor Packard Schmidt
Intermediate Composition
Amherst University of
Indiana
472-90-2006

Have you ever noticed that there are definite patterns to the things that can happen in your life? That is what this paper is about, the fact that things come in pairs of threes. You can see this phenomena closely if you look for it in the everyday events of your life. If you look care- fully enough you will see that it happens again and again, and if you look for it you can see a pattern in it's reocurerince that, definately seems to repeat itself over and over again, which for all intensive purposes will show you that there is a pattern that you always see hap- pening in real life. There are three examples of this. In my own life, plus the experience of my

roommate with her problems with guys that
 wouldn't   leave (100) her alone and they made
her life miserable, and my sister. In my own
life I remember first of all that there was a
really hard summer that I had last summer when I
was trying to get a job to help pay for my personal expenses and stuff for this year. I got
this job at the Pizza oven but, when I showed up
at work the next day they told me, that there
wasn't any job there for me any more, the company
had filed for bankrupt. Then I got another
job, at Pizza Hut, and that, seemed to
be a very good job with good pay and a good boss
and good coworkers and stuff. But I did'nt really get the job, I thought I just did, and I was
waiting at home with the application already
having been applied for and nothing ever happened. I just waited and waited, and I was clue-
less about when they were going to call me into
work, and it was very bad because, I could have
gone out and looking for something else for a
summer job while I was waiting and waiting for
this pizza oven job, but I didn't because, I
thought that I already had the job, but it turned
out that I didn't really. So I call them up and

they go ''Who are you'' but they said I could go on to the waiting list and if anybody quits or gets fired then, I could be on the waiting list. Which means that I would just be starting out all over again. So then I get another job after two weeks at this ice cream store that I always use to go to. This shows that there are things that always have a tendency to come in groups of three.

My roomate used to tell me that there are all kinds of things that come in three's, (300) and she ought to know! She has been going out with all sorts of guys, and there are all sorts of things that have happened to here and her guys, that show you that everything that happens in your life will happen in threes. I thought they were going to get married, but then he breaks up with her and I had to stay up all night with her crying and stuff. So upset I though she was going to end it all. So then she is going out with somebody else and they are un-seperable. Then I really though their going to get married and their going to settle down and have children and stuff just like the normal middle class that we all aquire to. The same

thing happens-they break up and she's all
upset. I told her not to worry. Maybe she was on
purpose going out with guys who would break up
with her and maybe psycologhically she knew
they were going to break up with her and things.
Then the same thing happened again. So you can
see that, sometimes, when things happen there
is a force that makes them happen in threes.

And my older sister, has had alot of problems
in her life. When she was in Junior High School,
she had a tormentic experience. And thats why,
she has so many problems in her life. The experience that happened to her was very frightening.
She was riding with this guy from the tenth
grade, who didn't even have a liscence or insurance or didn't even have his parents permis-
sion, and then, Whala!, he wrecks his car, which
was only bought from the Tuttle Chevrole the
other day before, on Foothills Bolevard, where
they went for years and years to buy every car
they ever did. Oh well. Like they say on television, friends don't let you get drunk. Only I
don't know if he was drink or not. It was totally
against the law and very dangerous to. Because
the guy was only in the tenth grade, and he

wasn't a very good driver. It was really a stupid
thing for him to do, just a few days after the car
was brand new, from his parents who really cared
about it and they sure didn't want anything to
happen bad. Well as you might be able to guess,
there was a wreck. He drove the car of the road
and into this wooden log kind of thing and I dont
really want to tell you what happened. But you
always say to include the details and, it will be
more interesting. Well I hope this is all very
interesing because it was all very frightening. There was a piece of wood that was sticking
through the windshield and it was sticking into
his neck. And she couldn't get out because the
crash was so hard that the doors would not open
and the glass cut off a piece of her face and you
can still see it if you look closely but she covers it up with makeup. And she had to sit there in
the wreck, and waiting for the Police to come and
open the doors. And theres this guy next to her,
the victim of his own wreckless driving. And all
she can do is look at this guy in the tenth grade.
He was all dead and stuff. I think that she was so
lucky that there was a seat belt and she was
wearing it. That's why even when she is really

partying she still wears her seat belt. And that
is why she has so many problems in her life, because of the frightening experience. Some
times we thought she was alright, but then she
comes home drunk for every night after night and
fighting with my father. because they were
afraid she would almost get killed again. Our
lives were a total MAIR. It was lucky for both of
them that my mother was already dead at the time,
because she would definately be dead now if she
wasn't before. And she was fignting with Debbie
so bad, I thought she was going to have an echo-
electric fit or something. We all liked her,
even when my sister was fighting with her until
her husband got transferred out of the western
hemisphere. I thought she was going to end up
with some big problems. But, she went ahead and
she graduated in elementary education, and now
she has this job in the school system, not teaching exactly, but more like being a helper to set
up all their programs, and very well respec-
tive. So it shows you that even if you think that
somebody is going to get in all sorts of trouble,
that sometimes they will surprise you and they
will turn out well respected. And it also shows

you that when things happen, they happen in threes. I and, my roommate and, my sister, are three people, and the things we have had happen to us have turned out to happen in threes, and that doesn't mean, that it's always bad, because sometimes everything always turns out alright in the end.

As I have illustrated, there are many kinds of things that sometimes happen in groups of three things. Of course you can say, that their are other things that don't happen in groups of threes. These things happen in groups of twos or sometimes in groups of fours or more, and sometimes the things that we are looking at with this theory will happen in groups of one. But in this paper I will concentrate on the things that happen in groups of three. As you can see there are many examples, because there is kind of a magic number, in the Bible, and in all sorts of other things where three is the most important number. That is why so many things happen in threes.

P.S. Dear Proffesor Schmitt. I hope you will except this paper, to get rid of my incomplete grade. I know that it's not very good, but I have been so busy that I didn't have any more time to revise it like you al-

ways want people to. I just hopw you can put
it in perspecetive with all the other work I
did that was alot better in your class. I
hope you have a Merry Christmas!!!!!
                              Yours Truly,
                              Sally Iverson

There was a time when I would have given this paper the F it
deserves, but then I would have gently guided the student through
the long revision process, which would have brought it up to a
C-minus or so, and everybody would have been happy. The problem is that it's just so much work. As it is, the only thing the
registrar's computer will ever know is that Sally's final grade has
been changed from a Z, meaning incomplete, to a B-minus.

I've already made the marginal notes, about run-on, frag, awk,
what?, sp, confusing. At the end of the paper I write:

Sally: Your paper would have some potential, I think, if you had
had the time to give it the attention it deserves. But it's clear to me
that it's rather a rush job, and I must say that it is far below the
quality of some of your better papers, including that one you did
about the four different categories of roommates, as well as that
narrative paper called "Gerbil Chaos Among the Amish." The
strength of this paper, despite its first-draft feel, is that it at least
begins to address the thesis you establish, and for the first few
pages, rough though they are, your thinking is reasonably coherent.
Toward the end, however, you really get lost, I think, and you never
really make it clear how your sister's admittedly ghastly experi-
ences contribute to the *thesis* of the paper. Plus, you raise questions
that you don't answer. Who, for instance, is Debbie? Anyway, I'm
glad you got the paper in, and I am happy to tell you that you've
passed the course.
          Paper grade: C —
          Grade for course: B —

Crossing the Strip back to the Westward Ho, I can hear the same monotone boom-boom of Toyota speakers drumming out another crack-music riff, on a note so low and heavy I can feel it thump in the air like the M-80s you can't get anymore. The address that Frank Iverson gave me for Sally is on something called Avenida del Sol, but he said he wasn't sure if that was right anymore; and he said that he couldn't get anything but an answering machine at the phone number he gave me. I walk back toward my room, through the casino of the Westward Ho, and back to the room blocks, where I will see if I can get her on the phone.

My room door is open; the chambermaid's stainless-steel cart stands outside on the walkway, so I walk back to the rear of the casino and find a row of pay phones against a wall next to the snack bar, in the peppery thick smell of that country gravy that tastes much better than it looks, which they serve over biscuits along with precooked scrambled eggs which they measure from a steam tray with an ice-cream scoop. The soft midmorning casino noise washes over me here in the corner of the building, the bells and the spitting of coins subdued somehow. I punch Sally's number in.

And then I hear that wobbling three-noted bosun's whistle of a failed call, followed by the shaky recorded woman's voice on a worn-out tape, the same voice all over the country: "We're sorry, your call cannot be completed as dialed or the number has been disconnected. Please check the number and dial again." I check the number, I dial again. "We're sorry . . ." I call 411 Information, and ask if they have a listing for Sally Iverson at 1906 Avenida del Sol, and they don't, which doesn't surprise me, because I think Frank said she was living with a roommate.

So I'll have to go to the campus and get her current address from the registrar's office. To kill a few minutes until the maid finishes up my room and I can change into something more professorial, I buy twenty dollars' worth of quarters from the girl in one of the elevated change booths beneath the "Quartermania" sign. I play a crisscross machine for a while, one in which every extra quarter lights up a new direction in which the machine can pay off: horizontal across the middle, across the upper row, the lower row, diagonal dexter, diagonal sinister. But I can't get interested. You have to be at least seventy years old to enjoy slot machines. I'll do my real low-rolling tonight, maybe in the Riviera, or anyplace else with a good facedown blackjack game.

The Westward Ho is mostly just a slot joint, having only one crap table. Most of the blackjack tables this morning are covered with a green plastic tarpaulin. Every few minutes, a voice on the PA system calls out, "Congratulations! We've just had another fifty-dollar jackpot winner!"

The dealers just stand there staring out toward the rows and rows of slot machines and poker machines, their brand-new decks of cards fanned out neatly in front of them in one or two arches, depending whether it's a two-deck game, a four-deck, or a six-deck, waiting for the first customer of the day. Most of the blackjack dealers here are Oriental girls—very pretty, but for some reason they never smile. They stand there motionless over their fanned-out cards, their faces as grim and serious as failed refugees who didn't get out of their countries in time.

Chapter 3

Once you get off the Strip it's just a town, medium-sized, flat, with a midday haze over everything, most of the drivers women, McDonald's displaying the regular thin golden arches, not those sizzling arches filled with a froth of white bulbs that you see at the McDonald's on the Strip between the Stardust and the Westward Ho.

Driving south on Maryland Parkway toward the UNLV campus, it could be any boulevard in any city in the west: the same 7-Eleven stores, the same Carl's Jr. hamburger drive-thru places, and on the Sunbird's radio the same chamber music, with the same popcorn static, that you would hear in any city large enough to have a National Public Radio station. I've been listening to some tidy ensemble piece that I had been thinking was Bach, but then a woman comes on and says it's something by Telemann; and I speak along with her in unison when she says it was "performed by the Academy of St. Martin-in-the-Fields, under the direction of Neville Marriner."

I pull into the UNLV visitors' parking lot just as "Adventures in Good Music" is beginning, introduced by the slow piano chords from Beethoven's *Pathetique* Sonata, which always sounds to me like "O Canada." Then Dr. Karl Haas comes on with his jolly, European "Hel*lo*, everyone!"

At the corner of the lot, a map of the campus stands on a pole, the buildings color-coded to a key along the side. I find the administration building, where I can get Sally's address from the registrar's office, I hope, and then I look up the English department and decide to take a side trip there, because I like to see what other English departments look like.

The UNLV campus is pleasant, green, flat, charmless, arranged around a wide common running down the middle among the uniformly new classroom buildings of stucco and glass. At the southwest corner of the quadrangle, the wide entrance to the College of Hotel Administration, with long rows of brown glass windows, angles into the configuration at a diagonal. Tall palms poke up from between some kind of willowy western trees. I suppose the flat layout of the campus must give the students less to complain about, unlike Amherst of Indiana, where every year I get serious papers about how it's unfair to make students walk up and down so many hills.

The cement walkways that cut across the quadrangle in all directions are crowded with moving figures in bright colors. They look different from the students in Indiana, most of the ones here from Los Angeles probably—the women shorter-haired, more spartan, many dressed like little children, with wide stripes of primary colors across their oversized T-shirts. A few have shaved or radically chopped their hair, for the chemotherapy look. The men seem chunkier, many with hanks of hair at the bottom fringe of their crew cuts and three channels dug into the temples.

Even on this coolish day, almost everybody is wearing shorts, which is what makes them look fat, I guess. Statistically, I know that Indiana and West Virginia and Ohio are really the fattest states in the country. California, where most of these kids probably come from, is the thinnest.

The English department takes up the whole sixth floor of the Humanities Tower, a sleek office building of brown glass and white stucco, with stilts holding up the outside of the first floor so that the indoor part of the first floor contains nothing but an empty information desk and a bank of elevators, surrounded by an empty paved area in the shadow of the overhanging second floor.

I walk around through the halls of the sixth floor, in my lucky herringbone jacket and my yellow corporate tie, looking like a professor on a not very important errand, hoping nobody asks me who or what I'm looking for, because I don't know exactly. I guess I'm trying to find out if working this close to the lights of the Strip changes the way academics walk down the corridors.

But it's just another English department: nicer than ours on the whole—airier, with a window of the faculty lounge looking west toward the red-and-yellow dome of the Thomas and Mack Center, and beyond that the northern end of the runway of McCarran Airport, and beyond the airport the ridge of gray hills in the distance. On the corkboards, the same posters, for graduate study at the University of Pittsburgh, for the University of Houston's Guadalajara Fellowships, for the *Playboy* Undergraduate Fiction Competition.

Down the rows of faculty offices, the same kinds of cartoons have been Scotch-taped to the doors: a graphic representation by means of an array of dots showing the potential power remaining in modern nuclear arsenals versus the total tonnage dropped in

World War II (we're even more doomed than I thought)—and Ronald Reagan, of course, his line-drawn image long outlasting his administration, Reagan at the hands of cartoonists so angry that I don't know how they get to sleep at night. I can imagine that the sketchers must have had to suppress the angry trembling of their hands as they rendered the old fellow's long, profoundly wrinkled, reptilian face decomposing at the end of a long neck like the neck of a turtle, his skeletal arm around a figure who looks like Tweedledum with smallpox but must actually be Manuel Noriega.

In English departments, Reagan will live forever; no matter how long the post office portraits have been packed away to wherever the old presidential portraits go, no matter how long his name has ceased to come up in the news—Reagan's cartoon face, cavernously shriveled, with a collapsed chin and long ropes of sagging flesh all the way down the neck, will continue to stare, as evil and stupid and subhuman as any artist in the running for the *Mother Jones* / Hunter S. Thompson Political Satire Award could contrive to make him, grinning from the doors of a thousand associate professors, adjacent to the Boycott Avon poster showing a shaved mouse with lipstick daubed on its back.

At the registrar's office, I find out that Sally has withdrawn from school. They almost don't give me her address, until I remember that I know her social security number, which makes me somehow legitimate. I write the address in my little pocket notebook, and walk outside among the T-shirts and rattail haircuts and the bright shapes of students getting out of their prelunch classes.

☆ ☆ ☆

This complicates everything—Sally out of school, maybe out of town. Chances are she's gone, like all the kids who drop out of Indiana and never come back, gone away into a world of frighteningly loud parties, of late nights speeding along the freeways of L.A, her boyfriend a little drunk but he can handle it; and besides, nobody in such a shiny black Nissan ever gets pulled over. We all know that the Lord protects dull boyfriends.

Back in the car, on KNPR, Dr. Karl Haas is talking about tranquillity, about the calmest moments in all classical music, and he has put something on by some Italian composer I haven't heard of before, a woodwind section slowly changing from chord to chord above a long series of sleepy string notes. The calmer the music gets the more nervous I feel, driving along Tropicana in the moderate lunchtime traffic toward the address they gave me, on Pecos Road, which I have looked up on my Holiday Payless map, somewhere out in this low sprawl of condos and little imitation Tudor villages, and multiplex cinemas, and the Renaissance Plaza at Eastern Avenue.

5900 Pecos Road turns out to be something called Pecos Villas, a complex surrounded by brown fences made of painted boards woven like an old-fashioned picnic basket. The sign at the entrance, probably lit up at night from between its two translucent faces like a Mexican restaurant, shows the P and the V formed by paintings of cactus plants growing in the shapes of those letters.

I pull through the one-way Severe Tire Damage gate and follow the signs, themselves cut from plywood into the shape of cactus plants, for visitor parking. The two-story buildings are supposed to look like adobe, with the butt ends of support logs forming a brown row across the top of the squarish structures.

The strings and woodwinds of Dr. Haas's tranquil morning are getting calmer and calmer, and now, except for a few sputterings of static, they have almost come to a complete stop. Over the far end of the parking lot I can see a gray-and-red Northwest 747 floating down on its final approach, wonderfully close and round, so close I can hear the distinctive 747 buzz of its engines as an undertone to the usual airy jet whine.

The apartment complex seems new, but there's already something crummy about it, like those low clusters of new construction you see on *Cops,* where the police are always battering the doors down in a *cinema verité* drug raid. The parking lot swirls with dust; the blacktop has crumbled around the place where the garbage truck comes and lifts the dumpsters up to empty them.

Standing out in front of Apartment 22 in my lucky gray herringbone jacket and my yellow tie, breathing hard for no good reason, I know I must look ridiculous, or unsavory, like a canvasser for the Jelly Donut Witnesses, or like the image of a slovenly detective so hackneyed even television won't use it anymore. I feel once more for the reassurance of Sally's term paper in my pocket, before I press the bell and hear its two-noted metallic chiming inside. The lens of the door viewer clicks open. A girl's voice, not Sally's, comes out of a little gridwork of holes cut into the aluminum doorframe.

"Can I help you?"

"Hi," I say into the same holes the voice came out of. "My name is Packard Schmidt. Does Sally Iverson live here?"

"Who are you, and what do you want?"

"My name is Pack Schmidt. I taught one of the classes that Sally was in back in Indiana. Can you tell me if she still lives here?"

"Who told you she ever lived here?"

"I checked with the office at UNLV, and they gave me this address."

"Bullshit," she says, her voice rasping over the tiny speaker. "They don't give out student addresses to strangers."

"I'm not a stranger. I have her social security number."

"Where did you get her social security number?" the voice asks.

"She was one of my students, that's where I got it. On the grade sheet."

"Why didn't you call first?"

"Because I didn't have the number."

"Are you some kind of private detective?"

"No, for Christ's sake, I'm not a detective. I'm just one of her old teachers and I'm here on vacation, and I thought I'd stop by and return a term paper she sent me."

"I'm looking at you right now and I don't see any term paper," the voice says. I take the paper out of my breast pocket and hold it in front of the little viewing eye in the middle of the door.

"It's right here," I say, knowing that she probably can't see a word on it through the door lens, so I start to read: "Things Happen in Pairs of Threes, Term Paper, Sally Iverson . . ."

"Where did you say you were from?"

"Amherst University of Indiana."

"And I'm supposed to believe you came all the way out to Vegas to give her a term paper?"

"No, I didn't come out here just for that. I'm out here on vacation, and I thought I'd stop by and say hello and return her paper to her. That's all I want. Can you tell me if she lives here?"

"Let me explain something to you, mister," says the speaker, just a bit less raspy. (I can hear another voice in the background: "Who is it?" "I don't know.") "I'm sorry to be so rude, but I can't help you. We don't let strangers in, and we don't give information to strangers. So you might as well just leave."

"What do you want me to do? Would you like me to slip my faculty ID under the door?"

"I'm sorry to be rude, sir. Maybe you're just a teacher like you say you are, but you don't look right, and you don't sound right."

"For Christ's sake," I say, whining rather than shouting, "What can I do to prove I'm not a cop?"

"You say you're an English teacher? Why don't you recite some English literature?"

"Are you serious? Will you let me in if I do?"

"Maybe. If it's not 'Mary Had a Little Lamb.' "

"Okay, I'll do it, but you're making me feel like an idiot."

There's something distinctly nasty about this place, with all its Camaros and ZXs parked in a row against the basket fence. I'm almost ready to give up and tell Frank I just couldn't find her, but if this girl wants me to recite something, I figure I might as well go along with it. So I start in on the beginning of the General Prologue to the *Canterbury Tales,* in a lilting musical tone:

> "Whan that Aprille with his shoures soote
> The droghte of March hath perced to the roote . . ."

And, of course, just at that moment somebody from one of the other apartments comes by on the walkway, two guys wearing linen sport jackets over T-shirts and wraparound sunglasses, the "Miami Vice" look, on their way to a cocaine deal no doubt. It has always seemed strange to me that the drug culture would imitate so slavishly the fashions established by plainclothes cops. And there I am, reciting Middle English poetry into the little speaker box on the side of the apartment door:

> "And bathed every veyne in swich licour
> Of which vertu engendred is the flour . . ."

The two cool guys stare at me as they pass, their eyes so dull that perhaps they can not think of a single cool thing to say to each other. They just keep walking, on the way to their coke-laden Japanese car. I don't even know whether they will be driving a Nissan or a Mitsubishi, but I know the Bose speakers will thump with a steady bass-drum note of red-rag child-abuse music.

"I can't understand a word you're saying, mister," the girl in the speaker box says. "How about something in *English?* How about some Shakespeare? If you've ever heard of him."

"Sure, okay." The first Shakespeare passage that I can think of is Sonnet One hundred and something; I don't know the numbers, one of the Dark Lady sonnets.

Edward Allen

> "My mistress' eyes are nothing like the sun;
> Coral is far more red than her lips' red;
> If snow be white, why then her breasts are dun;
> If hair be wires, black wires grow on her head."

Another 747, this one TWA, is bellying down with its soft whining buzz over the far end of the basket fence. It's lunchtime, the sun high in the haze, I'm getting hungry, and I'd like to be stuffing myself in the Stardust buffet and wasting a few more dollars on keno cards that will never win, but here I am for the first time in my literary life, perhaps the first time in anybody's life in the history of the world, bending over slightly to recite Shakespeare into the intercom of some cheesy apartment building.

> "I love to hear her speak, yet well I know,
> That music hath a far more pleasing sound;
> I grant I never saw a goddess go . . .

"Oh, wait a minute, I left out a verse."

"What, is that supposed to be some kind of love poem?" the voice says.

"Yes, that's right."

"He's just saying how ugly she is. What kind of a love poem is that?"

"Don't you see, he's making fun of all the phony poetic conventions that people were using in those days."

"That's not what it sounds like to me. It sounds more like he's making fun of her. Like he doesn't like her very much."

"Oh, but he does, that's the point. You see, after he goes through all these clichés, he finishes up: 'And yet, by heaven, I think my love as rare / As any she belied with false compare,' meaning that he recognizes the emptiness of the conventions. I'll explain the whole thing to you if you let me in. Unless you still think I'm some kind of troublemaker."

I hear the snapping of multiple locks being released, the door opens, and a tall, very pretty girl with full lips and slightly frizzy brown hair is looking me up and down. Behind her stands a shorter blond girl, the hair over her forehead bunched up with spray or mousse into those "broccoli bangs" that a lot of girls wear these days.

"I guess you might as well come in," the dark-haired one says. She is wearing bright red spandex bicycle shorts and a cartoon T-shirt that says, "See Dick drink, See Dick drive, See Dick die." The other girl has on a plain black turtleneck over the most torn pair of jeans I've ever seen, with a series of wide horizontal slits showing skin at the knees and thigh and hips.

"I'm Samantha," the dark-haired one says, "and this is Kristy. Sally's not here." I shake hands with both of them, feeling the smallness of their hands, so delicate and rubbery that I wouldn't dare give them the same robust handshake I use when I'm meeting colleagues at Indiana English Council conferences.

"It's nice to meet you—at last," I say. "You know, that's the first time I've ever had to recite poetry to get into somebody's house. Usually I get thrown out for reciting poetry." I laugh at that joke, but they just smile slightly.

It's one of those apartments set up like a trailer, with a narrow Sheetrock passageway leading from the front entrance to the living room, where I can hear that "Win, Lose, or Draw" is on, contestants shouting frantically, "It's a *steamboat!*" "It's a *sailboat!*" "I know, I know . . . it's, it's some kind of *pirate ship!*" "The *Pirates of Penzance!*"

They have poured me a cup of instant coffee. I sit on a tall stool at the kitchen counter, looking across at these two lovely young girls who have both lit up cigarettes. I know I must be grinning in that frozen Chinese way, the way I do with girls who excite me when I can't do anything about it.

"So . . ." Kristy says, leaning back against the avocado-colored dishwasher, one foot braced under her buttocks and her knee pointing out, like a ballet dancer's stretching exercise, "You're a teacher, huh? I guess I'll have to watch my fucking language."

"Doesn't matter to me," I say. "Say any fucking thing you want. So you're at UNLV?"

"Oh yeah, we both are," the other girl, Samantha, says. "On and off."

"What are you studying?"

"This and that. Travel and Tourism. Hospitality."

"I've heard that hotel administration school is pretty good."

"It's all right," Kristy says. She is doing most of the talking, while Samantha stands by the refrigerator staring at me.

"But anyway, what's the story with Sally? They said at school that she withdrew."

I'm looking around the apartment, trying to think what I'll say to Frank if I don't get to talk to Sally. It looks like a decent student apartment, not too dirty, no sign of drugs, though really, except for the thump and rattle of crack music, I wouldn't know a sign of drugs if it were under my nose.

"She dropped out temporarily," Kristy says. "She's going back in January. She just had to get a job for a few months."

Samantha says, "Are you a friend of her father's?"

"No," I say, and suddenly I understand how a polygraph machine works, because I can feel all of the pores of my skin constrict with the lie.

"Is Sally staying here now?" I say.

"I don't understand why you're so interested," Samantha says, her dark eyes twinkling. "Do you have a crush on her or something?"

I've always made a big distinction between having a crush on someone and indulging in a few fleeting sexual fantasies as most teachers do in a morning class, when the sorority girls have just put on their makeup, and I make them all do another freewriting exercise and I can sit there at the desk and secretly watch how beautiful they are while I collect my thoughts and decide what in the hell I can talk about today that they won't hate me for so they won't write me up in the computerized evaluations as a lousy teacher.

But the difference between a fantasy and a crush must be a false distinction, at least as far as Sally is concerned, because immediately I feel the hot tingle of blood rushing to my face.

"I think he does," Kristy says, with that exaggerated and cutesy tone of voice that people use with children and puppies. "Look, Sam, he's red as a beet. You do have a crush on her, don't you?"

"No, not really. I mean, she's very nice. But she's a little young."

"No, I don't think so," Kristy says. "I think she'd be flattered to know how you feel."

I try to push through this mysterious embarrassment, getting back to the real subject. "Can you tell me when she'll be back?"

"Not for a couple of days," Kristy says.

"That's too bad. I leave the day after tomorrow."

"Well . . . if you really want to see her, she's working at a restaurant. I can give you directions."

"Do they serve lunch?"

"Oh yeah," the dark-haired one says, grinning. "Breakfast, lunch, dinner, dessert. You name it."

"It's a real fancy steakhouse," Kristy says, "and it's out of town, about an hour away."

"And when you get there," Samantha says, grinning slightly, as if there's something comical about eating lunch in the first place, "just say that you're a teacher from her college, and ask the head-waitress to assign Sally as your waitress. Maybe they'll give you half price."

"Okay, I will. Thanks for telling me where she is." I start stirring around politely, as a signal that I'm ready to finish up the discussion and leave, although these girls are so pretty that I wish I had more of a pretext for staying.

"You know," Kristy says to Samantha, "this guy's kind of cute," and I feel my face begin to flush again. "What did you say your name was?"

"Packard Schmidt. You can call me Pack."

"So . . . Pack," Kristy says, fiddling with a strand of her blond hair, stuffing it into the rip in her jeans and gently pulling it out again, "you should come back sometime."

"That's very nice of you to say."

"No, I mean it," Kristy says. "I think you're cute. We'd like to make dinner for you." Again I can feel pins and needles all over my cheeks. We are all moving slowly toward the door.

"Come on, you're just making fun of me. You must have a million hotshot boyfriends at school."

"We're serious," Samantha says. "Give us a call and come back anytime. We'll make you a better dinner than they can at the restaurant."

"I don't have your number."

Kristy gently pulls the little spiral notebook from my shirt pocket, the same notebook in which she wrote the directions to Sally's restaurant, turns the page, and writes "Kristy and Samantha" and the number, in green pen, in the kind of girlish handwriting that is all loops and circles.

As I'm standing at the door ready to go, she says, "Just so you don't forget," and raises up on one toe, bringing her face close to mine. My head bends forward even without thinking, and I kiss her softly on the lips as she lifts her other foot behind her in that old-fashioned debutante style.

☆ ☆ ☆

I'm out in the car, with my ears buzzing, saying to myself, "What happened in there?" So many jets are coming in at this time of day that I can see them lined up a mile apart in a long incline out to the east, under visual flight conditions. I can taste something cool and camphorlike on my mouth where she kissed me. A loud Italian operatic baritone fills the space of the Sunbird, something I've heard before, but I can't say what it is.

I'm almost back to the Strip now, thinking over and over again about how friendly that girl was. I turn south and drive past the Tropicana, where the marquee, in floppy green-and-yellow letter-ing, announces the Folies Bergère—Dinner Show $19.95, Cock-tail Show $13.95, and Nonsmoking 21 pit. I can't wait to get down to some serious low-rolling tonight, but not at any nonsmoking table. Even though I don't smoke, I know that nonsmoking tables are bad luck. The best luck I've ever had has been at the table with some cigar-smoking creep next to me; the worst luck at a smoke-free table.

On KNPR, a cellist, perhaps Yo-Yo Ma, grinds out some frantic pentatonic business with a heavy bow hand, a piano backing him up. I'm following Kristy's directions (in her cute loopy lettering, like in the freshman placement essays I used to read, now called "first-year" placement essays—and if the lettering was cute enough I'd always assign the student to the smart classes), down the Strip to the first entrance on Interstate 15, already heavy with holiday traffic. I'd almost forgotten about Christmas, all the sta-tion wagons rushing through the flat sunlight, with bags full of wrapped presents stacked against the rear window.

Two exits to the south, among the mostly California plates now, and the roaring trucks, the motels have thinned out, and the land is mostly flat bushy stretches, and subdivisions for sale, then west on the two lanes of Route 270, and up a long slant, the Sunbird straining against its automatic transmission geared too low. Not a bad car on the whole, though—it's comfortable, and it handles better than my clunky old Volvo station wagon, which really I have no reason to complain about.

In this part of the country the whole geometry of land is differ-ent from anything I've grown up with. It looks as if a plateau of sand has been blown by the wind against the base of each mountain, the way snow behaves in Indiana when it drifts against a garbage can and hardens.

Miles away, from the gradually slanting high ground, I can still see Las Vegas, bleached white in the winter sun, looking more and more like a regular city the farther away from it I get, to the outer fringes of construction, among muddy pickup trucks with contractors' names on them; and farther up to where it's just speculation and no ground has been broken yet for subdivisions, nothing but the long scrub of creosote bushes and sagebrush giving a velvety fuzz to the surface of hills in the distance, the jagged spikes of yucca, and the arms of Joshua trees gesturing, like a cross between cactus and palm. The mountains all around in the distance have that wrinkled look to them, like the skin of a rotten apple.

It was Yo-Yo Ma. I'm getting good. A woman's voice has come on the radio, perhaps a student in the UNLV College of Broadcast Communications, a good husky breathy radio voice, but she hasn't learned to come down hard enough on the consonants. The nappy hills have closed in behind me, so I can't see Vegas anymore. The next piece of music on "Classical Afternoon" is one of Rubinstein's last Chopin recordings. It begins to fade out with a soft FM hiss, clears again, sputters, clears. I turn it off. I'm really up in the mountains now, the engine racing frantically, big sheets of snow nested in the concavities of the rocky ground on both sides of me. It's so cold that I have to turn the heater on for the first time. Higher up, toward Coyote Springs Pass, which leads over into the next valley, the ground takes on that bleak planetary look, little shadows of frost or snow trailing behind the exposed rocks, like the Mariner photographs of Mars—naked, uneroded rock chips scattered over the hard surface, as cold and lifeless as those pictures of viruses under an electron microscope.

Chapter 4

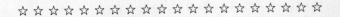

The steakhouse is located in a town called Pancake Flats, just over the line in Nye County, on the other side of Coyote Springs Summit, near the end of a long flat road that cuts off from Route 270 and runs for miles and miles toward a line of mountains that don't seem to get any closer, as in one of those driving games in a video arcade.

By now I'm so hungry that I can hardly think straight. A big sign braced up against a telephone pole shows the silhouette of a shapely cowgirl riding a bucking bronco, her hair flying, and her hat waving in her one free hand, and a cartoon speech balloon saying, "Howdy, pardner! Welcome to the MUSTANG VALLEY INN!"

I've always been told that the best restaurants are the ones that look the most unlikely from the outside, so given the looks of this place, I'm in for one of the best meals of my life. The restaurant is an odd-looking affair, a low complex of brown trailers joined together by the kind of fluted conduit material that you see between the cars of a train.

It doesn't look very busy, only a few cars parked in the gravel parking lot. Except for a few palms and scrubby willows planted as windbreaks, the place looks a bit like a minimum—security correctional facility, with a chain-link fence running around the edge of it, or like the temporary modular classrooms they put up next to Walter Johnson High School in the sixties when the population of Montgomery County, Maryland, doubled in five years.

It's hard to tell where the dining room is. There's just a gate in the fence saying ENTRANCE, and a flagstone walkway leading up to the front trailer. Somebody must have been watching me out the window, because before I can push the doorbell button, the gate buzzes and I push it open.

I've always felt weird eating alone in a restaurant in the off hours, now at almost two o'clock. I feel so conspicuous in an empty dining room, shoveling food into my mouth, while the waitresses hurry around setting up the dinner silverware at the adjoining tables. But it's too late now.

I open the front door—and there's no restaurant, just what seems to be the waiting room of a motel, with a chunky Spanish girl vacuuming the carpet, and a tall red-haired woman in her forties who says, "Hello, sir. Welcome to the Mustang."

"Excuse me, where's the dining room?" I say. "Am I in the wrong building?"

"Dining room?" she says. "What dining room?"

I can feel my face beginning to flush red again, and my heart thumps up in my throat, more noticeable on an empty stomach. "Oh, I'm sorry," I say, backing away. "I must be in the wrong place. I was looking for the restaurant. Do you know where it is?"

"What's your name, honey?"

"My name is Packard Schmidt. I'm looking for the Mustang Valley Steakhouse."

"I think your friends are playing a joke on you, Mr. Schmidt. This isn't a steakhouse—it's a cathouse."

I'm standing there with my mouth wide open. "You're kidding, aren't you?"

"I'm not kidding, honey. This is the best legal cathouse in the state of Nevada."

"Wait a minute," I say. "This is crazy. They told me . . ."

"I know, they told you this was a restaurant," the red-haired lady says. "We get that all the time. What convention you with, Mr. Schmidt?"

"I'm not with a convention. I'm just out here by myself, and somebody gave me directions out here and . . ."

"Well, your friends are having a big laugh."

"Does a girl named Sally Iverson work here?"

"She sure does, honey. Only her name is Natalie at work. You know her from somewhere?"

"I can't believe this," I say, starting to get angry, though maybe it's just the natural irritability of an empty stomach. I'd heard of these places, of course, but I never thought anybody pretty enough for me to care about would ever work in one. "Her friends sent me out here and said she was a waitress in a steak-house."

"You're welcome to visit with her. We've got the prettiest girls in the state. Guaranteed. Just make yourself comfortable on the couch and they'll be right in to introduce themselves."

"Look, ma'am," I say, "this is crazy. I'm not here to get laid. She's an old student of mine. I just want to talk to her."

"You can *visit* with her." She presses a button behind the desk, and I can hear a raspy bell ring in the back room, like an old-fashioned telephone.

So I sit down where she tells me, on a flouncy plastic-covered pink couch, with coin-shaped pillows whose countersunk buttons form little concavities in the cloth, the whole pillow sealed tightly in plastic as if in the vacuum-packing machine they use for steaks. The walls of the room are draped with pleated maroon cutains. On a side table are piled some Mustang Valley brochures, and some copies of the *Mustang Visitors Newsletter,* beside an ashtray full of souvenir matchbooks.

I guess all the pink and frilly stuff around the windows and the low lights on wood paneling are supposed to make people get excited. I don't think I've ever felt less excited in my life. I can hear the vacuum cleaner starting up again, off in another room, moaning its long syllable. I must be the least horny person who's ever sat on this couch. I can feel the thinness of the trailer floor, as if the whole thing were still on cinder blocks at the dealership, like the time I almost bought one, just after Cath and I got divorced and I thought I would have to sell the house.

A door opens, and five girls parade slowly, without music, into the room. All five wear solid-color evening dresses and identical white high heels—and there she is in the middle, Sally, in a deep blue gown, walking with a slight awkwardness on her shoes. The floor is so thin that I can feel the striking of their heels on the tightly woven carpet.

Sally doesn't recognize me yet; nobody's looking very closely. She looks different, her hair no longer puffed out behind a banana clip as she always used to wear it at school, but now fluffed out in every direction and arranged into bangs swept close from all sides against her face. Really, she's more beautiful than ever, sort of scientifically beautiful, as if she'd sat down with somebody and gone through all the possible hairstyles in the reference book of erotic fashion, until they fell on this one and a bell rang to say Yes.

They're all pretty, the madam was telling the truth, but they don't present themselves as well as they could. They just stand there in a line, shifting from high heel to high heel, looking bored, as if they've been pulled away from a very important television show.

"Ladies, would you like to introduce yourselves?" the red-haired woman says, as if she's reading off a card.

"Hi-I'm-Crystal," says a tall short-haired brunette (brunette is another word we're not supposed to use back in Drury Hall, no great loss, perhaps), and she says it with no pause between the words; "Hi-I'm-Susie," says a short wide-faced blonde with lipstick much too dark for the rest of her features; in the middle Sally, "Hi-I'm-Natalie," she says, and she looks up and our eyes meet and she recognizes me at last, I think. But I'm not sure. I can't read faces well. I can't tell whether she's frightened or just surprised, with her pale lips open just a bit, not to suggest a smile, nor with the frowsy slackness of a fellatrix, but with some tension in it, I think, though again I can't be sure. I've looked out for years over my classes and I thought they all looked happy, but then the computerized evaluations would come back from Princeton, New Jersey, and they all hated my guts, it turned out.

"Hi-I'm-Shantelle," says a sweet-faced black girl, a little too skinny, and the last girl, with long frizzy hair and remarkably large eyes, says, "Hi-I'm-Rhonda."

They all stand there for several seconds, bored, impatient.

"So," the red-haired woman says. "Which one of our lovely Mustang Valley hostesses would you like to visit with today?"

"I'd like to visit with . . . Natalie." The other girls stay motionless in their places as Sally takes a few steps toward me, looking alarmed—but I guess I look just as alarmed, my face flushed and my mouth still pulled into that tense meaningless grin.

"Just follow Natalie, sir," the hostess says. I get up and walk behind Sally, who hasn't said a word, behind her puffed-out blond hair and her slightly unaccustomed tiptoeing straight-legged motion of walking on high heels, down a beige wood-grain-paneled hallway so narrow that if we met someone coming the other way we would have to turn sideways, past the other girls' workrooms, the doors decorated with drawings and collages—of casinos and lines of showgirls in their enormous pink and yellow and baby-blue feather headdresses, stylized posters of painted faces, palm trees, girls' names in flowing longhand, names outlined in gold stars, "Paula's Playhouse," "Sandy's Sin-Bin," and at Sally's door a pink crepe-paper cutout in the shape of a naked woman blowing into a bubble-wand which has produced seven equal-sized bubbles with a block letter in each one, spelling out NATALIE.

She holds the door open for me, I walk in, she follows, shuts the door.

"Hi, Sally," I say.

She stands there, saying nothing, in her deep blue evening gown, the kind with a row of big diamond-shaped holes up the side where her bare skin shows through. Her brown eyes are shadowed and lined the way I used to love on the days when the weather was good enough for her to make it to my morning class.

"Dr. Schmidt . . ." she says, with a blankness in her voice, almost whispering. "What are you doing here?"

"I don't know. What are *you* doing here?"

She looks away from my face. "This is *so weird!*" She stares out the window, which looks out onto a courtyard of white gravel. "How did you find out I was here?"

"I didn't," I say. "I met your roommates, and they told me you were working here as a waitress and this was some fancy steak-house, and I bought it, of course."

"No way!" she says, smiling slightly for the first time. "You thought this was a *restaurant?*"

"Pretty stupid, huh?"

"It would be funny if it weren't so embarrassing." She leans against her counter full of cosmetics. Over the sink, a poster in Macintosh italics inside a serrated MacPaint border reads:

> *No kissing please.*
> *It needs to be stated,*
> *Kissing spreads germs,*
> *And I'm not vaccinated.*

This whole thing has happened so fast that the idea of getting excited seems unthinkable, even with all the accumulated hours I've sat in front of my class sneaking looks at her hair.

"This is just so weird," she says again. "They shouldn't have sent you out here. Dumb broads."

"I guess they thought it was funny."

"Well, ha ha ha," she says.

Just then someone knocks on the door, and a woman's voice calls: "Natalie, have you started your negotiations?"

"In a minute, Lana," Sally calls back through the door.

"That's the new efficiency policy," she says to me with a grin. "They don't want us to waste time bullshitting with our old professors."

"Speaking of bullshit," I say, "here's your term paper." I pull the folded paper out of my jacket pocket and hand it to her. "I'm afraid I could only give you a C-minus."

"No way!" she laughs. "You should have given me an F. That paper was total bogue. I was drunk and it was the middle of the night. You don't have any standards at all, do you?"

"I like to give people the benefit of the doubt."

She doesn't even glance at my red editor's marks and marginal comments, just looks out through the frilly white curtains again, into the bare courtyard where the sun is beginning to slant down with that sad Emily Dickinson kind of light that I always talk about in the Introduction to Literature classes that they sometimes let me teach when they have enough graduate students to cover all the freshman composition sections.

"So," she says, "now that you've found out about my sinful life, I guess you're going to give me the morality talk, right?"

"I hardly think I'm qualified."

"You're welcome to try the 'What are you doing with your life' talk. I get that one all the time too. Usually afterward."

"Look, Sally," I say, "it's not my job to give you a sermon. I'm just surprised, that's all."

"You're not mad?"

"I could never be mad at you. You know you were my favorite student in that class."

"Really?"

"Yes."

"But I was terrible. I hardly ever came to class."

"That just made it all the more fun when you did show up."

"Oh, Dr. Schmidt," she says, "that's really *sweet.* I never had a teacher say that before." She turns away, half hiding the window curtains. "But I'm still going to kill those broads for sending you out here."

"I don't mind," I say. "I'm glad I got a chance to see you at least."

"Really?" she says. "That's so nice. I was afraid you'd be shocked."

"I'm a little puzzled, but I'm not shocked."

"Maybe I'd like you to be shocked," she says, turning back to me, with a grin rising in her face. "Would you be shocked if I did this?"

She slowly pulls the stretchy fabric of her gown down below her breasts.

"What do you think?" she says. "Don't you wish I'd done

that in class?" Her breasts are perfect—small and firm, concave at the top where the taut skin holds them suspended. Just then, as if at the sight of a food source, my stomach growls audibly.

She stands close in front of me, her gown back over her breasts, and lays her head at the crook of my neck and shoulder. I can smell something different in her hair, not the soft airy lightness of a college girl's hair when she used to come into my office for conferences at which neither of us learned anything, but something more citruslike, penetrating, a sort of orangy, under-the-covers smell.

She pulls back a bit and looks in my eyes. "So what do you think, Dr. Schmidt? If I'm your favorite student, that means I should offer you this chance. You can have a session right now if you want. I'll give you a Mustang Special for the price of a French date. Anything on the menu. What do you think?"

"Sally, I'd love to, but I can't. You can do what you want, but I couldn't look your father in the eye."

"Okay, Dr. Schmidt," she says. "I guess I can understand that. But I'd like you to do me a big favor."

"Okay."

"I'd really like it if we could keep this our little secret," and I can feel the warmth of her breath up the side of my neck and into my ear. "I only want to do this for a couple of months, but if my father ever finds out, I'm afraid he's going to have another heart attack."

Another rap on the door, louder. "Let's go, Natalie. Time to log in the money."

"I'm going to have to kick you out now," Sally says. "You're sure I can't talk you into a session?"

"It wouldn't feel right."

"You're always free to change your mind," she says softly into my ear, her hands resting lightly on my shoulders. She hands me a piece of paper that looks like an old-fashioned valentine, two heart-shaped pieces of heavy pink paper, trimmed in lace, joined at the side.

"This is our menu," she says. "Will you promise to read it before you fly back?"

"I promise," I say. Then she leads me through the narrow inter-trailer passageways, back to the parlor and the front door, and the parking lot, where my rental car still shines in the afternoon sun.

☆ ☆ ☆

Driving back the eight flat miles of this road toward Route 270, my ears buzz, my stomach gurgles and squeaks. The Sunbird's little engine races, my mind races; and in the rearview mirror I can see my face, my double chin more visible than ever in the hard light of the desert.

When I turn my head slightly to the right I can catch for just a moment a trace of Sally's scent, there in the hollow of my neck and shoulder where she rested the fluffed volume of her blond hair and breathed in my ear about how she hoped I wouldn't call her father.

It's strange; for the past year, except for the dancers at the Petting Zoo in Lexington, no girls have even given me the time of day, and today, all of a sudden, everybody's trying to seduce me.

In the desert, even on Thursday, it always feels like Sunday afternoon, carrying that tentative and hopeless gold quality of light, and the sense of everything being too late to do anything about, so you just get in your car and drive around until you end up someplace worth stopping.

The Wagon Wheel turns out to be the only real casino in the village of Pancake Flats. Inside the Wagon Wheel, it's so small that to save space they have one of those miniature crap tables that looks more like an elevated mahogany bathtub. A few slot machines are churning away slowly, in that same filtered and scrubbed complexity of casino air. Bells, like underpowered telephones, keep ringing. The whole inside of the place is dark in that way that bars and nice restaurants have on the kind of day when even if you can't see a window you know it's clear outside and the sun is slamming down all day over the bare scrub.

The snack bar, strong with the odor of chili and grilled cheese sandwiches, is tucked into a far corner of the casino. As soon as I sit down at a two-seat Formica table, a trim little waitress in her fifties, with tired-looking eyes, brings me a menu and a glass of water.

"Have fun, sir?" she says.

"Excuse me?"

She points to the menu, which I have rolled up and tucked into my shirt pocket and forgotten about. It sticks out, round and pink, from my herringbone jacket. "The Mustang," she says, smiling. "I hope you had a good time."

"It was fun," I say, trying not to sound as stupid as I feel. I shouldn't have brought that thing in here.

"We get a lot of their customers in here. Try your luck here, maybe you can go back again."

"Thanks," I say. "Maybe I'll do that."

From the regular menu I order the daily special, meat loaf and mashed potatoes and green beans, with rolls and salad and coffee. Then I look around to make sure nobody is looking too closely, and I unroll the brochure that Sally gave me. It has taken on such a curve from being rolled up in my pocket that it won't sit on the table, so I roll it up the other way and squeeze it a few times until it flattens out more or less.

The folder, with the words "Pleasure Menu" drawn on the front in typography that looks like old western fenceposts, opens the a very pretty drawing of a naked girl lying on her back with one of her legs lifted, and in the space between her legs, the writing is set up just like the menu at Paolo's, the one nice restaurant back in the town of Amherst:

Edward Allen

Welcome to the Mustang Valley Inn

*We offer a wide selection of delicious pleasures
for gentlemen of good taste.*

Hors d'Oeuvres

Breast Massage
Bathtub Party
Lingerie Show
Body Paint
Whipped Cream Party

Daily Specials

Sweet n' Sour
Lana's Surprise (Do you dare?)
Jacuzzi French (With Snorkel)
S&M Rollercoaster
Psychodrama

Buffet Style

Full Horizontal French
Paris Police
Implements of Pleasure
Around the World French
Socrates Party
Eskimo Pie

Main Dishes

Doggie Date
Missionary Mania
Soixante-Neuf
Two Girl Sappho Show
Two Girl Play-Along
Fantasy Session

Desserts

Breast Shampoo
Peppermint Pussy Party
Action Shampoo

Perrier French
Hot Water Bottle Party
Instant Replay

Mustang Special—Unlimited choice of entrees and appetizers.
Time limit one hour. Special equipment extra.

If you don't see your personal desire listed, please ask!

Hablamos Español.   On parle Français ici. 口日本ワ犬人ノ目頂

I keep reading the menu over and over. It's strange to think that
the whole deal is legal, licenses filed at the sheriff's department
and everything, though I suppose it's a more honest transaction
than all the dollar bills I've stuffed into girls' panties over the last

year, at tittie bars like the Petting Zoo and the Baby Doll and the Cutie Pie. Not much difference, I suppose—but somehow having it not be a class A misdemeanor makes everything seem so mechanical.

In Lexington, Kentucky, which is the closest place that has tittie bars, it somehow makes it sexier to know that the gellicles could burst in any time with their guns, or that one of their bomb threats, like the one they had to evacuate the place for when I was there one night, could actually go off.

At the front of the Petting Zoo, which is just across from the Airport Red Roof Inn on Route 60, the place is marked by an outline in light of a girl dancing, her underpants twitching as the lights flash from one position to the other. Inside, it's horrible, music so loud I have to yell to the waitress, *"MILLER LIGHT!"* at the top of my lungs.

The girls dance on the raised stage in the middle of the floor— theater in the round, as it were—in a strobe light so intense that every stationary object in the place appears to be shaking. As soon as the strobes stop, a matched battery of transistorized laser light machines come on, all controlled by one central chip so that they generate identical patterns, frantically waving their filaments of green and red and blue and amber light through the atmospheric smoke of a room where I'm the only one without a cigarette.

When the girls are onstage, lifting their hair with both hands or swinging themselves athletically around on the polished brass firepole, the lights paint their skin in meaningless squiggles and brushstrokes, like something from "Laugh-In" in the sixties; and sometimes one of those thin shafts of light will ricochet for an instant off one plane of the slowly turning mirror-globe on the ceiling, and the pure light will catch me just right and explode in my eye like a cobalt bomb.

After each song, the almost incomprehensible disk jockey

chants, "Call your favorite *sex*-y lady over for a couch-dance, table-dance, slow-dance." If Carol, my favorite dancer, is there, I call her over. For thirty dollars she will lead me by the hand back to the couch-dance area, where there is no place to balance my beer, and she will dance in my lap, and kiss me with her cabbagey cigarette breath, and then bring her nipples close enough for me to kiss them, back in the gloom, away from the nightmare strobes, oh the swinger's life for me.

Then back home, always with a headache and my clothes smelling like cigarettes, through the patrolled darkness, past pairs of state police cars in the median of Route 64, facing in opposite directions, driver's window to driver's window, in that curiously intimate coupling. I set the cruise control of the Volvo to fifty-five, terrified of getting pulled over after my four five-dollar beers, back to the village of Amherst, and the house on Verossika Lane, and the college kids on both sides of the street staggering home to their slum apartments; and the dog, and the cat, both waiting to be fed.

Chapter 5

Showered, changed, with a crease in my mustard-colored slacks and the same lucky herringbone jacket, I'm on the town, the hero with slightly less than a thousand dollars, after losing three rolls of quarters on the four-reel progressive slots at the Wagon Wheel and gassing the Sunbird up at the Horrible Phelps convenience store in Pancake Flats before driving back across the mountains.

No waiting on line with the whiteheads in the buffet tonight. In the Hong Kong Trading Post in the Flamingo Hilton, one of several restaurants that line the carpeted walkway that runs parallel to the sidewalk outside, the keno girls keep hurrying from table to table, saying, "Good luck, sir." Thursday night begins to have a weekend feel to it, a livelier buzz in the air indoors, the Strip traffic heavier, the Toyota minivan taxis in more of a hurry, cutting nervously from lane to lane.

Frank Iverson won't be expecting to hear from me until tomorrow at the earliest, or even the next day. In the meantime, there's no point in worrying about what to do. Whatever happens, I'm going to be on somebody's shit list, maybe even my own. All I can do right now is have some fun and hit the tables. This is the night for it. I can feel the presence of luck, like a ghost, hanging over the huge signs, over the excited flowery torch of the Flamingo Hilton and the bright marquee of the Sands, hanging over the RT bus stops and the twin rivers of traffic, north and south, over the boom-boom of crack-music Toyota speakers.

I've been practicing every day on my office Macintosh: shareware craps, shareware blackjack. I even sent the guy who wrote the craps program fifteen dollars to qualify for free program updates, as his cartoon picture on the screen urges every time you open the program. The bastard deposited my check, and sent nothing.

☆ ☆ ☆

On the Strip, the wind has picked up, I mean literally picked up and grabbed on to anything small enough to fly: crumpled cigarette packs, newspapers, dust, and paper cups, all flying around in the light. Tourists hold their hands over their faces in a kind of hangdog salute, fighting through the wind.

It's a good sign, the Strip in the wind, as I walk north toward the blue-lit Torii of the Imperial Palace, because I know it is bad luck to play in the same place you eat.

The night is all tossed and mixed like a dry salad. Bodies move with a quick pace on the sidewalk; people's lightweight windbreakers are turning red, and green, and white under the Flamingo facade; farther up the Strip the signs for the Frontier and the Stardust busily flash, disappear, explode, grow. Because of the wind, the airport has routed the planes into an unusual glide path directly overhead—the heavies, they call them, luxuriously huge, bellying down with their big buzzing voices over all the nondescript sport jackets and unremarkable faces that crowd along the sidewalk from casino to casino.

At last I think I understand why the windows of the English department at UNLV face away from the Strip: if they had to keep looking at these lights flashing, miles away, in shades of hot lime and cool peach, had to keep looking at things being beautiful for no defensible reason on the nights they have to stay late at the office grading papers, I believe that all the angry cartoons would fall off their office doors.

You can walk up and down the Strip for hours without ever noticing anybody's face. It's a good town to be ugly in, which you will notice if you ever look closely into the crowds. People don't worry about how they look. The shined shoes and skinny ties of the Rat Pack days are long gone. A man could step up to a table with shit on his hat and nobody would complain. "We need something to turn this table around!" they might say, and the dealer would laugh and say, "Shitheads welcome."

In the Imperial Palace, breathing the same uniformly filtered and deodorized mildness of clean carpets and ventilated cigarettes, I walk up and down between the banks of slot machines for a few minutes, letting the sound wash over me, knowing that every second counts; every time I turn my head I cause myself to step up to the crap table a second later, every step I take I change the world. What a responsibility. In the distance the brassy clang of a jackpot, a whooping cheer from the close crowd around a hot roll.

Up in the ceiling, between the paper-and-bamboo light shades, I can see the black half-globes where the security people peek down to make sure we are not cheating. No academic honor code here. Everybody from dealers to floormen to customers is carefully monitored, which I shouldn't complain about really. At least you know the casino isn't going to try to cheat you. They make so much money legally that it would be insane to risk losing their license in a cheating scandal. It is amazing to think that this is the first time in history when you can be reasonably sure of a fair game. I've read somewhere that loaded dice were found in the ruins of Pompeii.

I step up to the least-crowded crap table, taking my place to the right of a country-and-western-type stickwoman with tightly permed blond hair who looks as if she would be more comfortable dressed in the square-dance outfit of the Frontier than wearing the chinoiserie, or maybe the japonaiserie, of her purple kimono uniform. The Imperial Palace doesn't really know if it is supposed to be Chinese or Japanese.

The last person rolling the dice has just "sevened out," that is, rolled a seven before he managed to roll his point number, so all the bets on the table have been taken away, the dice are about to be passed to the next player, the twin pucks that indicate what the point is have been moved to the side and flipped to the "off" side, and all the boxes and bars and diagrams on the table are empty except for the new pass-line bets that everybody is putting down. I put a hundred-dollar bill on the table in front of the dealer opposite me and say, "Change, please," taking my hand away, because dealers are forbidden to take money directly from a customer's hand.

The dealer hands my bill to the boxman, a man in a suit who sits at the middle of the table on the pit side where the players can't go, opposite from the stickman. The boxman is the boss of the table, the one who watches over the chips, supervises the two dealers and the stickman, makes change, and writes credit markers. He smoothes out my bill and stuffs it, using a flexible metal blade, into a slot in the table, while the dealer places four stacks of red chips on the table in front of me. Other people at the table are getting change, or "check-change," exchanging green twenty-fives and black hundreds for red fives.

"ALL RIGHT, A NEW SHOOTER, COMIN' OUT, GET YOUR BETS DOWN, WATCH YOUR HANDS!" says the stickwoman in a droning, liturgical voice, as she slides five dice on the end of her stick toward a bald-headed little guy to my right. The job of the stickman, or woman in this case, is to call out the numbers that have been rolled, for those who can't see, to handle the dice, passing them to the player by means of a long flexible L-shaped stick, and to collect and pay off the complicated-looking sucker bets in the middle of the layout, which I never play anyway.

This is a five-dollar-minimum table, so I take one red five-dollar chip and place it down on the felt top of the table two feet below the rail, in the "pass line" area, which is the most conventional bet. The new shooter picks the two dice he wants, taps them on the table twice, and lofts them backhanded in a high arc, and one bounces off the table.

"NO ROLL . . . TOO TALL TO CALL," the stickwoman chants. Somebody picks up the lost die, actually referred to in the singular as a "dice," and tosses it back onto the table, but before it can go back into play the boxman carefully examines it, turning over its six red facets, looking for damage, and also checking the code number, which is changed every day as new dice are brought into play, to make sure no "shapes," meaning crooked dice, have been slipped in. Unlike the white bevel-cornered kind you buy in a convenience store on a card with shrink wrap, casino dice have very sharp corners to make them roll more randomly across the table.

"COMIN' OUT!" the stickwoman says again. She means that this roll is what's called the "come-out roll." At this point in the game, seven or eleven, called "naturals," will win for the pass-line bettors like me; two, three, or twelve are "craps" and will lose. Any other number that comes up—four, five, six, eight, nine, or ten—is known as a "box number" and becomes the "point," at which time the rules of the game change completely.

The shooter lofts the two dice again, slightly less high, and they come up four and five.

"NINE-NINE-NINE-nine-nine-nine-nine-nine," drones the stick-woman. The twin pucks are flipped over from the black "off" side to the white "on" side and moved into the nine box in the row of box numbers in front of each dealer, the sixes and nines spelled out to avoid confusion, the identical setup on each side of the boxman. So now the point is nine, which means that I'm hoping that the shooter can roll another nine before he rolls a seven. If he rolls nine, the passline wins; if he sevens out, we lose.

With the point established, a flurry of side bets begins. Some players place the six and eight, betting that those numbers will show before seven; "Hard eight," some shout, tossing five-dollar chips into the "proposition bet" area in front of the stickwoman. There are dozens of possible side bets: one-roll field bets where you bet on the high or low numbers coming up, hard-way bets where you hope that one of the four even-numbered points will come up the "hard way," that is, with doubles.

You can bet on just about any possibility, but most of the bets are sucker bets. I just stick to the basic game, with the pass bets and the similar "come" bets, and I always take "odds" after a point is established, because the odds bet is the only bet in the casino that gives you an even chance.

The original bet that you put down on the pass line will pay off even money if the shooter makes the point he has established. But once a point is established, the casino lets you place an odds bet behind the original bet, usually up to twice the original amount; and that odds bet is paid off according to the actual likelihood of a number coming up before the seven. For instance, the hardest points to make are the four and the ten, with only three ways that the dice can add up to either of those numbers as opposed to six ways to make a seven.

But the beauty of the odds bet is that if the shooter does manage to roll that four, your odds bet will be paid off two to one. And the same goes for the other numbers: with four ways to roll a five or a nine against six ways to roll a seven, your odds bet on the five or nine will be paid off at three to two; and with five ways to hit a six or an eight, your odds bet on one of those points will pay six to five.

I'm starting at this table slowly: just a simple five-dollar pass-line bet and ten dollars behind it for double odds. The dealers are frantically moving chips around, taking bets from all sides, alert, tense in their high-pressure job; and the stickwoman keeps the two active dice on the table, waiting for the betting to be finished, when she can pass them back to the shooter. As the dealers' hands fly over the table with stacks of chips, the stickwoman stirs the two active dice with her shepherd's crook of a stick, fiddling the dice back and forth on the felt, from one side of the L-shaped crook to the other, like a hockey player dribbling the puck; then when all bets are in she pushes the dice back to the shooter, who grabs, taps, lofts . . .

"THREE CRAP!" the stickwoman says. On the come-out roll, three would be a loser, but on a point roll, it means nothing. The dice come back to him, he shoots, they land five and two.

"SEVEN-OUT, LINE AWAY! PAY THE DON'T AND THE LAST COME BET." And the table breathes a collective sigh of "Shit," while all the bets that covered the table are whisked away by the fast hands of the two dealers. A beautiful blond cocktail waitress has just come around to take orders.

The way it works is that the shooter keeps the dice until he sevens out, at which point the next player in the clockwise direction is offered the dice, and now that's me. Some players refuse the dice and pass them on, but I love to shoot. Meanwhile, a white-haired guy has come up behind the stickwoman, tapped her gently on the shoulder, and taken over for her.

"A NEW SHOOTER, COMING OUT!" the new stickman says, less priestly than the former caller, with more of a musical lilt to his voice. I pick up two of the five dice he slides to me, shake them quickly in the space inside my closed fist, and shoot. I like to shoot with a low forehand, rolling the dice around the semicircular far end of the table, making them hug closely against the pyramid-baffled foam-rubber lining around the inside edge of the table. I hate people who waste time "setting" the dice, very slowly moving them to a particular number on the table surface before they pick them up and shoot.

"YO ELEVEN, WIN-NER!" And since this is the come-out roll, the pass bets are paid off at even money. I shoot again.

"THREE CRAP!" And the bets are snatched away.

"Yes!" a skinny young guy with short brown hair growing in all directions at once shouts from the far end. The dealers are paying him off. I can see that he's playing the "don't-pass" line. What this means is that he's betting against the shooter, in a reversed game. For him, a crap wins, a natural loses, and when a point is established, the "don't" bettor, or "wrong" bettor, is hoping for a seven to come up before the point. "Wrong" bettors are usually the kind who like to antagonize people. Often, as in this guy's case, they are drunks.

"COMING OUT, HANDS UP!" The stickman slides the dice back to me. Even though my last throw was a loser, I still keep the dice. You only lose the dice when you seven out.

I shoot again, the skinny kid shouts, "Come on *crap!*" The dice tumble around the far edge next to the "don't" player.

"SIX, EASY SIX!" Now, with a point established, the real betting starts, the odds and the come bets and place bets and the hard ways. People are shouting, "Place the eight!" "Hard six!" "Ten dollar C and E!" and "Dollar Yo!" The dealers' hands fly over the green table surface like a wild and incomprehensible game of checkers, while the crush of noise, of voices and machines, and the formless muffled sound of thousands of feet on the carpeted floor goes on and on all around us.

I put my ten-dollar double odds behind my original bet on the pass line, and then I put my five-dollar chip in the come bet area. A come bet works the same as a pass-line bet, except that a come bet begins a separate game of its own; and for that bet, the next roll is just like the come-out roll, as if no point had been established. If the next roll is a crap, the pass-line bets won't be affected, but the come bet will lose. If a seven comes up at this point, the come bet wins, although the pass-line bets will lose. And if a point number is rolled, that number becomes a separate point for that come bet, and the player can take odds on it the same as he would on a pass-line bet.

The kid at the other end of the table is getting on everybody's nerves. "Come one *seven!*" he says. "Seven out!" People are giving him dirty looks and edging away from him, even though nobody has said anything. I've tried playing the "don't" a few times, but I had the sense to keep quiet about it. It's boring, really, unless you are a drunk and like to get people angry.

"SIX IS THE POINT, SIX IS!" the stickman says as he slides the dice to me and I roll . . .

"FIVE, FIVE, NO-FIELD FIVE!" The stickman has a name for every number, and five, not being one of the outside, or "field," points, is usually referred to as "no-field." More side bets; the dealer across from me moves my chip from the come-bet area to the edge of the five box in front of him, meaning that this come bet will pay off now if a five is rolled before a seven. I toss him two five-dollar chips, which he catches backhanded as they bounce off the table, and he places the odds bet on top of the original bet, slightly off-center. The pace of the table is picking up, money all over the place. I roll . . .

"TWO CRAP!" And again . . .

"FIVE, NO-FIELD FIVE!" And very quickly the dealer pays off my winning come bet, returning twenty dollars along with the fifteen that were up there. I put up another come bet, and shoot . . .

"WINNER SIX!" And the dealers' hands fly, paying off everybody's pass-line bets and the odds, and the pucks are flipped over again, back to the "off" side in the "don't come" box.

"Shit!" says the kid at the far end. He's dressed in some kind of green industrial uniform such as you see in catalogues of work clothes where smiling models with perfect teeth pretend to be having a great time digging ditches.

"All right!" the guy next to me who sevened out is saying. "We got a shooter here! We got a shooter dice!"

"COMIN' OUT, COMIN' OUT!" I shoot . . .

"THREE, CRAP DICE!"

"Yoooooowwwwwwwwww!" says the drunk at the other end of the table, with one fist curled in toward his chest in an end-zone victory posture. All around the table, people are glaring at him.

"You wanna keep it down over there, sir," the boxman says, giving the kid a hard look. Dealers hate "wrong" bettors even more than the other players do, because they are invariably lousy tippers. The bets are put down again. The dice come back to me . . .

"NINE-NINE-nine-nine-nine-nine-nine-nine-CENTER-FIELD   NINE!" And with another point established, a flurry of hands and chips, more paper money fluttering onto the table, *"Change one hundred!"* the dealer shouts, loud enough that the pit boss over in the roped-off area behind him can hear, *"Change fifty!"* and paper money is stuffed with the steel blade into the slot.

I put up the odds on my six come bet from the last roll, and keep rolling, a few more come-bet numbers, a crap twelve, and finally . . .

"NINE, WINNER NINE!" A shout around the table. "WINNER NINE, TAKE THE DON'T, PAY THE LINE!"

"God *dammit!"* says the drunk, but nobody cares now. We're winning. The cocktail waitress comes back with her tray full of complimentary cocktails. Usually I just tip the waitresses fifty cents, but this girl is so cute, and her hair so soft and fluffy-looking, that I slip her a whole dollar chip from one of my six-to-five payoffs.

The cocktail waitresses who bring free drinks to the players are always the sexiest-looking employees in the whole casino. And there's a reason for it: with pretty girls around, guys want to bet more. It must be related to some kind of mating display: a baboon gets a red ass, a willow ptarmigan puffs up the air sacks on either side of that slit in the middle of his chest where it looks like his guts are starting to come out, and a human male puts down another ten dollars on the pass line and makes a bet for the dealers.

"Dealer bet!" I say, while the waitress is still looking, and I place a red five beside my own bet, which I have raised to ten dollars. The dealer bet will go to them as a tip if the point wins.

That's my strategy, with or without the waitress around: bet more when you're ahead, cut your losses when you're down, never chase the money that isn't yours anymore. And every few hands make a bet for the dealers.

"Dealers on the line!" the stickman echoes. "COMIN' OUT! SAME SHOOTER, SAME DICE!"

"Keep it up, pal," other players are shouting. "You're doing great!" I shoot . . .

"FOUR, EASY FOUR!" And the pucks are flipped over again and slid to the four boxes. I know everybody's disappointed, because four and ten are the hardest points to make. I put down my twenty dollars for double odds, swallow, shoot . . .

"EIGHT-EIGHT-eight-eight-eight-eight, IT CAME HARD." A come number pays off, and I put up another one, for ten.

I'm ahead now, by how much I don't know, and I don't have the time to find out. I've stashed a pile of chips in my right-hand pocket, leaving in the rack in front of me only those chips I'm willing to risk before I quit if the table goes cold. Voices are shouting, "Get that *four!*" and the wrong bettor at the end of the table says, "Come on, *seven out!* Come on, *sheriff!*" I roll, fast along the corner of the round-ended table, I can't see it, a great shout from the other players, and the stickman sings out, "WINNER FOUR!"

The thing about craps that intimidates so many people is that it's a noisy, vocal, extroverted game. Even the hottest blackjack table stays almost silent. But a hot crap table, with the occasional exception of an oddball "wrong" player, feels like a bunch of old friends flying off on an adventure together, like a stunt plane with everybody riding in it together, like one of those rafts you can buy a seat on to run the rapids of the Colorado River. After a few points, all the players are bosom buddies.

Money and chips fly all over the table now. I made fifty dollars on that one roll, and the two come numbers are still up there, sixty dollars still hanging, with the odds off on the come-out roll.

Usually I've seen the hot tables from far away, when I was playing at another table, and even then, from two or three tables away, you can feel the excitement. And now I'm in the middle of it. The dealers' hands fly in a controlled frenzy of adrenaline. Dealers love a hot table, even if the casino is losing, because their tips come from winners. The pit boss is watching, standing behind the boxman, looking with a mild curiosity. People are putting down black action now, hundred-dollar chips, I can feel the table breathe with one common breath. I'm up to thirty dollars on the pass line. "COMIN' OUT, SAME GOOD SHOOTER!" I shake the dice, exactly the same as I have been doing, shoot . . .

"YO, ELEVEN, WINNER!"

I keep going; and over the next few minutes I make two more points, six in a row, I think, my bet on the pass line and two come bets up to fifty dollars now, with double odds, action on almost every throw now, everybody winning, except the "wrong" bettor, who has fallen silent.

I'm way ahead, how many hundreds of dollars I don't know. All

I know is that my keeper pocket is so full of chips that my lucky gray herringbone jacket hangs crooked on my shoulders. It's bad luck to count your money in the middle of a shoot, I think; and besides, I don't have the time to do it.

Craps is the only game where you get so busy you forget to drink. My vodka grapefruit, which for some reason they call a Greyhound in this town, sits untouched in front of me on the shelf below the chip rail.

These tables move so fast that you can hardly look away. Except for all the sucker bets in the middle of the layout, which don't mean anything anyway, it's the simplest game in the world— coming out, seven wins; with a point, seven loses; just you against the dice. But now even the garbage bets are winning: the hard eights, the crap-eleven bet, the "horn," the "yo-eleven."

"COMIN' OUT! SAME BIG SHOOTER!" I roll a four, put the odds down, roll again, and again, winning a few more come bets, then I shoot again, watch the red cubes go spinning along the round racetrack shape at the far end of the table, one comes to rest with the five, and somehow I know this is it, there's the two.

"SEVEN-OUT . . ." A collective wince, and a grunt of breath exhaled. And then they're clapping. "Good shoot, pal!" They're giving me an ovation, and I'm grinning like somebody being congratulated at a faculty meeting for winning the Hoosier Press Award for Academic Excellence. We're all hundreds of dollars ahead, even with the inevitable final loss. The guys who were putting down black action are up by thousands, although I'm always too busy to pay much attention to other people's bets.

My keeper pocket bulges and sags, and I'm ready to leave if the table gets cold again. Quit on the downturn after an upswing— that's the rule. I measure out a small row of red fives in the rack in front of me, going back to a minimum bet; I'll build it back up again if the table stays hot.

What most people do wrong is that they try to force the game, and they don't know to walk away from the table a winner. My philosophy is to quit when a hot table turns cold, and not to lose everything I've won by being greedy and forcing the bets. The term in the business for winnings re-bet and lost back to the house is "churn." Casinos love it. For myself, I prefer to let the dice decide whether I keep playing or not. They're smarter than I am.

The next two shooters seven out on their first point, and I'm gone, tossing two reds to the dealers. "Thanks, guys."

I try a blackjack table, and lose three five-dollar hands in a row; and I know that that's it for the Imperial Palace. So I walk, my keeper pocket bulging, over to the row of barred cashier's windows, carefully scoop the chips from my pocket into a plastic coin cup I picked up in the slot-machine area. Standing in front of the cashier's window, I slowly count out the chips, arranging them in twenty-five-dollar stacks, until it comes to six hundred and ten dollars.

Just to see those bright-faced hundred-dollar bills come flashing out of the cashier's drawer, as lightly and quickly as if they were singles, makes my heart beat faster. Hundred-dollar bills have a very soft look to them, especially on the back, with their wide borders and light green scrollwork.

The giant room rings and churns as I walk to the door, which I can hardly find, because they purposely set up the casinos so you will get lost and find yourself at the tables again and lose all your money. But I finally find the right exit, out onto the Strip, and push out through the heavy glass door, feeling the square shape of my wallet riding awkwardly in my back pocket.

☆ ☆ ☆

Outside, I'm walking around in the dark, in the simmering crowds. It's cold, my head buzzes. With tonight's winnings, I've got a wallet full of hundreds, plus all my traveler's checks back in the room, folded and stashed in the inside of the cap of my deodorant, because I've seen on a hidden camera episode of "60

Minutes" how the chambermaids will look everywhere, including in your shoes.

Just across the Strip, the Mirage volcano is going off again, with a breathy hiss of propane spewing out from underwater among the jungle of palm trees. The crowd stares, oohs and aahs, snaps pictures, the yellow flames flickering against their pale clothing. Even from the other side of six lanes of traffic, most with their windows open and funky bass lines blasting, I can still hear the dragonlike rasp of gas, and I can still feel the heat of the flames on my face.

There is a special way people walk when they have won money. It is not a strut, nor anything purposeful—rather, a kind of intensity, a kind of solidity, to the way arms and legs work together. If I were a mugger, I think I could spot my marks by the confident scissoring of their legs, and the slight, involuntary jauntiness to their steps.

Then a face catches the corner of my eye: stopped at the light at the Strip and Twain Avenue, in the lane closest to the sidewalk, a deep maroon Cadillac Seville idles softly. In the passenger's seat, beside a large man with slicked-back hair, sits a beautiful dark-haired young woman, who I instantly can tell is a prostitute—I'm not sure why, perhaps the sculptured smoothness of her makeup, or the way she looks straight ahead out the windshield with her well-defined lips slightly pursed, simultaneously bored and alert, looking up toward the letters of the Frontier sign filling up from the bottom with red, draining, filling with white. She never glances at the guy sitting next to her.

As I cross on the pedestrian walkway in front of them, I catch her eye and grin. It seems that for one moment the understanding of what's going on passes silently between us, unnoticed by all the other shuffling nighttime figures. She neither acknowledges my glance nor avoids it, just sits there, prim and casual in her flawless foundation and dark eyeliner, with her hair gathered together on top into a kind of elevated knot, then falling down, sprayed and scalloped, on both sides of her face.

Boom boom go the speakers on the little polished minitrucks that can never carry anything in the back because people would steal it. Everything rings and churns and flashes; and suddenly my stomach goes cold, with a trembling chill from the crotch all the way up to the throat, with the realization that I am not going to try to talk Sally out of her new profession, no matter how ridiculous it is that she should be doing it. I know now that it was never going to turn out any other way. Somewhere between my legs I knew it all along, from the moment Sally cuddled against me and let me smell her hair, and talked about keeping it our little secret, which is always a sexy thing to say for some reason; and I knew that one way or another, whether by virtue of a hot table or a hot Tele-Cash machine, I would end up back at the Mustang, getting myself excitingly washed in her little sink.

My heart bumps like a Toyota speaker; I know at once that this is the moment. I stop halfway across the Strip, walk back to the sidewalk on the northbound side, and flag down a taxi back to the Westward Ho, where I don't even go up to my room, just transfer from the taxi into the Sunbird and then come out following the taxi back over the speed bumps.

☆ ☆ ☆

From the Interstate, I can see the giant red-lighted blades of the windmill in the middle of the miniature golf course at the Scandia Family Fun Center. Although it seems a little cold for miniature golf, the blades keep turning and turning like a slow eggbeater, whipping the night up into something you can bite into, like one of the steaks the Mustang doesn't serve. Tonight it doesn't matter; I'm going on a full stomach.

And all the time there's this little voice inside me saying I shouldn't be doing this. Or that's what a gentleman is supposed to hear in a situation like this. And really, I'm listening for it, but I can't hear much. The second I saw that hooker's face in the Cadillac, everything went silent.

I know that a man in the English department should be expected to do better, even when he doesn't want to. He should advise everybody in the world to major in English, and always give students that handout listing all the careers open to English majors: air traffic controller, bakery clerk, corrections officer, door-to-door salesperson. And if a girl should get into prostitution, we're supposed to rescue her. On television, an English teacher should be expected to beat the girl's pimp over the head with his briefcase, not to go driving out into the desert to fuck the daughter of his racquetball partner.

But these are only thoughts in traffic, and they fly around my head as insubstantial as crack music without the bass line. I can feel a cold thrill at the bottom of my spine. A loud operatic baritone fills the darkness of the car, something I've heard before, but I don't know much about music. I guess I don't know much about anything. All I know is that choices don't mean much anymore. I spread my legs apart and let myself imagine that I am being pulled over the mountains by a string tied around my dick.

I wonder about Sally's situation. What she's doing in a job like that I don't know, and maybe she doesn't either. It's her business, I guess, and if the government says she has the right to sell, in the only local-option state in the country, then I have the right to buy.

I know she can't be on drugs, not if what she said about weekly blood tests is true. But I should say something to her, or at least I should ask her what's going on to make such a nice girl from such a nice family do something that I'd never look twice if a poor girl on drugs did it. But actually I don't care. Even if I like her, I still don't care. A chance is a chance, and every year my chance gets smaller, every year I can feel my capacities going downhill, as the morning Chi Omegas get more achingly beautiful week by week.

Even so, maybe I should say something to her about making

her money and then getting out, like a gambler at a hot table. I've read somewhere that most hookers are broke when they finally quit. That's what seems cruel—not the principle, but the money, the bread-and-butter economics, not all this morality stuff.

The problem is that it's a bad job. But you have to admit it makes the world a better place. It will for me, at least, after all those years of eight o'clock classes, with those gorgeous, bored, polished faces staring up at me and me staring back at them until sometimes I get lost in the middle of some convoluted sentence that I can't find my way out of either grammatically or logically.

There's a program about that coming up next week at the Modern Language Association convention: "Pedagogical Fluency: How Teachers Find Their Way Through Their Own Rhetoric." It's the only session description that interests me, although I thumbed though the whole fat program on the flight out here.

Why I even bother I don't know. The only reason I go every year is that the university pays my way. Most of the stuff in the discussions is pretty predictable: how terrible Reagan was, and how much everybody hates him. Oh a long life to the Gipper, dim as he was. On a night like this I can forgive him everything but his choice of a running mate. And I know that when he is gone, a hush will fall over panel discussions; entire publishing houses will fold; a whole symphony of opinion go silent.

For the level of my own classes, none of the theoretical stuff matters much. I don't need to learn about Foucault and Jonathan Clark; I don't need to know the manner of punishment that some speakers hope will befall Bret Easton Ellis in revenge for the cruelties he has concealed beneath his lists of brand names; and I probably won't get thirsty enough to attend the Marxist cash bar following the symposium about new ways of incorporating Race-Class-Gender into remedial composition classes.

☆ ☆ ☆

The Pancake Valley opens up in front of me with its flat spread of lights. Wind buffets the car; now I'm scared about what's coming—scared in that icy tingling way that has excitement and desire and a dry mouth mixed in.

The Mustang looks busy. Every one of the interconnected trailers, every corner of the fenced space, glows under some kind of yellow floodlights. At the entrance to the parking lot, on a short pole, a red light flashes. One of those very tall Mercedes buses with the entire upper portion made of glass, like a railroad observation car, is parked in the gravel lot. As I walk up to the waiting room, I can hear rapid voices and laughter and music.

The place is packed, with about forty Japanese men in business suits, some with their ties loosened. None of the girls are there. Japanese instrumental music blasts from a boom box, a simple, almost mechanical pentatonic pop song in a minor key. Somebody has hooked a microphone up to the speaker. Two men sitting on a couch are singing into it, in soft harmony—something about *anata* and *watakushi,* which I know means "you" and "me." A bar has been set up on a white-draped table. The girl who was vacuuming earlier today is pouring drinks for the men crowded around the bar.

One of the men walks up to me where I'm standing, just inside the front door. "You want something?" he says.

"I'm here to see somebody."

"I can't hear you. Who you rook for?" he says, with a challenging edge to his voice. Whatever this party is, he seems to be the boss of it.

Trying to speak as loudly and as clearly as I can over the Japanese boom-box music without sounding like a kindergarten teacher, I tell the guy, "I WANT TO SEE THE WOMAN—MUSUME, ONNA-NO-KO—WHO WORKS HERE, AT THE DESK."

"Too busy! You go 'way!" Just then a soft chime rings. One of the girls who was in the lineup with Sally this afternoon stands in the doorway that leads back to the cubicles. The man who was talking to me hurries over to her side and points authoritatively at the boom box, which goes silent as the microphone is brought to him.

"Moshi-moshiii!" he shouts into the microphone, waits until most of the talking stops, then fires out something else in rapid Japanese, pauses, then announces, "Mus-a-tang Va-ree ho-se-tess, *Kari-si-taru!"* It takes me a moment to remember that her actual working name is Crystal, which they have Japanicized to Kari-si-taru. Several of the men, holding some kind of blue index cards, rush forward and palaver in the doorway like stockbrokers until the boss takes the card from one of the men, who follows Crystal down the hall as the music comes back on again, and the two singers resume their harmonizing in midsong.

The man walks back toward me. "You talk to boss woman, okay?"

I start to say something, but he has already turned around and is pressing the buzzer on the desk over and over again.

Then the red-haired woman whom I talked to this afternoon walks in, looking at me with surprise.

"Mr. Schmidt!" she says. "What are *you* doing here?"

"I wanted to see Sally . . . Natalie." We are both raising our voices over the chattering laughter and the simple up-and-down pentatonic phrases of Japanese pop music.

"Didn't you see the sign on the gate?"

"No."

"It must have blown away. I'll put another one up. It said, 'Reserved for Private Party—West Coast Charters.' "

"I'm sorry, I didn't know."

"You should have *called,* honey. Mr. Tanaka—he caters these things out of L.A.—he has the whole place booked all night."

"Oh, really?" I say, sounding stupid again.

"You've had bad luck today, haven't you?"

"What do you mean?"

"First you thought this was a restaurant, and then you come back and the place is booked." The chime rings again, the voices go quiet. She looks at me and smiles. "We'll get it right one of these days, honey."

The music goes silent again. Sally appears in the doorway, in the same bright blue evening dress with the diamond-shaped holes up the side, and her hair shines in the light off the paneled walls. She holds her mouth in the same prim, self-contained expression that I saw on the face of the girl in the Cadillac, staring ahead, attentive but uninterested, not meeting anybody's eye, until she sees me, and her eyes go wide. Over the murmuring voices I can't hear what she says, but I can see her mouth form the words: "Dr. *Schmidt?*"

"Moshi-moshiiii!" the caterer chants into the boom-box microphone, says something rapid in his own language, and shouts, "Mus-a-tang Va-ree ho-se-tess, *Na-ta-ree!*" And again they crowd forward until I can't see her anymore.

"Maybe you'd better try the Silver Garter, honey," the red-haired woman says. "We won't be open to the public until tomorrow."

"Can you tell me," I say, lowering my voice and bending forward, the way people lower their voices when they talk about minorities if minorities are in the room, "what time . . . Natalie will be on duty tomorrow?"

"If she's here, she's on duty. But you'd better go now, honey. He's gonna yell at me for leaving the gate unlocked."

☆ ☆ ☆

I'm driving fast along the flat pavement toward Route 270, because I can still see that girl's prim face in the Cadillac, and I don't want to lose the feeling of this being the night of all nights. As soon as I get back to town I want to call up Sally's roommates Kristy and Samantha and have just as much fun as I would have had with Sally. More, maybe; I've never been with two girls at once. As a matter of fact, except for the occasional kiss on the breasts at the Petting Zoo, I haven't been with a woman since the divorce.

I slump back in the bucket seat, move my legs apart, and try to make myself imagine once again that the car is being pulled along

Edward Allen

by the string around my dick. It pulled me all the way out here to get embarrassed at a Japanese orgy; now it's pulling me all the way back, to an American orgy, I hope. My head throbs, not with pain so much as an overload of thoughts. My heart beats deeply; the area between my legs pulses with a chilly desire. All the way back along Silver Trail Road, I can see the red light of the Mustang pulsing in all three rearview mirrors.

Chapter 6

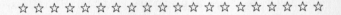

Sometimes I wish I were the kind of person who could have moral crises. I could sit in my rental car, agonizing with my head in my hands, about what to say to my friend Frank, and I could congratulate myself on the similarity between my own situation and the famous crisis in *Adventures of Huckleberry Finn*, with Huck's letter to Miss Watson—a scene that I always used to spend two whole class sessions talking about.

But one of the problems for me is that I'm reasonably sure that there is no overriding moral irony to my situation, no great truth that remains hidden from me, as it is hidden from Huck, no roomful of sophomores, or rather second-year students, applauding me when I tear up the letter to Frank Iverson and decide to go to hell and do the wrong thing, which everybody but me knows is really the right thing.

It's a dead issue anyway, as far as Samuel Clemens is concerned. I finally had to stop teaching that book last year after the administration ruled that minority students had the right to boycott any book whose language they found racially offensive.

I guess I even knew that whatever happened with Kristy and Samantha last night wouldn't make any difference, except maybe to interfere with my later performance. What did happen made me want to see Sally even more. As soon as I got back from Pancake Flats, I called the number that Kristy wrote in my notebook in her pretty green handwriting, and got their answering machine—a sexy, giggly recording with the two of them speaking alternate lines.

"We're sorry, we'd really like to talk to you." This was Kristy, I think.

"But we're busy all night tonight," said Samantha, lower, less breathy.

"Why not give us a call tomorrow," said Kristy.

"You'll be glad you did," said Samantha, and then in a kindergarten kind of singsong they both said in unison,

"Have a nice daaaay!" and giggled, and made kissing sounds with their lips. I was calling from the row of phones to the rear of the Stardust, by the rest rooms, using a pocketful of quarters from the slot machines. It was so cute I called four times.

After I called the girls and couldn't reach them, I had just enough time to catch the eleven-o'clock show at the Stardust, called "Incandescent!" It was weird to be searched going in, but the animal-rights activists in this town have made so many death threats against the operators of the parrot acts and the dog acts that the casinos don't want to take any chances.

As usual, the girls were beautiful, their eyes were painted, and their breasts were naked. For the eight-o'clock "family" show, they keep them covered. In the audience, a lovely young girl wandered, not tall enough to be a showgirl, carrying one of those old-fashioned cigarette trays electrified with a moving caravan of tiny bulbs, her body spangled in glowing cyalume bracelets with yellow chemical light shining from inside the soft plastic, wearing a tiara that flashed with electric light and twirling a light-generating yo-yo.

In one production number, the dancers appeared as dark silhouettes moving before a wall of white light. We took a trip through the back streets of Paris. Then, after the ventriloquist and his foul-mouthed dummy insulted each other for a few minutes, there was a scene that if the wrong people saw it they would be up in arms about how Racist and Sexist it was, those words that once you get hit with them you're off the lecture circuit for life.

It was an adventure, believe it or not, in African Ooga-Booga Land, though not in blackface, of course, the showgirls wearing those straw-fringed oval witch-doctor masks, jumping around with their spears and their straw shields, having captured the loveliest of the showgirls and tied her to a Styrofoam stake for a human sacrifice.

And the strangest thing is that she was not rescued, just writhed there in a foam-rubber device that closed around her body makeup like a nut cracker, very sexy I'm ashamed to admit (I have no future). She stood above a pile of straw with yellow lights flashing under it. Oval-masked natives waved their battery-powered torches, and odd-smelling powdery smoke began blowing out into the front row where I had slipped the maître d' ten dollars to seat me.

And that was it. No rescue, no Tarzan. No Ooga-Booga showgirls routed. The curtain closes on a human sacrifice, and then, when it opens again—Bobby Berosini's Orangutans.

☆ ☆ ☆

In the early afternoon, the sunlight up here on Route 270 is so bright against the chalky ground on both sides of the road that I almost wish I'd stopped somewhere and bought a pair of sunglasses. But I think that sunglasses are more appropriate for people who drive Camaros and do drugs.

So this is it; my hands tremble on the steering wheel. Or maybe one of the front tires needs to be balanced. In Indiana they would say it "needs balanced."

I love how being a little scared makes everything sharp, defined, like the sawtoothed ridge of hills, over in California, on the other side of the Pancake Valley, precise in the winter sunshine.

That's what was wrong with being married to Cath: everything was too safe, too familiar. Our bedroom on Verossika Lane began to feel like the same room we watched television in. Sometimes when she was asleep, and breathing in a deep bronchial rumble, I would lie awake and think about the nude-dancing bars along Route 60 by the Blue Grass Airport: the Baby Doll, the Petting Zoo, the Play Pen, Bubble's Hideaway—places where I'd already started going whenever I could think up an excuse to drive to Kentucky by myself.

Lying there beside her silent heat, I would think about the theory I had come up with—how sex was more a quality of light than a quality of flesh, something cold and off-balance flying around in the stomach on a summer night when one of the girls would sit outside the entrance to one of the white stucco buildings in an iridescent purple bra and panties, her skin flawless in the high-intensity floodlights.

But really, Cath wasn't that bad; and not being afraid had its good points. She never yelled at me when I woke her up by nibbling on her breasts, even though her friend Lynn from the Women's Studies department had written an article in the *Faculty Newsletter* advising any wife whose husband fondled her body when she was asleep to call the state police and charge him with spouse rape.

☆ ☆ ☆

"Entering Nye County," the sign says. As I drive down the last few miles of incline, I can almost feel the air lighten into something permissive, past the Desert Green Golf Club, past Caleb Cowles Realty in its little trailer close to the road, past a rainbow-colored billboard: JESUS IS LORD OVER PANCAKE FLATS. I wonder if they mean that on general principle or if it was put there specifically as a battle cry against the pretty girls down the road.

My mouth is dry, so I drive on past the Silver Trail turnoff, toward the center of town, such as it is, and stop for a can of soda at the Horrible Phelps convenience store. Inside, it's just a regular place, full of mothers and their kids, and some of those video poker machines that I have never gotten any good at playing.

I can't get over how normal everything looks, just a few miles from where Sally sits, probably watching television with the other girls, maybe filing her nails. Kids are getting ice cream on a stick. I wonder if the kids know what I'm doing there, if the mother can read it on my big face, or if she even cares, in Nye County, beautiful name, a name in which you can smell a prostitute's hair—a county full of regular little mommy-families with swings in the backyard, and crayon drawings on the refrigerator, in the secret village of Pancake Flats, where a man may touch a prostitute, where a man with a wallet full of hundred-dollar bills can come driving across the mountains in the Christmas season with visions of sugarplums dancing in his head.

Wonderful county, with its little secret. Driving out on the long road, past the turf farm and the alfalfa farm, I wonder how long it can last. In front of a double-wide trailer a teenage girl is jumping vigorously up and down, her head flopping from side to side. I can't tell if she's dancing, or if she's mentally defective, or if she's trying to shake water out of her ears.

In a county like this a father can push his kids on the swings a mile from the inn, and someday in the car, driving past the sign, they will ask, "What's a Mustang Inn?" and maybe he goes into some circumlocution about pretty girls who get paid to play with rich men; and the kids will wonder about it, and perhaps for years to come they will imagine a girl in a bikini and a man in a pinstripe suit sitting together in a sandbox, playing with Tonka trucks.

☆ ☆ ☆

"Hello, Mr. Schmidt, welcome back!" This is the same rangy red-haired lady who was here the other two times. Everything seems quiet, the Mustang parking lot is nearly empty, the same Spanish girl vacuums the front room.

"Just sit down, sir. The girls will be right out," the red-haired woman says.

"That's not necessary," I say. "I just want to see Sally. Natalie."

"It's rules, honey. We have to do the lineup." She presses the raspy bell; the girl shuts the vacuum cleaner off and trundles it out through the doorway. I sit down on the same tightly tufted pink couch. This room is becoming very familiar, with its pleated maroon curtains and imitation Louis the Fourteenth or Sixteenth or whatever kind of flouncy sofa.

Nobody's here yet. All I can hear is the vacuum cleaner starting up again, off in another room, with its long syllable, the oldest sound in the world. I used to be afraid of that sound, used to sit up on the couch at my grandmother's house with my legs folded under me when the maid would vacuum with her old brown Hoover, its one eye lit up like a cyclops. What a thing to be thinking about.

I get up and walk around, looking out the window. Outside, in the slanting afternoon light, my blue Sunbird sits, jacked forward rakishly, it seems, as if it's proud to be in this parking lot.

"Please sit down, sir," the madam says, and just then the door opens and the same crew of girls parades out, looking a little tired, and reciting: "Hi-I'm-Crystal," "Hi-I'm-Shantelle," "Hi-I'm-Natalie," "Hi-I'm-Rhonda," "Hi-I'm-Susie."

Back in her room she seems a little shy, not meeting my eyes. "So you came back," she says blankly. "I wasn't sure if you would or not."

"Yeah . . ."

"I saw you last night. Sorry you had to come out for nothing."

"That's okay. It was interesting."

She lets out a long hissing breath between her glossed lips. "God, I'm still tired."

"I guess that must have been a hard night."

"I can't complain. It's good money for those parties."

"What was that thing where they announce your name in front of everybody?"

She smiles for the first time. "They get turned on by that. Rituals. We call it the 'Honorable Tittie Ceremony.' They do that because it's the only way they can remember our names, so that way they can compare notes about us on the bus all the way back to L.A."

"That's weird."

"It really is," she says with a chuckle. "This whole business is weird. Half the guys I had last night didn't know a word of English, so the boss had to run from room to room translating. Every time one of the guys needs something translated, they open the door, with their pricks hanging out, and yell out at the top of their lungs, *TANAKA-SAN,'* like a banzai warrior, and he comes running in and they jabber at each other, and then he goes, 'Mr. Namaguchi would rike to know how much you expect payment for sit on face.' "

The room seems narrower than yesterday. I can still hear the sad old vacuum cleaner sound down the hall, and the *bunngg bunngg* of a super-low-frequency bass speaker reverberates through the wall. She's leaning back against the "No kissing" poem.

"So am I the first customer of the day?" I say.

"You are if you want to be."

"You don't sound very enthusiastic," I say.

"I'm just tired. I'll be enthusiastic if you want. Terri taught me how to do a really good orgasm."

"You don't have to do that."

Edward Allen

"I notice you haven't said 'uhhh' very much today. Do you still go 'uhhh' all the time in class?"

"What do you mean?"

She grins and looks at me from the side. "I used to count, when you were lecturing; one time you went 'uhhh' a hundred and fourteen times in a one-hour class."

"I didn't know I was that bad."

"Well, *I* might as well tell you, 'cause nobody else will. They're probably still making the 'uhhh' pool."

"What's the 'uhhh' pool?"

"You know, everybody puts in a dollar and whoever comes closest to guessing how many times you go 'uhhh' gets it all."

She sits down on the bed and motions me to sit beside her, patting the pink quilted comforter, the way people pat the place where they want a dog to sit. Her eyes seem a little red, but she looks great anyway, with a sort of iridescent gold shading around them, and her blond hair is brushed forward against her cheeks, flipping up slightly at the ends. I can smell the same citruslike fragrance of her hair. "Well, anyway, Dr. Schmidt . . ." She looks down at the floor, at the pink plush carpet.

"Please . . . call me Pack."

"That sounds so *weird*. But okay . . . Pack," and now she sounds like she's reading the words off a card. "What would you like to do, and how much do you want to spend?"

"I want to do what you told me about yesterday," I say, my voice getting soft and my stomach shaking. "The special."

"Oh, that's right," she says. "Well, here's the story. . . . Pack, I was kind of wrong what I said. There's a minimum that we can charge for an hour session. I asked Lana about it, and she goes, 'Sorry, two hundred and fifty minimum.' "

"What does that cover?"

"Anything, basically. Except no equipment, no extra girls, and no Socrates."

"Socrates?"

"You know, Greek. Up the ass. I don't do that."

"Neither do I."

She tells me to stand in front of the sink and to drop my pants. There's a special light, waist-high, that she turns on. She sits on a low stool and carefully examines me.

"Not much to examine, I guess," I say.

"Oh, I like it," she says, smiling. "I have much more muscular control with a little guy. So tell me, did Tracy Apple pass your class?"

"Yeah, she did all right. I think I gave her a B-minus."

"No way!"

"What do you mean?"

"You're a sucker, Dr. Schmidt. Pack. She copied her term paper from the *New York Times*. And she bragged about it. I can't *believe* you didn't catch her."

Sally presses the liquid soap dispenser beside the sink and begins to wash me, the soap slippery in her warm hands.

"Oh, I like this already," I say, and she looks up at me with the same mischief-making smile I used to love when she was in my class.

"I wish I'd copied *my* paper from the *Times*. I worked a whole forty minutes on that piece of shit."

"That long, huh?"

"You know what your nickname is at school, don't you?" she says.

"I don't know if I want to hear."

"I'll tell you if you won't be mad."

"I won't be mad at you."

"They call you 'Professor Pack-of-Shit.' "

"I've never heard that."

"They also call you Dr. Dirty Jokes."

"That one I *have* heard."

After she dries me off, she collects the money, for which I have to fumble in my dropped slacks, and she leaves the room, walking gently on top of her high heels, to log the money in.

"Make yourself completely comfortable," she says, "and don't get under the covers." Then she leaves.

I know that to get comfortable means to get completely naked. There's no hook to hang anything on, so I just lay my lucky jacket and my pants and shirt on the carpet, against the wall. Then I sit there naked on the pink bed, waiting. It's warm, my heart pounds, thinking of Sally on her way back to this little room. Looking down toward my feet, over the expanse of my stomach, I can see how much I've been eating on this vacation, stuffing myself at the buffet tables.

The remarkable thing is that for all the times I've been thinking about it, this will be my first time with a woman since Cath left. The closest I came to getting lucky was when I went to the Faculty/Staff Great Books Discussion Group, where I met a young lady named Laurie who was a computer operator in the library. We went out to dinner a few times, and I liked her and everything, but I was afraid to let things go too far. Lately there's been so much talk around that town about date rape that I was worried that if something did develop and if she had any regrets the next day, or the next week, I could wake up and find the state police standing over my bed. So until somebody comes up with a legally valid sexual consent form for people to sign, it seems better to stick with tittie dancers and not to risk anything on a friend except maybe dinner and a good-night handshake.

So it's been a long time. And even when I was still with Cath, our last months were pretty chilly. Poor Cath. She let herself go to hell much too early, let her skin and hair grow dull like one of those people who believe it's a crime against the planet to eat egg yolks. At thirty-five years old she let the peach-fuzz hair start growing wild from her chin and upper lip. The nights when she was in a good enough mood to do anything, I used to try to get myself excited by pretending she was one of the dancers at the Petting Zoo. I would think about Carol with the laser lights drawing frantic squiggles all over her skin, and how her nipples would always have a slightly bitter, soapy taste to them.

That's another thing that will be gone soon. I read in the *Indianapolis Star* just before I came out here that the attorney general of Kentucky has forced a law through, to go into effect midnight on New Year's Eve, that the dancers must maintain a distance of two feet between them and the patrons. Meaning no more lap-dancing, no more slipping a five-dollar tip into Carol's iridescent blue panties and sneaking my finger all the way down into the wetness between her legs.

It scares me sometimes, the way everything I love is more and more hemmed in every day, how everything is becoming smaller and smaller, like an island with the tide rising around it. I suppose the same water will rise into this room someday. I suppose even the state of Nevada will bow down someday as the black shoes come tromping on the unstable trailer floor, as the Latter Day Saints come marching in, all of them smiling, always smiling, like a happy pestilence of crickets flown in from the streets of Salt Lake Stupidity, happy as the church group in the town of Amherst whom I have heard chanting their slogans about family values in front of Keystone Video, or the committee, from the same church I think, that organized a campaign of threatening letters to get the Smurfs taken off the air, on the grounds that Papa Smurf practices black magic.

Sally takes a long time to get back. The electric heater hums and ticks along the floorboards, the light outside slants down over the bare courtyard. In the ceiling mirror I look like a big white blob.

The door opens, and there she is, still in her blue evening gown, with the diamond-shaped windows up the side.

"Okay, Dr. Schmidt. Ready for your fantasy?"

"Oh, Sally, I sure am!"

She stands there and quickly takes off her bright blue gown, and she is wearing nothing under it. There's no in-between; suddenly she's completely naked except for her high heels, no bra and panties to work off slowly the way the topless dancers do.

She moves closer to me, standing in that forward-shifted balance that looks so beautiful for reasons I don't understand. Some of my colleagues would say that the look is sexy because the shoes make her less mobile, thus less free, and that's what excites terrible people like me. Maybe they're right.

I'm looking at her smooth body moving toward me, all pink and silver, as Amy Lowell would say.

"I have to tell you I feel really weird about this," she says. "I've been here for six weeks, and this is the first time I've had stage fright."

"That's okay, Sally. I feel a little weird too."

Everything happens very slowly. Her nipples move close to my face, as soft and vulnerable as the nipples in the "Incandescent!" show last night. Like the turning of a baby bird's head, my mouth moves forward, and for a moment the softness of one of her nipples touches my lips. I can taste on my tongue the slight oily sharpness of whatever she has bathed in.

She pulls back. "We're not allowed to do that."

"Why not?"

"It's not safe."

"What can I do?"

"You can touch them, but you can't kiss them."

She sits down in front of me on the bed, leaning against me, and I hold her from behind, her small breasts cupped in my hands, my face buried in her hair.

"Oh, Sally." I'm kissing her on the neck, my face buried in her hair.

"This is really strange," she says.

Her floodlit warmth moves closer to me, the skin so soft I can hardly feel the friction as I move my hands along her body, along the curve of her side, and down to her legs, into the reddish hair between them.

"That's another rule. Can't do that either."

"You certainly have a lot of rules here."

"It's weird, isn't it?"

"You'd better show me what I'm allowed to do."

She looks at me, smiling, with a flicker of boredom perhaps, the way she used to look up in class when I tried to make jokes and nobody ever laughed, and then I would try to do what Johnny Carson does and make the class laugh at how badly I was dying up there. In the angular afternoon light coming in the trailer window, I can see the iridescence of the makeup around her eyes, perhaps formulated from pulverized fish scales, as I heard once in an ecological horror lecture that Cath took me to.

But I don't care. If that is what happens with pulverized fish scales, then I like pulverized fish scales: the way they bring some of the sea's own brightness into a trailer in the middle of the desert, traced softly around a prostitute's eyes.

She opens a little drawer next to the bed, tears the foil packet open, and unrolls the white condom onto me, with its strong latex dispensary smell, flicking her hand gently up and down to get me started. She looks me in the eyes, smiles, wiggles her shoulders so her breasts wave back and forth playfully, then whispers in my ear, "I'm gonna show you why I'm the best booker in the house."

In her mouth, the loose condom wrinkles and folds, making an irregular squilching sound against her moving lips. I'm breathing hard, watching her blond hair plunging up and down in my lap, resting my hand on the back of her hair, following her motion.

"Oh, Sally! Would you do me a favor?"

"What?" she mumbles with her mouth full.

103 ☆

Edward Allen

"Would you look up into my eyes like they do in the porno movies?"

She looks up at me, and it's the most beautiful sight in the world—except in porno movies the girl isn't usually sucking on a wrinkly white condom. The whites of her eyes seem luxuriously big as they look up into my eyes.

"How's that?" she says, and goes on pumping her blond hair up and down. There is something about eyes looking into each other that the people who make porno movies understand—a warmth, a friendship between faces, an electricity that becomes just as important as the graphic stuff. That's why those extreme close-up shots in the adult videos of somebody's huge dick pile-driving in and out of an anonymous cunt for five minutes have never done much for me, which even more than not being a lawyer disqualifies me from the Supreme Court. Usually it's not even the same people as in the rest of the movie.

I've gotten more or less out of the habit of renting those things anyway, now that Keystone Video has bowed to the demonstrators and closed their adult room, so now you have to drive all the way to Louisville, where they make out-of-state renters put down a thirty dollar deposit.

She keeps looking up into my eyes, her mouth going squilch-squilch-squilch on the wrinkly white rubber sheath, her face big-eyed and innocent like a little student at my feet waiting to receive the knowledge that I have made a living pretending to have been entrusted with.

I touch her smooth moving cheek with the backs of my fingers. She holds onto the base of what the writers would refer to as my "manhood," and her head nods up and down, a smirk visible at the upper part of each stroke before she plunges down into a blank full-mouthed stare. In the ceiling mirror I can see how trim she is, how evenly the tone of her untanned skin reflects the light, and what a gone-to-seed slob I've become.

104 ☆

"Oh, Sally, you're so pretty!"

"Mmm-hmmmm . . ." she says, making my back arch with the vibratory thrill.

"I'm so glad you were in my class. You're the most beautiful student I've ever had."

She stops then, flicking her hand up and down on the loose condom. "I paid to get into that class."

"Why?"

"Because you let everybody cheat. There are people who have preregistered for your classes five times, and then they charge fifty dollars to let someone take their place."

"They won't let you do that."

"They don't know. All they know is that Robin Maples dropped the class at one-thirty and Sally Iverson came into the English department computer room at one thirty-one. We even had our watches synchronized, like in a James Bond movie."

For a minute I see all those pleasant faces in the class ranged in front of me at eight o'clock in the morning—the silently dreaming athletes, the invisible faces behind the *Daily Arrow,* the girls in their broccoli bangs and their banana clips. I knew I had a reputation for easy grading, but I had no idea things had gone this far down. I am just sick about it.

"Ready for the next phase?" Sally says.

"Oh, yes." I feel the cool tickle as she rolls the condom off me, smudged around the middle with her pale pink lipstick. It catches a few hairs, and I say ouch. She gently unrolls another condom, this one greasy with lubricant, probably that spermicidal Monoxodil stuff that's supposed to be very safe.

And then my beautiful student is in my arms on the pink quilting of the unopened bed. Even through the greased condom she is remarkably warm, with just the right balance of tightness and looseness that caresses from all sides at once without squeezing. She looks into my eyes, amused, curious, maybe a little bored.

"Oh, Sally. You can cheat in my class anytime. I'm so glad I know you."

"Do you like fucking your favorite student?" she says, in a sort of baby-talk voice. "Does my cunt feel good?"

"It's wonderful."

"Do you like me?"

"I love you," and for that moment it's the right thing to say, and I mean it. "You know what I wish?"

"What?" she says.

"I wish you were my girlfriend."

"I'm your girlfriend right now."

We roll on the bed for a minute more, she looks off into the paneled walls, and soon the rhythm builds, and I'm grunting and breathing hard. If we were in a movie they would bring in two people at this point with more stamina and let them slam face-lessly against each other for a few minutes, then cut back to full body shots of us at the end. What is most remarkable about the whole thing for me is the length of that treasured interval between the moment of inevitablity and the moment of release.

"Oh shit," she says after I stop moving. "I forgot to do an orgasm. I wanted to show you that."

She washes me again, gently, and cleans herself between the legs with a washcloth. It's only been a little more than half an hour, so I have plenty of time if I want it. The problem is that once is my limit these days. Sometimes it's more than my limit.

Sally sits at her table, touching up her foundation with a small sponge.

"Sally, that was so nice," I say, sitting down on the slightly mussed comforter, with my back leaning against the wall and my feet sticking out over the edge of the bed. "I know it's a really strange situation, but . . . I'm really glad we got together."

"Well, good, Pack," she says, a bit distractedly. "I'm glad I made you feel good."

She sits down, her back leaning against me. We're both still naked, though she has stepped back into her shoes. "So what's it like?" I say. "Do you like it here?"

"It's okay," she says. "I guess. Mostly it's just boring. It's kind of like getting paid to be in jail. We have to stay on the premises for three weeks and then we get one week off. That's tomorrow, I can't wait, I'm going off shift. That's why I'm so tired. And there's so many rules. You can even get fired for talking about Harold."

"Who's Harold?"

"He's the ghost. Some old guy who died of a heart attack with one of the girls here, supposedly. They say he died before he could come, so he's haunting the place, trying to get off."

"That's funny."

"Lana doesn't think so. Some girls actually quit because they were so afraid of Harold. If she catches you talking about him you can get fired."

"Do you get a lot of creeps?"

"They're not too bad. Some of them are cheap, though. Not like the guys I used to get doing parties in Vegas. That's where you make the money. I was going to do that for six months, and have my whole college fund paid for."

"Wasn't your father paying?"

"He was, but I just couldn't go along with it. I love him, but he doesn't know how to let up on people. He actually made out these Xeroxed forms for me to fill in, about my progress. That's why I quit."

"I still think you should call him. I know he wants you to come home for Christmas."

"Maybe I will," she says, getting up. "I've got the tickets he sent me. But I'm not going back to school until I have my own fund. I can't quit this now. I had to wait thirty days for my license here, and before that I had to wait thirty days before I could even apply, because I got arrested."

"What for?"

"What do you think?" she says with a grin. "I robbed Fort Knox?" She pulls her gown over her head and then starts brushing her hair in the mirror. I start picking my own clothes up from the deep-pile carpet.

"The escort service sent me and this other girl to Caesars, to this guy who's supposed to be some rich Arab from L.A—I don't know if he was supposed to be an oil shah or some big terrorist or what. Everything's going great, and we all agree on the money and start stripping down for him, and then, *Whala;* 'Abdul' breaks into a Brooklyn accent and goes, 'You're both under arrest,' and the door from the other room opens and about a dozen cops from the pussy posse come in.

"It was really a *mare.* They kept me in the waiting room until four o'clock in the morning, and then they let me go with a warning and said they'd put me in jail next time. So anyway, for a long story short, I said the hell with this—if I'm going to do it, I might as well do it legally and not worry about this shit."

"Well, if you ever get sick of this business and you want to quit, you can come and stay with me, 'cause I think you're really nice."

"Are you a fall-in-love?" she says, with the same mischievous grin.

"What's that?"

"It's the same as a Romeo. It's a customer who falls in love with one of the girls. Lana encourages us to cultivate them and to be real nice to them, because they come back again and again. I've only been here for two shifts, and I already have this guy in Oregon, he's been sending me a dozen roses from Teleflora every week."

"I don't know, maybe I am a fall-in-love. You probably think it's a little pathetic."

"I think it's cute." She cuddles against me, warm through the rayon of her gown. "But anyway, you'd better go."

I give her a book of Westward Ho matches, with the phone number on it. "Call me tomorrow if you want. I'd really like to take you out to dinner. At a real restaurant."

"Sure, okay . . . Pack. Maybe so."

"Oh, Sally, you're so sweet." I'm holding her next to me, and even through the rayon dress I can feel the softness of her skin. "I want to give you such a big kiss."

"No kissing."

Chapter 7

It was the first time in twelve months that I've ejaculated in the presence of another vertebrate. Wonderful how such a plain fact makes things look different all the way back to your motel: the black seismogram of hills backlit by the diffuse light of the city beyond them, the ghost shapes of Joshua trees passing in the Sunbird's headlights, and then the bright basin of Las Vegas as it comes into view on the other side of Coyote Summit.

Even the show I went to that night seemed prettier, as if the faces were smiling directly at me. It was called "Bravissimo!" and it attempted to tell the history of the world—topless—in a series of connected musical numbers: starting with dancing cave people, then the Pyramids, the fall of Rome, the Black Plague, the New World, and happy times on the riverboats. To the whistled tune of "It's a Long Way to Tipperary," quarter-sized Fokkers and Sopwith Camels buzzed and circled above our cocktails.

They even reenacted the story of the *Hindenburg*, except the model they used had no swastikas on its tail fins. It began with a production number on the suspended gondola, people swinging their ornate beer steins in time to the aircraft's rolling, some dancers dressed as distinguished gentlemen, in homburgs and monocles, shots of cloud and ocean projected on the rear scrim. Then night, lightning, as the prerecorded French horns of a large floating object blended with harps and trumpets, and a faraway voice reported the stately mooring process: "And there she is, folks, gracefully approaching the mooring tower . . ."

Suddenly real fire bursts from a nozzle in the tail, the music breaks into frantic distorted guitar riffs, the famous voice, at first almost expressionless: ". . . it burst into flames . . ." and then as his shock rises and he shouts and sobs about the humanity and all the passengers, the showgirls dash across the stage with paper hoses.

I thought about Sally all night, and I was still thinking about her when I got back from the sausage-and-eggs buffet and the phone rang. I was afraid it would be Frank with a million questions, but it was her. She said the Mustang limo was going to let her off downtown that night and that she needed me to take her to the airport.

Amazing. I never thought she'd actually take me up on it. Just to think of somebody that pretty calling me up at my own motel, even if it's only for a ride to the airport, makes me feel as cool as the people I look down on, as suave as some guy with designer stubble and a black silk jacket sitting behind the wheel of a car in which not even the license plate is made in America.

And why me I don't know. I'm sure she knows plenty of guys with real Japanese cars and real designer stubble. Maybe she's flattered that I didn't give her the "you've got to get out of this business" talk. Maybe she needs help with her comma splices, though in this town it's not a priority. Even room-service menus contain terrible spelling errors. I would hardly even be surprised around here to find dangling participles in the Gideon Bible.

☆ ☆ ☆

From the bar I can see her walking with her luggage, past the velvet-roped cordons in front of the Union Plaza check-in counters, where clerks stand alone at this slow hour, or look down at their paperwork. Suddenly she looks like a student again, just the way she used to in my class, as she moves down a long corridor between two rows of dollar slot machines.

She's wearing jeans blanched to a bonish pale with sort of spiderwebby patterns that the bleach or the acid has left in the denim, and above it one of those quilted patchwork jackets of rabbit fur. I wasn't sure before if she had one of those or not, because I always got her mixed up with all the other girls in class who drove me crazy on class mornings.

The back half of her hair is pulled back the way she used to do it in school, puffed out behind a long vertical clip. Not a hooker anymore, not a Mustang girl, just a nice girl who accidentally happens to be beautiful and it's no big deal—a nice girl with a nice blue-and-white garment bag strapped over her shoulder and a matching blue-and-white carry-on-size bag in her hand, walking through a crowd of the uneducated to meet a man who those people not too absorbed in their machines might think is her father.

Maybe we even look like father and daughter, she with her generous nose that somehow does not take a thing away from the sculpted sexiness of her face, and me half bald, all the bulk that has been lost from my hair having collapsed down into the space beneath my own nose, becoming a food sponge of a mustache, now with little extra bristles coming out of it here and there because I forgot my trimmer.

Only fathers don't kiss their daughters on the lips—not in my family, at least. It is strange to imagine at this moment what Frank would think if he could see this all-around nice guy and dependable racquetball friend kissing his daughter on the lips, with just a discreet mutual application of tongue—and all these fat guys with cigarettes standing around watching in their pink-and-blue ski jackets.

We walk down a long aisle between rows of horizontal tabletop poker machines that play "Happy Days Are Here Again" every time someone gets jacks or better. The players move their hands so quickly as they poke the betting buttons that they look like secretaries at their typewriters. Two old ladies in this row have their own portable oxygen bottles with clear plastic tubes taped under their noses.

These poker machine players are the hard cases. I heard a psychiatrist say on the local news last night that ninety percent of the compulsive gamblers in this town are addicted to video poker.

Sally holds my arm as we go out past the last of the crap tables, not very busy, only a few dispirited shooters clumped around them, through the faraway musical wash of the machines spitting out quarters, out through the front doors and into the space under the marquee, the underside of which is lined with thousands of blinking light bulbs.

I was all ready to run her down to McCarran right now, but it turns out that her flight isn't until tomorrow. "I would have stayed with Kristy and Sam," she says, "but they're already out of town for Christmas. And you were so nice to me yesterday that I was hoping you might have room to put me up."

She kisses me on the cheek right there in front of all the taxis. It occurs to me that this is the first time in two years that anybody has kissed me for any reason other than politeness or profit.

☆ ☆ ☆

On Fremont Street it's broad daylight, as usual. They always say you could read a newspaper in this light, but they never say why anyone would want to. Every surface that faces the street is lit, even the front window of McDonald's, and the golden arches fill with the same white froth of bulbs that you see inside the outlines of the letters in the Sahara sign down on the Strip. Everything flashes and twinkles, making people's faces turn different colors in the light.

I would have parked in the Union Plaza parking lot, but one of the things I believe very strongly about downtown is that it is very bad luck to park in the same place you are playing; and for myself I believe moreover that even if you aren't playing and are only there to pick up somebody at the bus station, it is particularly good luck to park at the Four Queens, because one night last year on a previous visit I had a good night in Binion's while parked at the Four Queens.

The lights have a different quality here in the middle of downtown. To the south, on the Strip, the individual signs are more impressive, more kinetic, standing alone in the dark: the Stardust, and the Frontier, and the Dunes, all going through their complicated sequence of darkening, filling up, changing colors, agitating, flashing, frothing, going dark again. Here on Fremont Street, in the section the tourist magazines call Glitter Gulch, the individual signs are less elegant—just whites and colors and a quick twinkly oscillation to their goings on and goings off; but there are so many of them, packing so many tubes and bulbs so close together, that the cumulative effect is that of a town in which every vertical surface has been patched and sheeted with its own color and motion of light.

You could walk up and down this street for a year and you'd always find so many lights to look at that you would never notice how ugly everybody walking along the street is. And even if you did notice, it wouldn't be more than a few seconds before your eyes were drawn back to the light, frothing and flashing, even in the pawnshops and the T-shirt shops and the place where they advertise Ray-Ban sunglasses for $39.95, and the liquor stores where the half-pint bottles are gathered on stacks behind the cash register—light everywhere, from the pitchforky red letters of the Union Plaza at the west end of Fremont Street, with caravans of light seeming to pour out from the sides and the bottom of the sign, to the yellow tubing of the Golden Nugget, to the staticky crownlike structures at the corner of the Four Queens.

We walk past the old Golden Gate Casino, where I used to go for the quarter crap game, moving against the one-way Fremont Street traffic, past the Pioneer, with its famous cowboy, Vegas Vic, outlined in red and yellow and blue tubes of what most people call neon—although I don't think it's actually neon gas in there. I think neon produces only red light, like the old "Eat at Joe's" signs you see in Warner Brothers cartoons whenever anybody gets shocked by an electric eel.

"Howdy, pardner," he says from a speaker, barely audible over the traffic, "welcome to downtown Las Vegas!" Years ago he used to boom out "HOWDY PARDNER!" so loud that he drove everybody crazy, so his voice was silenced, and now they've just started experimenting with turning it back on.

Vegas Vic has been having trouble lately with the machinery in his elbow, so tonight his arm does not wave, as it is supposed to, but his face still winks and unwinks, and the glowing cigarette twitches up and down in his mouth. I wouldn't be surprised if they soon extinguished his cigarette, the way they got Surgeon General Koop to confiscate Mr. Potato Head's pipe.

That's the only kind of cigarette they're likely to get rid of around here—the kind that doesn't make any smoke. The real cigarettes, the ones I have to breathe the smoke from, will never disappear, except from the Silver City Casino, where I don't dare to play anymore because I always lose. Nevada has the highest rate of cigarette smoking in the country. You'll never find a non-smoking section in any casino restaurant, any more than you will in a truck stop, only a few no-smoking two-dollar blackjack tables, which are no good because the worst players always play there, including the occasional hose-nose, the oxygen bottle taking up an extra seat; and they do things like stand with fifteen against the dealer's king, which screws up the rest of the deck for the decent players—plus, it's just bad in principle. The more you hate smoke, the better luck you're going to have breathing it.

Sally hangs on to my non-luggage hand, like a little girl, like a daughter, even though she's really somebody else's daughter and maybe a neutral observer would say I'm treating them both like shit. Maybe it's true.

I wish she had never seen this town before, so I could show her around, and watch her eyes pop open when we turn the corner from the Strip onto Fremont and look down that tunnel of reds and blues and whites where you have to be very careful or you will not be able to see the traffic lights.

Across the street, the slot joints have their door partitions open so you can walk in and out of their bright and clanging interiors as if in a penny arcade on the Atlantic City boardwalk. The fluorescent cowgirl over Kate's Corral sits, with her legs crossed, on a sign that shimmers like those surfaces of windblown disks you used to see on billboards. She grins and jiggles her blue-booted calf up and down. Unlike Vegas Vic, of whom her own shape is unashamedly derivative, she does not smoke.

Next to Kate's, a place called Sassy Sally's flashes and bustles, a sign above the main entranceway reading "Double Jackpot Every 15 Minutes" and the white numerals of a digital clock counting down the minutes—now zero, and a red light pulses like an old-time ambulance, and everything gets brighter, like the pinball machine back in the Wolverton Student Center at College Park when we hit enough of the trip-wire sensors to make everything go into the 500 When Lit mode.

Voices are singing from Sassy Sally's loudspeakers out into the street, to the tune of "Abba Dabba Dabba Said the Monkey to the Chimp":

Double-double-double-double-double-double-double-double
Jackpot time is here!
Double-double-double-double-double-double-double-double
Payoffs will appear!

As we walk past Slot Paradise, on this side of the street, a girl, not very pretty, in an apron with hundreds of dollar bills trapped beneath a layer of plastic, tries to hand us coupons in the form of two-foot-long dollar bills.

I'd forgotten how nice it is to walk down the street next to a pretty girl. The world shapes up differently, and the dent you make in the sheet metal of the universe fills in behind you as gently as the way the ocean closes in behind the stern of the presidential yacht.

The last year with Cath didn't qualify as pretty-girl territory. But now, what a thrill to give that slightly dumpy coupon girl the polite brush-off, to smile and tell her without saying anything: I am Professor Pack Schmidt with an off-duty prostitute on my arm and more money in my wallet than I came to town with, more money than you're wearing under the clear plastic of your shill uniform, and I don't need coupons, and I don't need a souvenir key chain, or half price on your shrimp cocktail with jumbo shrimp the size of maggots, because I am a man staying in a motel room with clean sheets, and not some poor quarter-crap-table casualty wandering around full of my own problems in the vicinity of the bus terminal.

That's one of the things about downtown that makes it immediately different from the Strip: for all its flash and prime rib, downtown is very much within smelling distance of the wrong side of the tracks. Just a few blocks south of Fremont, the bottom-of-the-barrel motels line the streets: the Blue Star, with the O missing from "Motel." The Brittany, the Cactus Rest, Howard's, the Scotsman, all occupied by big old cars resting low on their tired frames and doors that don't match their quarter panels, parked in the horseshoe-shaped courtyard—big, low, dirty drug cars. Half the time when you drive by there's a Metro cop with his lights flashing in front of one of the motels, for a dope complaint or the ever-present domestic violence call.

Streetwalkers, all rotten teeth and bony elbows, wobble out onto the sidewalk to flag a car, then hurry back into the cars or into their motels, whenever they think the cops might be coming. They are particularly wary because some of them have already tested positive for AIDS, which makes it a felony if they get arrested again.

Although all forms of prostitution are illegal in Clark County, Metro more or less leaves the ugly ones alone, unless they block traffic. It's the pretty girls they're trying to stop. You get a few blocks off Fremont and all these sad cases, too poor even to afford wigs or dental work, are blowing guys in cars all over the place—girls in skirts that don't fit, their bodies emaciated. When people talk about jumping somebody's bones, with those sad cases that's about all there is *to* jump.

Adjacent to the motels, under the tall thin-windowed form of the Clark County Detention Center, the bail bond offices line the streets. E-Z Bail Bonds. Jail Busters Bail Bonds—Get out of Jail Quick. Honest Bob's window says, "I'll get you out of jail if it takes a hundred years!" Cartoon pictures of guys in prison stripes holding on to those vertical bars, or a bird in a hanging cage, or a parrot in stripes flying from a sprung door. A few blocks off Fremont you realize that it's a city like any other city, not just an amusement park, but a real town, kids driving around with no insurance and shooting each other to death over a dollar's worth of crack.

☆ ☆ ☆

Just as we cross to the corner of the Golden Nugget, a police car pulls to a stop on the street, and a cop shouts over at us,

"Heyyyy, Sally!" with such bounding warmth that for a minute I wonder if maybe he's some long-lost friend of hers from back home in Indiana.

"Hey, Sally!" he says. "Come on over and visit with me." He's a young black guy, in his early twenties he looks like, with very precise features. He's sitting in the patrol car by himself. Everything he says has a twinkle to it, as if there is some very funny joke underlying the whole conversation.

"Wait here," she says to me, and walks over to the patrol car.

"No, Sally, your friend too! I wanna meet your friend," and he beckons me over, like someone trying to get a timid cat to come to a bowl of milk, so I trundle over, carrying the bags, my face starting to get red.

"Have I got your name right, Sally?" he says with an inquisitive smile. She nods.

"What was that last name again?" Friendly. He sounds more like someone in a singles bar than a cop hassling a girl for what I imagine this must be about. He has the delicate face of a lounge singer. The only thing that spoils it is that his cheeks are covered in a nubbly texture of those razor bumps that some black guys get.

"When was it that we picked you up, Sally? Was it September?" She nods.

"And now you're *working* again," he says, with an exaggerated sadness, almost whining.

"I'm not working," she says very softly.

"Okayyyy . . ." he says. "Maybe I'm prepared to believe that. During an eclipse. So this must be your dad. Right? Mr. Iverson, I presume," He reaches out the window of the patrol car to shake hands, his eyes twinkling, his tan uniform crisp inside the black-and-white, his badge twinkling Christmasy against the yellow bulbs of the Golden Nugget.

"He's a friend of the family," Sally says. All along the sidewalk the uglies and the Oriental tourists are staring at us as they pass. A few have stopped, waiting to see us get hauled in, I suppose.

"Ah yes!" the cop says, smiling even wider now. "The old friend of the family."

"Lonnie, I'm not working," Sally says. "And you're just hassling me."

"What are you doing for a living?"

She straightens up a little and says in a very small voice, as if she's reading from a card, "I'm a registered hostess in Nye County, license number AB-60492. I'm on my way home for Christmas."

"Let me see your sheriff's card," he says. She rummages in her purse and then hands the sherrif's card to him, a plastic-encased rectangle about twice the size of a driver's license.

"So you've gone legitimate, huh? No little jobs on the side with . . . friends of the family?"

"No," she says. "I wouldn't risk my license. And anyway, you shouldn't be hassling me." She starts smiling again. "You're just afraid of the Crips. If you guys weren't so scared of the Crips you'd be busting heads up north and you'd leave me alone."

"Sally, Sally, Sally," he says, letting out a sigh. "Don't you worry about the Crippies. We'll take care of the Crippies. You just take care of keeping your own self out of trouble, okay?"

He looks over at me, his eyes still twinkling. "Let me talk to you for a minute . . . mister friend of the family." I walk over close to the car window.

He takes my driver's license, looks it over, and starts chuckling in low, conspiratorial tones, as if he's about to tell a very off-color joke. I guess what scares me about him is that he's so young. Lately I've been having trouble getting along with people younger than me: eighteen-year-old bank tellers scowling behind clip-on ties, the Amherst security guards young enough to be my own son if I'd ever had one, even the checkers in Mr. Dollarsaver when they give me dirty looks for putting the Doritos on the conveyor belt first and leaving the canned food for last.

"What do you do for a living . . . Packard?"

"I'm an associate professor of composition and technical writing at Amherst University of Indiana. And I'm also faculty adviser to the campus chapter of the Crips."

"What is all this *Crips* stuff?" he says, raising his voice for the first time.

"Just a joke. I'm sorry." I didn't want to make a dumb joke like that. But they just come out sometimes, the way they used to come out of my mouth in class, in the days before I learned to watch myself.

"Well, Packard, I'm required under the circumstances to ask you a few questions."

"Okay."

"Are you a registered ex-felon?"

"I'm a registered Republican. Is that close enough?"

He laughs and says, "Now that's funny, Packard, but it doesn't get us anywhere. You see, they have this rule: I'm supposed to ask the question, and you're supposed to answer it. Okay?"

"Okay."

"Are you an ex-felon?"

"No."

"Are you aware that it's a misdemeanor in Clark County to patronize a prostitute?"

"I'm not patronizing a prostitute."

"Now there you go again—not answering the question," he says, then, smiling, "You sound like you're running for the Supreme Court. All I'm asking you is are you *aware?*"

"I guess I am now."

The guy is still smiling, but I can see that if you look into his face long enough the twinkle of humor disappears, leaving underneath a little man who is slightly too proud about making it out of the ghetto for his own good. Not that I would have wished for him to stay down, with his poor mother and all his half brothers on welfare. I suppose it's an appropriate revenge, after all the history of slavery and rape and low-tech lynchings, that black authority figures should now be hired to help supervise the private lives of white women.

More people are standing around now, younger ones mostly, imagining they smell blood, and neatly dressed Japanese tourists keeping up a soft commentary in their graceful language.

The smiling cop has one more question, and I guess I'd better answer this one straight: "Do you have any warrants, subpoenas, or outstanding traffic tickets against you?"

"Not that I know of." Even that was probably too vague, because Lonnie holds on to my driver's license and asks for my university ID—blue for tenure, I explain.

"We're just gonna run a little check, *Pack*ard." The guy keeps hammering down on my first name as if it's the most freakish name in the world. Maybe it is a silly name, but I'm glad I'm not called Lonnie.

"If it comes back with no felony record and no outstanding warrants, I'll say good night," he says.

Something beeps inside the patrol car. The cop gets out for the first time, hands me back my license and my faculty ID.

"Okay, Sally," he says. "You can go, but watch yourself. You know the rules. Maybe he doesn't, but you do."

"You shouldn't have stopped us, Lonnie," she says. "You stopped us for nothing."

"Whaddya want, girl? It's a slow night. You be careful now," he says with a broad grin as he powers the window up.

Suddenly Sally shouts at him.

"Hey, Lonnie, *look!*" And she presses herself against me, shimmying her breasts against my camel's-hair jacket, and wiggling a long tongue in the vicinity of my ear. The moment she puts her tongue and her breasts against me like that, about a dozen Japanese flashbulbs go off, from all directions, some shutterbugs even crouching professionally on the sidewalk. Lonnie just looks down at his dashboard, waves, and pulls back into traffic.

☆ ☆ ☆

After we're back in the car, passing through the dark neighborhoods of bail bondsmen and '78 Oldsmobiles, I ask her why she made a scene like that on the street.

"I don't know. I just wanted to tease him. Fuckin' pussy cops. If it weren't for them I could be making three times as much as I am now. And I wouldn't have to live like some kid in military school."

"Is it strict over there?"

"Herb and Lana are okay, but the county rules are crazy. We're not supposed to leave the premises more than once a week. And then when we do, we're not allowed to go into any bar or casino or theater in Nye County. The only place we can even go to play a poker machine is in RK's Supermarket, and then people stare at us. It's not something you'd want to do for more than a few months."

"And then what?"

"Then I'll go back to school. But I can't let Daddy support me. He's got this problem about supervising everybody else's life. He should have been a pussy cop."

"That's a mean remark," I say, but then I shut up when it occurs to me that I've paid for sex with the guy's daughter. I can still feel the tingle on the skin of my face from being stared at by Japanese newlyweds. It should have gone away by now, but getting yelled at by someone ten years younger than me takes longer and longer to get over every time it happens.

That's a feeling that goes back a few years, specifically to the day I almost lost my job on charges of sexual harassment. I've never been able to look at young people in the same way. It wouldn't have been so bad if the students from the Community Fairness Committee had brought some administration with them, or the department chair, who used to be my friend, or even security—but what made it bad was that it was only students, all of them very polite, crowding into my office, where I did not have enough chairs for them.

What they were there to talk about was contained in the letter, a copy of which had already gone to the ombudsperson: the charge being that I had told a joke in class so dirty and so offensive that it constituted sexual harassment. So there was nobody upon whose authority I could rest, or protect myself behind, just students, appearing in the mandated balance of race and gender: one white male, one black male, one white female, one black female, and as a representative catchall for everybody else, one Korean guy who did not say a word.

It occurs to me that I probably should list the blacks first, or the females first, in describing the composition of the Community Fairness delegation. However, of those two options, I don't know which one would be preferable.

It was a stupid joke to tell, on that rainy and hopeless morning when I hadn't done my homework, I admit that—about the woman who asks a guy on the bus to give her his seat because she's pregnant, and when he asks how long she's been pregnant she looks at her watch and says, "About forty-five minutes."

But if the people in the administration who responded to the complaint could have seen that class, they would have realized that it was a desperate situation. If I had thought it would do anything to liven that class up, I would have been willing to drop my pants and take a shit on the desk.

And it turned out that the person who complained was a guy. I guess he wanted to show everybody how sensitive he was to women's issues. He was so sensitive that I had to spend eight hundred dollars on a lawyer from Indianapolis who did nothing. I finally had to eat crow in the student newspaper, the *Daily Arrow*, paying for the space at that, with a letter I know by heart:

Dear Students and Community Members:
Last month a regrettable incident occurred in my 301 class. In an
ill-advised attempt to inject some levity into the class, I recounted
a joke that I now realize was both vulgar and sexually discrimina-
tory. I would like to thank the concerned students who apprised me
of the offensiveness of this joke; and I would like to state my firm
committment never again to let my humorous impulses express
themselves in a way that other community members find offensive.
Free speech is important; humor, I think, is important—but the
Amherst ideal of community must come first. Let me say again that
I am truly sorry for my offensive outburst.

Sincerely,
Professor Packard Schmidt

There is something very strange, I want to tell you, about being
confronted by young authority figures in one's own office. Everything gets serious, concentrated, shrunk down to a period of a few
minutes, the way the diffusion of sunlight is shrunk down by a
magnifying glass to one burning point in which my face gets red
and my mouth goes dry and I notice my water glass is empty. I
know that in a situation like that it would be rude, or even provoc-
ative, to ask if I could go out to the water fountain.

☆ ☆ ☆

It's early, and we're both getting hungry. All the nice
casino restaurants are listed in the tourist handout, some of them
so fancy that they don't even have a keno board on the wall. We
just have to stop at my room, so I can change my clothes. Casino
Center Boulevard runs into the upper part of the Strip in a sharp
angle just above Bobby Stupak's, and I drive down to the cascad-
ing electric mushrooms of the Westward Ho and back into the
barracks-camp darkness among the speed bumps—and all this
without a single flashbulb going off in our faces.

Chapter 8

After we get back to the room from dinner, Sally wants to hit a few tables, but I'm a little nervous about churning what I've won back into the casino bankroll.

"That's okay," she says. "We can play with this," and she pulls two hundred-dollar bills out of her purse.

"No, we can't," I say. "Don't you know a gentleman never lets a lady gamble with her own money?"

"This is just crazy money, Pack. My regular money I can't draw out until the first of the year. I made this on the way over here."

"Doing what?"

She's holding the two bills with extreme delicacy, waving them back and forth like silk handkerchiefs, smiling, almost a bit shy now as she looks back and forth, from the money, to me, to the mirror in which she already knows she looks great. Her voice as she answers this question is small over the forced air and the general back-of-the-Strip hum, a little embarrassed, but not in the least ashamed, as if it had to be done for the good of the country and nobody else in the platoon had the guts to do it.

"I blew two Japs in the limo."

"Sally!" I say, as if I had a right to be shocked. "I'm shocked."

"Don't worry," she says. "I cheeked both of them."

"What does that mean?" I say.

She looks away from me as she talks, out the window, through the gap in the pleated drapes that cover the whole south end of the room, but there's none of that depressed sound in her voice that you hear when people talk about their weird sex lives on Sally Jessy Raphael.

"It means that we put the rubber in our cheek, and then when we go down on the guy we just fit it over him with our mouth, and in the dark they think they're getting it bare. One of the great technological advances of the nineties."

She tucks the two bills into a pocket on the inside of her woven straw pocketbook.

"Then after he comes we sort of drool and make a lot of spit, and he thinks he gave us a mouthful of come. And when we spit it out the window, the rubber goes too. You can see them on the road if you look. So are you thoroughly disgusted now?"

"No. I'm interested. I'd like you to give me a demonstration."

"That's why I came over in the limo instead of asking you to pick me up," she says. "I knew I'd get a couple of Cadillac dates. Something about being in that car, in the dark, up in the mountains—it does something to people."

"Well, at least I'm glad you're being careful."

"You have to, anymore. Even if you're working under the table you have to. I can't kiss anybody I don't know, and I wouldn't fuck anybody bare. Not even a Jap, and they're clean people. Not even you."

"What do you mean?"

"Especially not you," she says, looking up and grinning again like a student who has gotten away with cheating on her term paper.

"Why not?"

"Because you go to tittie bars. You can catch anything there."

"Who says I go to tittie bars?"

"Everybody in school. They've seen you. Some Kappa Sigs I used to know were in the Petting Zoo one night and they said you were drunk, and you were up at the edge of the stage, and putting five-dollar bills in your mouth, and the tittie dancers were picking the bills up in their cunts. They all know, Pack."

"Bullshit. How could they see in the dark that it was a five-dollar bill?"

"Because they know that the girls won't do that for a one, that's how."

"I'm glad to know I have so much privacy around that school."

"That's why they turned you in for telling dirty jokes that time," she says. "Alan Barrish and his crowd found about it, and they said they were going to teach you a lesson. Because you taught that Intro to Lit class without including a single black writer. So they got that guy in your class to watch out for anything you said wrong."

During this conversation our mouths have begun once again to turn in the direction of each other—a tentative motion, with a palsy of indirection to it, like those shaky time-lapse pictures of plants following the light.

"They taught me a lot of lessons." Inches now. "But I can't remember any of them."

☆ ☆ ☆

After dinner we walk up the Strip, toward the towering clown in front of Circus Circus, who holds an illuminated pin-wheel in his hand that seems to spin by means of a dark sector that goes round and round. His name is Lucky, and his brain-damaged grin has always reminded me a bit of the faces of the gaping little bears in the old Bear Wheel Alignment signs at gas stations which you don't see anymore. Toward the back of the hotel, which we can see down the side of the huge main building, the pilotless monorail car glides above the bars of light, toward one of the back towers.

"Want to go in here?" I say, turning toward that huge casino shape, with the white lights lining the underside of the marquee. "Maybe it's late enough that the screaming babies have gone to sleep."

"I'd better not," she says. "They have something called a 'family values' policy. Just like what they have at the Ex and the Remo and Bobby Sleazebag's and all the new places. No registered hostesses. If they spotted me I could lose my license."

"Why do they care? If you're not working."

"Because anything sexy is going to drive away the slot players," she says. "The slot players make so much money for the hotels that the hotels bend over backward for them. So the real gamblers get fucked. Plus, now the casino has to report anybody who cashes in more than ten thousand dollars. The real shooters go to the Cayman Islands anymore."

"That's depressing," I say.

"It's terrible. In ten years there won't be a live game in this town—just slots. Slots and Tots. And oxygen tanks. You might as well be in Laughlin." She pronounces the name of Nevada's senior citizen boomtown with a twist of contempt that must indicate a long-running joke.

"That's why the Circus and the Ex never have tittie shows," she goes on. "Slot players are either newlyweds with screaming kids, or else they're *old*—and old people and newlyweds are the two kinds of people that can't stand having pretty girls around."

"They must really hate your guts."

"Well, *thank you!*" she says, slipping for just a moment out of the blasé hooker mode and into the small-town-girl cuteness that she grew up with. I can even hear a distant Appalachian echo of her long-gone south Indiana accent.

Now that I think about the last time I was in Circus Circus, I realize she's right—that between the geriatrics and the couples too young and too uneducated to afford baby-sitters, there's no room for anyone in the middle. You can walk in there at four in the morning and the slot zombies are still dragging their poor toddlers from machine to machine, and the kids scream, or slobber, or they get agitated with fatigue the way some kids do and start dashing around the place, turning around without looking, and running, always, into my legs.

☆ ☆ ☆

We play for about twenty minutes in the Riviera at a five-dollar table, but suddenly Sally pushes her green chips to the dealer and says, "Color me out." I try to get her to stay, since she's been winning, but she just says, "Let's go. I just thought of something I need you to do for me."

Out front she flags down a taxi, and we ride up past the El Rancho and the Sahara, and the chilly closed flume tubes of Wet 'n Wild, past Bonanza Corner, under the round pumpkinish orange of the Union 76 sign, where the World's Largest Gift Shops blaze with a yellow light against their shared parking lot, with a dark spot in between the gift shops where the World's Largest Adult Book Store used to be until it was closed by the Department of Justice because its owner was accused of selling pornographic films not protected by the official imprimatur applied to *Long Dong Silver.*

Just to the north of these stores stands the Desert Vision Community of Praise, which was featured a while ago on "60 Minutes" when members held a parking-lot service in which they burned copies of the new JC Penney catalog, in protest against the pantyhose pictures.

Sally won't say where we're going. The taxi takes us farther up the Strip, past the cartoonish shape of Bobby Stupak's Vegas World. Now the big towers of light have shrunk down to scrabbly little motels, here in the district of missing letters, where cavity-ridden hookers stand in the doorways of their rooms at the Sulinda Motel, and the Yucca Motel, and the Tod Motel.

L'Amour Wedding Chapel stands in the dark, all pink and fluorescent. At the Cupid Wedding Chapel, the sign says, "Happy Marriages Start Here." For a minute I think she's going to try to take me in here. That would be okay, although really the gentleman is supposed to ask.

☆ ☆ ☆

It turns out that all she wanted was some Polaroid Time-Zero film packets, and White Cross Drugs at the top of the Strip was the only place she knew would have it. She said she needed some picture for a contest she was entering with *Hustler* magazine.

So here we are back in the plain little Westward Ho room, and I'm playing Richard Avedon with a Polaroid camera that Sally told me cost less than the two packets of film she just bought. I crouch down against the corner of the bed for a low shot, saying, "More sizzle! More sizzle! Yes! Dahling, you're beautiful. Fluff your hair out! Lick your lips. Ah, that's gorgeous!" With every flash of the disposable flashbar the film comes pushing out of the front slot of the camera with a high electric squeal.

She's leaning back against the long mirror, pouting, agitating her hair back and forth, pulling away from her body the shoulder straps of this deep blue underwear arrangement she has on, with guy wires under the breasts and complicated straps and ruffles around the bottom where the matching blue stockings are held by a pair of suspenderlike things that reach all the way from the tops of her thighs to just under where the wire runs across in a semicircle under the lighter fabric that covers the breasts.

I'm lining up the half-developed panels on top of the dresser. The color isn't great, a bit cold and blue-shifted. Skin doesn't have any softness to it, and her face is blurred in some of the exposures.

"Make love to the camera! Seduce the camera! The camera is the man you love most in the world If you don't get him into bed with you this very minute you'll lose him forever."

She moves closer to the photographer, her blue satin stuff half off by now, making these seductive, open-mouthed expressions with her face such as I've never seen outside the cassette of a rented videotape. There really is something thrilling about taking sexy pictures in a motel, like all the other motels people have taken pictures in, letting the camera find its own way around her as she walks, and stops, and crouches down on the floor, just pure motion, just for the sake of how pretty it looks. She's really got something—I can see that. In fact, I'd like to tell her sometime that if she gets her nose fixed she might have a chance with the Eileen Ford Agency.

Some of the pictures come out little more than abstractions, blond hair flying through a blurred space of floral wallpaper. One of the pictures catches its own flash in the mirror, showing my shape blurry through the glass and half my head vaporized in the white fireball of the flashcube. We try a close-up shot—she says the magazine wants this kind of stuff—with me pointing the camera down into my lap and her eyes looking up into the camera, with a lot of whites in them, and her mouth wrapped around a white condom.

It doesn't come out—the face is just a white sheet with two red eyes blazing out from it. We try again, but it's even worse, just vague ivory cloud shapes from ghostland. Finally I try holding the camera on my shoulder next to my head, so it will be a little farther away, and with my other hand I partially block out the unpopped next cell of the flashcube. It takes a few tries, but at last we capture that classic picture, with only a minor case of red-eye reflecting back into the lens.

☆ ☆ ☆

Early in the morning the phone rings. It's Frank, and he's in a jolly mood.

"I just wanted to tell you, everything's okay. I heard from my daughter. She's coming home for Christmas. So you don't have to keep looking for her."

"I'm glad to hear it, Frank," I say, in what must sound like a sleep-laden mumble.

"Hey, I didn't wake you up, did I?"

"No, Frank. This is Las Vegas. We always get up at the crack of dawn in Las Vegas."

"I really appreciate your efforts to find Sally, Pack, I really do."

"I'm glad."

"And I'd like to have you come over for a little gathering on Christmas Eve, if you can make it."

"I'd love to. That'd be great."

"You're coming back tonight, aren't you?"

"Tomorrow," I say, lying. Somehow I'm afraid that if Sally's flight and my flight come in too close to each other, there will be some kind of old home week around the baggage carousel.

"Don't forget our game Wednesday."

"I'll be there." I had forgotten it, actually. I'd rather stay away from him if I can, but then again I've been eating at the slob lines and refilling my plate three times, and I need to get back into those steamy old courts and sweat away some of that weight.

Sally wakes up, rustles around on the other pillow, looks over at me in the half-blocked-out gray morning light coming in where the drapes don't fit together. I put my finger against my lips for silence, but she's not really awake, her eyes cloudy and not quite there, like a dog's eyes. She turns over with a soft groan.

"What's that, Pack, you got somebody there with you?"

"No. I'm all by myself."

"I heard somebody."

"That was just me."

"You got some Vegas broad in your room, don't you?"

"Come on, Frank. I don't do that."

He's laughing. "You got lucky at the crap table, didn't you? You got lucky, and then you got lucky. Well, I'm glad. You've talked about it enough." I can hear the glee in his voice, like a younger brother teasing his older brother about having a girlfriend. How strange it is to think that he's two years younger than I am.

"I wish I got that lucky," I tell him.

Now he wants to speak to her. "Come on," he says. "I want to hear what a real showgirl sounds like."

"Frank, there's nobody here but my own dirty underwear."

"Come on! Put the phone up to her ear." Sally's awake now. "Hiya, sweetheart," he says in a chuckly voice. We're both listening in now, the sides of our heads forming an acute angle around the phone receiver. "Take care of my buddy Pack, huh? Show him a good time. He deserves it. He did me a big favor. And he needs to work off a little weight too, so I can beat the shit out of him in racquetball without worrying that he's going to drop dead."

Sally lies there with her mouth open, little twitches visible around the edges of her lips where the impulse to say something keeps pricking her face in momentary twinges. Finally she turns away, shaking her head.

"Frank, I hope you're enjoying yourself."

"I'm just glad *you're* enjoying yourself," he says.

Sally has now crouched away under her side of the covers, her back presenting a blank arch toward me and the phone receiver.

"Just tell me one thing," he says in a tone of amiable, stifled conspiracy.

"What's that, Frank?"

"Is she pretty?"

The instant I put the phone down it rings again. "Good morning. This is your wake-up call. Thank you for staying at the Westward Ho." I've always wondered what happens if you're on the phone at the time when the wake-up timer goes off.

Chapter 9

Never fly in a plane the day after you have strenuously failed to ejaculate. The change in cabin pressure will sit beneath you like those midwestern snowstorm shapes in the middle of the day, and you will find yourself jounced around on top of some remarkably sensitive turbulence.

I've been drifting off to sleep, with the sun in my eyes and my hook-shaped earphones tuned to the channel called "Oldies in the Ozone," and wondering about all the other people in the Christmas season who must be looking out of airplane windows today at the same cottony untouchability of winter and remembering whomever they had to say goodbye to.

There is a classic moment that always happens when people who like each other go to the airport at Christmastime, a scene that sneaks up on you in every movie—so that the moment Sally and I realized that we were temporarily each other's girlfriend and boyfriend was the same moment we realized that it was time for the people in rows fifteen through twenty-eight to board the aircraft.

Before going through security, it was just an adventure in the world's fanciest terminal; now it was that classic moment in an airport—of a semi-girlfriend going home and her semi-boyfriend about to follow on another carrier. I don't remember what we said, except I do remember getting kind of carried away and saying that I loved her, which was true.

She said I was being "nave," but I said I didn't care.

"Pack, I can't be your girlfriend."

"I know," I said, and we hugged each other, and kept our kisses modest enough that people watching must have thought how sweet it was that a father and daughter could love each other that much.

It was Christmas in the airport and it still is, as it remains Christmas up here in the subdued brown-and-beige decor of Northwest Airlines, with "Ruby Tuesday" and "Jingle Bell Rock" and "It's My Party," where even the tops of clouds, looked down upon from where nobody belongs, have taken on that same fleece bleached white as the cotton fluff Cath and I used to spread out under our own tree to set the presents on, until we got to the point where we couldn't think of any more presents nice enough to distract us from the fact that we didn't love each other.

It's bad luck to watch somebody fly out of sight, especially when she's flying Continental. And even if the plane doesn't crash, it's bad luck for me next week at the Modern Language Association meeting in Philadelphia, because I have a side trip planned into Atlantic City, a room reserved, and a small bankroll that I know won't last long once the town gets crowded and the pit bosses start raising all the table minimums. Still, the place has been good to me a few times, when I didn't deserve it.

And now, up in the disturbed pressure, the pain sits like a lump at the bottom of my coach seat. But I don't mind. I would rather suffer with blue balls for the duration of this flight—if Sally could be the one to have given them to me—than to have even my wildest fantasy come true.

☆ ☆ ☆

Even walking through the gate tunnel to get off the plane in Indianapolis, I can feel how different the air is—saturated, pneumoniac. In winter the afternoon hangs so low for so many hours over Indianapolis that everybody tries to ignore it, nobody looks up much, you notice it getting dark and you put on your headlights and that's about it.

But it's not bad. This is the part of the country that all the hotshots ignore, which makes it easier for the not-so-hotshots like me. People who wear Gucci loafers and carry five-hundred-dollar briefcases call this region "the Flyover."

That wired feeling of not having slept well in a motel in Vegas fades away as soon as I spend a few minutes outside, waiting for the van to pick me up from Park 'n' Fly, in that ringing space, sort of outdoors and sort of indoors, on the other side of the glass door from the baggage area. The airport is packed, of course, full of that wonderful soft din of taxis and suitcases and well-behaved children. You can hear the shuttle buses overhead, letting people off at the departure level, from which they will presently zoom down a ramp and circle around the inner airport circle to come back and pick up the arriving passengers.

☆ ☆ ☆

What is it about an airport that makes me love it? Even the lowliest telephone pole and traffic cone exists with one of its corners in another dimension, in another whole climate of the country.

Everything seems conditioned by the closeness of travel. When we think of these same objects existing at home, we will know that nothing is the same, that this curbstone is not their curbstone, this traffic light their traffic light. To be in an airport always reminds me of one of my favorite lines, from Faulkner's *As I Lay Dying*. If it weren't for all that stuff about Dewey Dell trying to get an abortion (which some of the kids in class have been instructed to write to their parents about if it comes up in a lecture), I would love to go back to teaching that book, especially because of what Darl says toward the end, about the Bundrens' wagon, but applicable to every 727 at every gate of this terminal: "There is about it that unmistakable air of definite and imminent departure."

"As I Die Reading," I found out later the students called that book, when I assigned it, along with "Absolute Tedium," and "The Bore," and the somewhat more farfetched "Drowned in the Brewery."

☆ ☆ ☆

I've always noticed in this state that you can tell where you are less by the official direction signs than by whatever the kids have spray-painted on blank surfaces. Here, still in the city limits, weird symbols and formulae have been daubed onto the outside walls of the new condo-communities. Red and black. A weird hieroglyphic of numbers and initials with red circles around them, lightning bars converging on a black triangle. The code language of the gangs, numbers crossed out but still pointedly readable, sets of initials with arrows in them and drops of blood leaking out of them—some hasty but exacting drug blueprint that makes me click down the door locks and check the gas gauge.

Then, out of town, beyond the lights of the Goodyear plant and the dark shape of the closed-down Hoosierland Packing Company, something else takes over. An extraordinary mildness imposes itself upon the discipline of spray-painting. Now it's just kids, loyal to a band called METALLICA, pledged in fealty to THE DOORS, whose logo, in imitation of a hand stencil, they have copied. And even more traditional: I LOVE MARLA. CLASS OF 88 RULES!

The Flyover. Kids who still fall in love. PARTY ALL YEAR! And then my favorite, painted on the side of a bridge over Route 74 just a few miles before I have to get off it and pick up the two-lane highway for the last ten miles down to Amherst. It's been there for years, and it makes me smile every time I pass. SKEETER LOVES IT!

Even though it's full dark by now, as I come through the slight roll of the land outside Dartmouth, there's a look in the air that says its going to snow, although it's not always telling the truth. When it snows in the town of Dartmouth, or when it looks as if it is about to snow, a dome of manila-colored light, in the peach color of the third copy in the set of snap-sheets you fill out to drop a student from class, hangs in the air a few hundred feet over downtown. If you were lost in a car out in the farm roads you could find your way by that light, to hamburgers and beer any night of the week but Sunday.

The signs change again. We are in walking distance of a college town. "U.S. out of Costa Rica!" proclaims the Front Street bridge, as it has for most of the time I have been working in this town. "Hands off Panama!" on the plywood sheets in front of the building where the Hangar Six nightclub has closed down and Domino's Pizza is in the process of taking it over.

In front of the Ford Brothers Real Estate office, a banner reads, "√ US OUT," and since it comes so soon after the plywood slogans, I always read it wrong, as if it's another demand about where we should get out of. Farther on, in the vegetarian district, on a slab of concrete painted over and repainted so many times that you can see cracks in it like the cracks in a desert mud flat: "Meat Is Murder! Go Total Vegan or Die!"

The dog comes out of the kennel, even though he has a reservation to go back in just a few days. One of the saddest things about when Cath and I split up was that she couldn't keep him. She always liked him better than I did. But her new guy has this monster of a dog that she was rightly afraid would eat an under-sized half Irish-setter like Dog-man.

"Hey, Dog-man," I say to him, as I let him off his leash in the backseat, "gimme a kiss." But he just sneezes and sticks his nose into a corner of the window, as a signal to me that he wants me to open it a crack. The problem is—we're just not that interested in each other. I've tried. I know that a man is supposed to love his dog. I've taken him for walks. I've taken him down to Florida. And I don't dislike him. But we look in each other's eyes, the way a man and his dog are supposed to do, and then we both look away.

☆ ☆ ☆

Winter is personal. Nothing much happens. Nobody tries to take it away from you; nobody tries to make you like it more than it deserves to be liked. You come home to it from someplace warmer, and it just sits there, old, neither welcoming you back nor making fun of you, just marooned in the air, bringing out a slight graininess of static in the songs on the car radio, a fine sand in the strings of Scriabin, and Mendelssohn, and whoever else nobody in any of the other cars is listening to. WPBK, the local NPR station, is located, as usual, down at the staticky end of the dial. The station is run by the university, and it's pretty good, mostly, except for all the talky "public interest" programming that they feel obliged to put on, like "Psychological Horizons," "Native American Music Festival," and "Global Malaria Watch."

The only alternative to that stuff is WZPY, the golden oldies station, whose playlist is so dominated by Diana Ross and Olivia Newton-John that one could almost forget that there used to be something called rock and roll. Once in a while you might get lucky and stumble onto the last verse of the Beatles' "Yesterday," about as close to heavy metal as the station dares get. Sometimes you might even come upon a Beach Boys song. That song will be "Good Vibrations."

Vacation hangs over a college town like a cold fog. When I

open my eyes in the morning in this house on Verossika Lane, I come awake with a start, like falling out of bed. With no traffic on Union Avenue, the house stands quieter than I ever hear it the rest of the year. Without the usual traffic noise to shield me from it, the electronic bell tower in front of Lawrence Hall, pealing the Westminster chimes tune with fake bronze undertones added by computer to its synthetic timbre, seems just a house or two away.

But I'm not complaining. I like the way the air goes into my lungs when I go out running on these days. I like the nights, when I can walk into town and have a few beers in Wiggly Wog's, and think about all the sorority girls who hang out there during school, and the overflow customers waiting to get in on a busy night, even when it's below zero, trailing out into the wind like the tail of a kite, sharp bursts of voices flying across Broad Street to their friends waiting in line to get into the Dirt Bag or the Full Court Press.

Now only the music of Christmas echos up and down the deserted Broad Street, Johnny Mathis and Perry Como and Nat King Cole caroling from the little horn-shaped speakers hung on the same light poles from which the steel-reinforced festoons of lighted greenery arch across the street, mostly empty, except for an occasional townie car cruising dispiritedly down its one-way length.

The tape deck that controls the carols is located at Courthouse Square, which is the main intersection of town, and which most people in the university call Cathouse Square. Every lunch hour when school is in session, the sidewalk here fills with gray-faced social workers, and ex-students who never moved away, and a few undergraduates who finished eating early—all standing vigil for Justice in Palestine.

Today as I run past, there stands only a tiny plywood house, taller than it is wide, like a child's drawing of a house, on the back of a low flatbed trailer, with portable wooden steps leading up to it. Inside, Santa Claus holds office hours from noon to four. Mostly he just reads the newspaper. I don't think I've ever seen a kid go in there.

I wave to Santa Claus as I run by, on this street where I never like to run during school. He waves back, although he doesn't know who I am. His beard is off, resting down on his chest. I turn, chugging up the hill past Kinko's and the army-navy store where they never have anything I'm looking for, and then up to the flat part of town where the dogs bark all day in their chain-linked front yards.

I've noticed something unusual about running in dog neighborhoods: that one dog will never stop barking at me until another dog farther along the street has started. They hand me off, as it were, from dog to dog, the way the regional air traffic control stations hand over a transcontinental flight from Sioux City Control to Cheyenne Control.

Sometimes I get sick of that noise. But I have no right to complain. These running afternoons are what I have to do to pay for all my visits to the Riviera slob line, visits timed to fit between the moment when the keno girl takes my money and the moment after the board has filled out when she comes back and says, "How'd you do?" and sometimes I say, "This is a keno game, honey—how do you think I did?"

Right now I'm trying to balance the need to get myself in shape with the need to have some strength left over tomorrow, when Frank and I have a racquetball game. Lately he's been impatient about my level of physical fitness, always getting his friends in the high blood pressure support group to send me low-calorie recipes. I'm the only other racquetball player in the English department, and though he always beats the pants off me, and then teases me about it, he's very protective. If I get hit by the ball he comes rushing over, asking me if I'm all right.

I have not seen a single person walking, have looked blankly into the few cars I passed, and I didn't recognize anybody. In fact, I don't believe I've spoken to a person face to face since stopping at Mr. Dollarsaver on the way back from the airport and the kennel with Dog-man in the car. I don't usually like to leave him in the car alone, with the Animal Liberation Army active on campus, but I figured during vacation he should be all right. I parked around the back, and he was still there when I came out. What they like to do is break into people's cars when they see a dog locked inside, and then let it out, usually to be lost, or run over.

☆ ☆ ☆

Frank Iverson is one of those people for whom an early heart attack was a piece of good fortune. When I first knew him he was much heavier than I, one of those jolly, bearish kind of cigarette-smoking slobs you see striding in heavy tweed jackets through the halls of almost every English department, moving with long steps, a broad face half hidden behind the black bristles of a beard, his voice a little too loud for some reason.

All this time his diminutive colleagues worried about how he was getting along, with a dead wife and two live daughters, as well as about all the extra work that such a person's heart must have to do when he climbs the stairs.

Now, two years after being carried on a stretcher out of his Introduction to Milton class, the guy has cleaned up every mess he ever made. He has quit drinking, quit smoking, has trimmed himself down to a viable shape—not shrunken in the cadaverous way some dieters get after a brush with death, but with his former bulk intact, compacted, something like the bouncers in the Dirt Bag.

He walks with very little excess motion past the rows and rows of offices in Drury Hall. Like most Miltonists, he keeps his academic specialty scrupulously isolated from the other parts of his life. He has kept that slightly agressive, needling way of speaking to people, coming down hard again and again on whatever weakness in someone else amuses him, though he has given up, along with his drinking, the slob side of his humor, the dirty words he used to try to shock people with; and his old belly laugh has been compacted as radically as the belly from which it originated.

On the court he's a monster. Every time he misses a shot he loses his temper and roars obscenities at himself. You always know when Frank Iverson is on the court, if you're walking down the hall outside of the row of courts with the round windows cut into their doors. You can hear, above the resonating plop of hollow balls caroming off the walls, above all the foot noise and stray voices and racquet noise: *"FUCK!"* Then a few more wings and bings, and plops of racquets. *"GODDAM SON OF A BITCH!"* And so on for the rest of the hour he has the court reserved. He has learned always to bring a spare racquet. I've seen him smash one against the wall when he missed a shot.

But as I said, he likes me, and he always sticks up for me, not because there's any great shortage of racquetball players, but because I'm one of the only ones who still play the kind of powerhouse, smack-it-off-all-four-walls game that he likes. The other players, mostly from the College of Engineering, play this effete little spin game full of dink shots and overly precise corner work.

I'm doing better than usual today, trailing, but within range. I don't know why he's not murdering me. Perhaps I have built up a reserve of glycogen from all those buttered rolls in the buffet lines. I'm trying to keep from getting any more tired than I am, so I keep calling time out after almost every shot and pretending to adjust my headband.

"So," I ask him, to kill time between points, even though it's not usually proper to start a conversation during play, "did your daughter get home all right?" Since he's asked me so much about her, I figure it would sound strange if I appeared to forget about the whole thing.

"Oh, yeah," he says, not even breathing hard. "She's back. She said hotel school was boring. I could have told her that."

He serves the ball high up into the corner of the walled court. I move in and hit it hard off the front wall, and it comes straight back to him so fast that he's stuck in the middle for a moment and can't get set up any better than to make a high defensive shot that I run up on and wing down the sideline just out of his reach.

"Shit-fuckin' BASTARD!" Then immediately he calms down and says, "From what I heard, you've got some girls of your own to be interested in." His eyes twinkle behind his plastic eye protectors, a pair of narrow white lensless rims outlined in the shape of a narrow Lone Ranger mask.

"Who's that?" I say, as Frank hauls back for a smash serve that I can barely see as it pops off the front wall and caroms off my right shin.

"Geez, I'm sorry, Pack," he says, rushing over like an ambulance, all his rage over the previous point long forgotten. "You okay? You're not hurt, are you?"

In racquetball you only get a point when you're serving. This has been a tough game, because we're just trading serves, mostly without doing anything to affect the score.

"Time out," I say. "Water break." This is actually very bad form, to call a water break in the middle of a game, but this is the first time in months I've had a chance to beat him, and I need to conserve my strength. As we walk up the empty hall toward the fountain, past the doors of the basketball practice courts, our court shoes echo down the cement-block walls with a high, underwater, Jacques Cousteau sort of sound.

"So how was the action?" Frank says. "You gotta tell me about it."

"Oh, I did all right. I didn't come back owning any casinos, but I came back ahead."

"I don't mean that action. I mean those show girls you were fooling around with."

145 ☆

I really want to get him off this subject, but it's hard to get Frank Iverson off any subject. "Look, Frank, I can't afford to fool around with show girls. If I could afford to fuck a Vegas show girl, then I sure as hell could afford to quit teaching *Fun with Dick and Jane* to the Future Truck Drivers of America."

Back on the court: "Mother*FUCKER!*" I'm about to tell him some John Wayne movie type of thing, like "Save it for the MLA," but then he turns to me as friendly as you could ever ask for, and says, "So she wasn't a show girl. Big deal. But I know you had somebody in that room. I could hear her in the background. She sounded really sexy." He has stopped the action to bend over his shoelaces, as he usually does when he loses a point.

His eyes are narrow behind his protectors, sweat sprinkles off the mixed black and white hairs of his beard, and he winks, and laughs, and returns my serve way over in the far corner, but I get to it, sticking my racquet out more by instinct than plan—for an accidental drop shot that he doesn't start for in time, so that his return just bloops high off the wall right to me, while he's still moving forward, and I put the ball away with an easy passing shot.

"Fucking *ASSHOLE!* Iverson, you gotta LOOK at the MO-THER-FUCK-ING *BALL!*" He has crowded himself into the front corner, and his voice echoes in every direction, until he bursts from his punishment corner and whales the hollow blue ball so hard against the side wall that it splits completely in half along the middle seam. The two dead grapefruit halves of the ball lie wobbling on the floor.

"Iverson one, ball zero," I say, in a singsongy voice like an old-fashioned tennis umpire. I shouldn't have said that, because now he gets quieter, his anger focused onto the game. He's winging the ball every chance he gets down the side where I can barely reach it, even making dink shots up into the front corner, which he usually doesn't have enough patience or control to do.

No swearing now, just grunts and the squeak of his heavy black Reeboks against the hardwood floor.

He wins, finally, though I walk out of the court happier about how I played than I usually do. As we head down the long hall to the faculty locker room, holding our racquets and towels, he's still needling me about the mystery woman. It bothers me, but of course I can't let myself react. It's not that there's any risk he could find out what happened; I just don't like the squelched and unstable tone my voice gets when I have to tell lies over and over, especially on the campus of a university whose honor code I have signed a pledge to uphold.

"So what was she really, a call girl? An escort service?"

"She was the chambermaid, Frank," I say, still wheezing from the last hard points. "I tipped her a C-note and she couldn't control herself."

"C-note? You're even talking like a high-roller. Right out of Damon Runyon. I got the horse right here . . ." He chants, more than sings, this line, in a low throaty voice, then stops. "Or maybe I should say: I got the *whores* right here." His laugh rings through the empty corridors of painted cement blocks, carrying a trace of his old pre-infarction heartiness.

From stall to stall in the shower, he keeps up the questions, though I can't always hear him at the times when the water is coming down on my face.

The locker rooms here used to have the kind of ordinary communal showers you see everywhere, the ones in the faculty locker room arranged with eight showers around the edge of a big square room with the tiles of the floor sloping down to a central drain.

Now the shower room, as well as the locker area, is a maze of partitions, made of the same bright orange textured plastic as the molded stackable faculty-meeting chairs we have to sit in for two hours every two weeks. The reason for the partitions is that in

October the state senate was in such a hurry to outlaw the topless bars in Indianapolis and Fort Wayne that it wrote and passed a series of antinudity statutes that were so strict that they ended up prohibiting almost every conceivable form of nonmarital undressing.

We're all waiting for the big test case which will come up as soon as summer starts: when the first four-year-old girl swimming topless at Beverly Shores Beach in Lake Michigan is arrested for a Class A misdemeanor. In the meantime, the university's lawyer suggested putting up the partitions, as well as closing down all the life drawing classes in the art department, mostly as a way of protecting its own interests and making some sort of show of good faith in the admittedly unlikely event that any arrests should occur in the future.

"I got the whores right here," he chants again, voice booming over the water sounds.

"Frank, if you don't shut up, I'm going to call Richard Lugar's office. You know what he said about 'dirty-mouthed professors.' "

The locker area too is partitioned, big sheets of plastic every three feet reaching out to where the benches used to be where you could sit down to change your shoes. I've been told that the school's counsel recommended these partitions not because of the topless law, but rather in observance of some other poorly worded provisions of the anti-gay-bar ordinance that the state senate passed around the same time. One would have thought, however, that even our own legislators would be smart enough to know that if the faculty of our university really wanted to suck each other off in the locker room, these cubicles would make it easier.

"Just tell me one thing," he says. "Was she pretty?"

"Frank, I really find this conversation tedious. No offense."

"What happened, something went wrong?"

"No, nothing went wrong," I say, thinking back suddenly to Sally's face, the way she looked up at me that last night with as much warmth and understanding as I've ever seen, as if to say that she was the first girl in the world to realize that not all guys are eighteen years old. At about this point I realize that there's no way I can get him off the subject, so I might as well humor him.

"It was great. You should try it."

"Oh yeah?"

"They've got legal cathouses out there in the next county over from Vegas. Zero AIDS rate. No cops. No Richard Lugar. I've even got a menu at home that I'll show you." But suddenly I remember that my souvenir menu from the Ranch has Sally's handwriting all over it, in that sexy green ink that's always turned me on for some reason.

"If I can find it," I say. "I think I lost it."

It's getting dark outside. The cement blocks of the gym begin to take on that golden indoor look that they get around this time in the afternoon.

"I'd like to meet that girl that you had in your room, that's who I'd like to meet. What was her name?"

I should have told him to go to hell, or said I didn't remember, but suddenly I find myself in one of those situations when I have to tell a lie and I can't even think of a plausible sounding name. In the rush of my thoughts the names all come out sounding like Mildred, or Millicent, or Millimant, from whatever that play is that everybody hates to read—*School for Scandal,* I think; I always have trouble with the eighteenth century. Finally, the only thing I can come up with is Natalie.

"That's a cute name," he says, and swings the door to his locker shut with a bang. The reason he slams it like that is not that he's angry, but that the noise helps him to remember whether he has locked it or not.

☆ ☆ ☆

I tried every story I could think of to beg off, but when you're living alone on vacation, with only a dog and a cat to apologize to if you get home late, you don't have many excuses for not coming over to somebody's house when he asks you. This is especially true in a university that has an honor code, where I would feel awkward, even in a nonacademic matter, if I said to a colleague that I was feeling sick or I had to go to the dentist or I was meeting some young lady for a date rape. His house is just on the other side of Drury Hall from the gym, which makes it easy just to ride back home with Frank and then later walk back to my own car.

Frank has one of those old two-story frame houses that in a town like this become either student slums or marvelously comfortable family houses. Bright bulbs form an arch around the door, and more bulbs frame the front windows that look out onto the porch. It's one of those old, wide porches that since the invention of air conditioning don't get used for much anymore except as storage for old bicycles and the cans and bottles to be picked up by the Earth-Action Recycling Project.

Sally's there, as well as her sister, Janna, whom I know only from the C-minus pages of Sally's term paper. Janna is dark-haired, with a wide, kind, not very pretty face. When I shake hands with her, I look discreetly to see if she really has that scar from the terrible accident. Sure enough, there it is, a lightning-shaped seam in the flesh, barely visible in the dim Christmas lights.

"Hello, Dr. Schmidt," Sally says, as we carefully shake hands. "It's been a while. I liked your class. I'm sorry I didn't work harder."

"That's okay, Sally," I say, sounding almost as wooden as she does, "How's UNLV? Does Jerry Tarkanian still chew on those towels?"

The housekeeper brings the drinks, diet Coke in long bottles for the girls, a bottle of Coors Light for me, and a nonalcoholic Cutter for Frank. After what Cath told me about the Coors company harassing employees who use birth control, I don't approve of drinking the stuff anymore, but it would be tacky to make a fuss about it in somebody else's house.

I've met the housekeeper before. Her name is Hillie, an unsmiling middle-aged black woman, with huge matronly breasts forming a shelf at the front of her barrel-shaped figure. As soon as she goes back to the kitchen, Janna says, "Daddy, I wish you'd tell Mountains to stay out of my clothes. She's really getting on my nerves."

"Don't call her that," Frank says. "I've taken enough flak in this department for having her at all. If she hears you talking like that, you'll hurt her feelings."

"I don't think Mountains has any feelings," Janna says. "She's a robot. Not like Debbie. Debbie had some class."

"Remember that time," Sally says to her sister, "when I was in the shower and Mountains was outside the door and I thought it was you, and I go, 'Hey, shit-nose, bring me a towel,' and she just came waddling in the door and handed it to me. If that had been Debbie, she would have gone, 'Don' you be talkin' to me like dat!' " And now the room goes silent, because Hillie has appeared from the other end of the room and we have been caught laughing at a racial punch line.

"So," Frank says to Sally. "You two have something in common. Professor Schmidt is a big Las Vegas enthusiast."

"Oh, really?" she says.

"Yeah, he said he had a wild time out there last week," Frank says, his eyes twinkling behind his salt-and-pepper beard. I can see he's having fun teasing me.

"The next time you go out there," he says, "I think I'm going to come along. And I want you to fix me up with your friend Natalie."

Fortunately, Frank is too busy enjoying himself to notice the reaction to his last remark. Sally and Janna both bring their heads up as abruptly as if a rock had just crashed through the window. I can feel in my face that I have turned either bright red or ghost white, with the same galvanic tingle that would send a polygraph machine off the edge of the paper. As Frank laughs, I help Sally and Janna wipe up the puddle of diet Coke that Sally has dribbled onto the coffee table.

Chapter 10

Christmas Eve is better when it's overcast. With a gloom clamped over the town, the quality of Christmas can be seen more easily to radiate out from the clapboard houses with their windows flashing on and off.

Midtown Marathon has already switched on its white fluorescent lights in the overhang above the self-service pumps, so that the men in car coats squeegeeing their windshields seem bathed in a holy glow, like the figures in a crèche—although in this town all public nativity scenes have been banned.

From one end of Broad Street to the other, Julio Iglesias sings "The Little Drummer Boy." On the corner diagonally across from Santa Claus, the traditional Peace Tree has been decorated all around up to a height of five feet with letters from the children of Amherst's sister city of Cienfuegos, Cuba.

If I understand their itinerary, my parents are not far from that island right now, watching the water glide past their deck chairs on the *Brunhildefjord*. Usually I go to their house in Florida for Christmas, but this year the deal they got through AARP for the Caribbean cruise was too good to pass up.

Here and there along the street I can smell a whiff of dinner, the boiled celery smell of dressing, or the tofu-and-lentil smell of the many macrobiotic households.

I've been thinking about Sally, trying to remember if I still feel anything, or if this is just one of those classic situations of finding out that your friend's daughter is a hooker and fucking her anyway and then everything goes back to normal.

It is a town that has gone half silent, except for the little pockets of people who have stayed around to get drunk and sing songs and hug each other and eat vegetables. All over town at noon it's dark enough that folks have switched on their Christmas lights.

In my camel's-hair coat, with a white shirt and a tie, and my good brown slacks, and my brown wing tips which I just polished to a high glaze, I'm walking all the way to Frank's house, a Christmasy thing to do, I think, past McDonald's, closed, a strange sight in the height of the afternoon, as if even the constancy of business that underlies a college town and protects us from poverty has taken a vacation for a day.

Here and there among the student hovels, among the brown-and-yellow flags from whatever country we are doing something wrong to, paper posters announce: "Habati-Gani. Have a Strong and Proud Kwanzaa." This is the new holiday that most of the African studies faculty are promoting, so as to avoid the Eurocentric racism that has become associated with Christmas.

On Sloan Street, usually called Slum Street, the Ecumenical Liberation Outreach is putting on its yearly banquet for the homeless, but not many people have shown up. Amherst has plenty of poor people, but the homeless mostly find their way to Indianapolis, where they are far less welcome than they would be here.

Across the face of the old house which has become the ELO Community Center, a long banner has been stretched, printed in the kind of mechanical lettering you see on the giant Happy Birthday signs you can order in flower shops. This sign reads: THE ELECTION WAS RIGGED! NOT A PENNY TO CHAMORRO AND HER CONTRAS!

Far up in a third-floor window, a hand-lettered sign proclaims: CHAMORRO'S CONTRAS ARE DESTROYING THE RAIN FOREST!

A handful of very thin men and women in loose corduroy coats and pea jackets are flipping a Frisbee around in the dry grass of the lawn that slants uphill to the next retaining wall. I can tell they are not homeless, because homeless people do not become expert Frisbee throwers. Only college students who never leave this town can ever get that good with a Frisbee.

As they flick the disk from corner to opposite corner of the square they have formed, the chords of a song from last year's Jackson Browne album roll from a basement window beneath the church, a thick ensemble sound, full of mournful piano arpeggios and a sweet ringing Gibson Les Paul coloratura:

> They promised us we'd get nice things from Santa,
> A toy bomber for every mile of trees.
> We tried to warn them but they couldn't see
> Anything but their own propaganda.

Now I'm starting to get the Christmas spirit. My stomach growls with the hunger of skimping on breakfast to make room for dinner. My breath puffs out in front of me on the sidewalk. Just seeing how drab and gray those kids are, kids who don't care about clothes, kids who lie on their mattress-beds thinking about all the things they are angry about—they make me thankful I'm an American slob in shiny wine-dark Florsheims.

But maybe that's not fair. Maybe they're stupid, but they're not so evil that they don't deserve somebody to tell them peace on earth, and happy Kwanzaa, and good will toward the kind of people who make me want to move away and spend the rest of my life in a Holiday Inn. They wave to me, because it's Christmas, and I wave back because it would be very rude not to.

☆ ☆ ☆

There are no lights at Frank's house. At first I figure the electricity has gone off. I clump up on the wooden porch, cross to the front door, stretch out my hand. "Happy Kwanzaa!"

He stands there, staring, blank as a closed window.

"How's everything, Frank?" I say, a little less heartily.

And now the slightly off-balance feeling that I felt ever since I mounted the porch steps and saw him motionless in the doorway without a trace of a smile has crept up on me. And at the moment when it becomes clear to me what has happened, I can see his face release itself from the theatrical blankness in which it was shrouded, into a cold scowl that could swallow up every curse word over every bad shot he's made in a lifetime of racquetball.

Very slowly, very softly, he begins to speak.

"You stink," he says. He almost sounds as if he's laughing. "You . . . miserable . . . piece . . . of . . . *garbage.*"

"Frank, what's the matter?" My knees are weak, I feel myself swaying on the porch boards, my cheeks tingling, my face pulled back into a mirthless grin.

"I don't have to tell you anything about what's the matter," he says, so softly that I can barely hear him. "I think you should be the one to tell me what's the matter with you. What's the matter with the kind of man who fucks his friend's daughter and doesn't even have the simple human decency to admit it?"

"I don't know what you're talking about," I say, but the bumps in my voice give me away.

"You don't know what I'm talking about," he says, tenderly, almost a singsong. "You don't know what I'm talking about. You stand here in front of my face," and now his voice rises for one word, from barely audible to the level of his loudest curse on the racquetball court, "you stand here on my property, in front of my face . . . *SMIRKING!"* His voice falls again. "And you don't know what I'm talking about."

I can feel myself sweating under my collar.

"You don't know what I'm talking about," he says again. "Then I guess you'd better just stand here until you think of something to tell me. Maybe you can tell me what kind of film you used to take these pictures." He holds a few of those Polaroid shots up, including the messed-up one with half my face in it, as well as the one of her looking up into my eyes after we got everything straightened out with the flashbar.

"Oh shit."

"What?" he says, with that peculiar, tickly, provoking tone of a tough trying to start a fight. "What was that? What did you say?"

"Frank, there's nothing I can tell you."

"What did you say just then? What was that you said?"

"I said, 'Oh shit.' "

"Do you think you have any right to use that word?"

"I don't know."

"I asked you if you think you have any right to use that word."

"I don't know if I do or not." It occurs to me that he is dominating this discussion the way he dominates a racquetball match.

"Do you think you have any right to use the word *shit*—when you buy a night with your friend's daughter?"

"Frank, I'm sorry."

"Sorry? You say you're *sorry?* You ruin my daughter's fucking life, and then you take pictures for souvenirs. I think you're a piece of scum."

"I didn't ruin her life."

"Well, you ruined yours!" he roars, so loud that his voice echoes through the long porch, and the dome over the portable barbecue

cooker that he's not allowed to use anymore buzzes in a low subharmonic with his voice.

"Frank, I'm sorry."

"And don't think I missed anything. I know all about it. Hillie found the pictures, and her goddam *prostitute's* license that you probably encouraged her to get, and then I made her tell me the whole story. She admitted everything. I know about the term paper that you took to—what is the expression—her *crib?* And I know how you blackmailed her with the grade on that paper."

"That's not true."

"So you're denying the whole thing, huh? Right to my face?"

"I'm denying that part."

"And then you fucking tease me about it. You mock me in front of my daughters. You make me make a fool out of myself in front of my own daughters, and all the time you're taking pictures of my own daughter sucking your cock!"

I can tell now that he's gone past the stage of asking questions or finding anything out. Now he's just working himself up. I can feel the nausea of this afternoon like the motion of the *Brunhilde-fjord* under my mother and father's deck chairs, down where I wish I was, except that I'd be the only passenger under sixty.

Nobody seems to be in the house. I'm wondering what he's done to Sally. For a moment I feel a flash of my own anger as it occurs to me that whatever happens, she deserves it. She was the one who left those pictures around for that . . . maid to find. I actually said the word "nigger" to myself, which I don't feel good about. It's not fair to Lynn MacEntire, who has an office two doors down from mine, it's not fair to B. B. King, and it's especially not fair to Janet Jackson.

"And if you're thinking of trying to break into my house and snatch her away back into prostitution, forget it," he says. "She's voluntarily committed herself to Wabash Pines Hospital."

"Voluntarily," I repeat, as expressionless as his own voice was earlier in this discussion. "Have you found a doctor to diagnose her as mentally ill?"

"You *challenge me?* You *fuck* my daughter, you hold her term paper over her head so she can't get out of sucking your cock, and then you *challenge me?*"

"I didn't challenge you," I say, my voice pushed back in my throat. "I just don't think she's crazy. If anybody's crazy, it's me."

"You know what they call it when a teacher uses a grade to blackmail a student into having sex with him?"

"Frank, I'm sorry about what happened. The whole thing was a mistake, and I . . ."

"You know what they call it?" He hasn't moved in all this time from his place blocking the doorway, his hands stuffed down in the pockets of his heavy chinos, leaning backward and forward on the soles of his new yellow work shoes.

"You know what they call it?"

"I didn't blackmail anybody."

"They call it *rape,* that's what they call it!" and he shouts this word so loud that it echoes off all the other white clapboard houses up and down the street. *"Rape!"* he roars again, but the sidewalk is empty. Most of the neighbors have gone away someplace else for Christmas.

There's nothing I can do. I can't calm him down. I can't walk away. I just have to listen to everything he says. He's half off his rocker, maybe he's even drinking, I don't know—but all I can do is stand here and listen to it. Most of it's true, too. I didn't know that before. There's nothing wrong with a forty-eight-year-old man going out with a twenty-one-year-old woman. But to appear to have used that paper as a pretext, whether I really did or not, and I don't even know if I did—maybe that will appear to be a little unethical.

With a shocked sinking as if the boards of the porch had given way, it occurs to me for the first time that I have lost my job.

"How could you *do* this *thing* to my family?" he says, moving away from rage, back into dumb shock. "Have you no decency? Have you no common . . . human . . . decency?"

"I'm sorry."

"Is there anything that you wouldn't stoop to, Packard? Is there anything in the world too low even for you?"

"Frank, I'm sorry."

"Do you know how much I hate you?"

"Frank . . ."

"Do you want to know how much I hate you?" His voice rings the length of the porch. I don't really want to know how much he hates me; in fact, I have a fairly good idea, but instead of standing there like a whipped horse, which I should do under the circumstances, I say the wrong thing once again: "A lot?"

And now he's back into the cold shivery shocked voice.

"I just can't believe what I'm hearing. You make a joke at a time like this. Is there no level to which you will not sink, Packard? Have you no *shame?* Have you no simple, human respect, Packard, at a time—like—this?"

I've always liked Frank Iverson when he's not being a jerk, but I've also known for a long time that he doesn't have the most original imagination in the world. Just last month, when he introduced a talk by the writing authority Donald Murray, he called him "a man who needs no introduction—but he's going to get one anyway." And now I realize that he's even found it necessary to go to an outside source to find a shape for his moral indignation. He's taking most of his words, as well as all of his tone, from an old kinescope that anyone who watches those self-congratulatory documentaries about great moments in television journalism has seen a dozen times: that still-exciting moment in the Army-McCarthy hearings when Joseph Welch stands up to Senator McCarthy, his voice thick with a kind of weary dismay mixed with cold fury: "Have you no decency, sir, at long last?"

(The next chapter in the documentary invariably concerns what a great job they did covering the assassination of John F. Kennedy.)

"Frank," I say, trying to get him back out of the brave confrontations of the fifties. "I made a mistake."

"You know what you are?" he says.

"Frank, I'm—"

"Do you know what you are?" Again, he's running this discussion like a lopsided racquetball game, forcing me to be the straight man, to play Larry to his Moe.

"What am I?"

"You're a felon, that's what you are. A *felon*. Don't you like the sound of that word?"

"No."

"You should. It's a venerable old Norman word. You'd better learn to like it, because that's what you are. I've already called Sam Brunton, and told him what kind of *felon* he has working in this department. I've called the police and my attorney, and there's going to be a full investigation of all the times you've told abusive jokes in class and all the times you've blackmailed your students for sexual favors." He sounds like he's reading this out of a transcript of Oprah Winfrey.

"Felon," he says again, wrestling the word down to the ground with his mouth. "I really like that word. *Felon.*"

"Frank, I've been trying to apologize. I've been trying to tell you I was sorry, that it just happened and it was stupid, and we don't have any intention of doing it again. I know that's not enough, but it's all I can do right now.

"But I hope you understand that now I can't even say that. I was hoping we could deal with this like former friends in a civilized university. But now I can't say anything until I've talked to my own lawyer. I really didn't want to turn around and walk away from you. But I don't have any choice anymore. The only thing I can do is leave, and the only thing I can say is merry Christmas."

That was particularly stupid to say—merry Christmas. His fist flies out of his pocket and smashes me in the face, and I go down. I go straight down, not sprawling backward into the porch railing like John Wayne, but just crumbling in place, as if there had been a lever in my face connected to the joints of my knees, like the target in the clown-dunking booth at a county fair.

I have been dumped on the ground so fast that it seems there's more gravity than usual, making my legs crumble instantly. I think that a person watching would see a man going down as fast as in the old piece of news film from the Tet Offensive, when the Saigon chief of police shoots that kid in the head.

I'm down in a heap, but still perfectly alert. He got me along the side of the jaw with the flat of his first joints, but it doesn't feel as if he broke anything—just a dull, generalized ache.

He stands above me for a minute. "I didn't want to do that. I've got a Ph.D. in English and I really thought I could control my fucking self and not punch you in the mouth." He sounds as if he's almost crying. I'm ready to get up, but I'm not sure if I should. Strangely, I taste no blood, just a region that feels like novocaine wearing off.

"I'm sorry I sunk to your level and hit you," he says, then reaches his hand out to help me up.

I guess it's strange to say "Thank you" when somebody helps you up after knocking you down, but it's hard to break the polite habits of a lifetime. He obviously was brought up in the same kind of household, because he automatically says, "You're welcome," then stiffens and adds, "You can get off my property now."

I back away, keeping my eyes on him.

"I thought I could fucking control myself," he says, walking in the door. "You gotta fucking *control yourself,* Iverson!" And he slams the door so hard that the glass shatters all over the green Merry Christmas welcome mat. "You'll pay for that door!" he says.

As I hurry across the porch, toward the steps down to the

walkway, I can hear him slamming things around inside. If I didn't know he was a member of the American Gun Control Caucus, I would be half a mile down the street by now.

Some kind of crockery smashes. Chairs fall over. Then the big window shatters and the roast turkey comes flying through, a big one, slams against the porch railing, and rebounds at my feet, spinning on the grease of its breast. I know it's a horrible thing to think about at such a time, but I'm so hungry that I'm almost tempted to snatch up a handful of dressing out of its ass.

☆ ☆ ☆

Everything that I hated about this town half an hour ago has taken on a new angle of light, now that I have spoiled my place in it: the snowless expanse of ground, the student rentals with couches set up on the front lawn, and the dogs, the beautiful dogs with their voices ringing through the afternoon when everybody else is either gone away to someplace more interesting, or eating, or getting drunk, or watching football. To be part of a town—how much more important that is than to hide in the middle of a city. In a town you have to be nice to people because you see them all the time, and if you get caught with their daughters, the stink from that fire will hang over you from one end of Sloan Street to the next.

All I can do is walk home. Even though most people do their Christmas shopping in Cincinnati, the stores over on Broad Street are still open, in hopes of a season-saving last-minute rush. Once in a while I can hear a note or two of Crystal Gayle, "Chestnuts roasting on an open fire," clear for a few seconds, then lost behind a building, or drowned out by a pack of townie cars.

It's a beautiful street, Slum Street. I never noticed much about it before, the way the houses on the downhill side of the street let the gray walls of their basements stand bare where the ground falls away, the way the old cars lined up facing me squint in their own archaic and unmistakable grimaces.

Even the Victorian headquarters building of Ecumenical Liberation Outreach seems to have retained a modicum of its ladylike dignity. The Frisbee throwers have all gone inside. The only sign of life is the music still playing from the meeting-hall window, another Jackson Browne song from later in the same album, with mournful crushes of the piano, and a two- or three-voice chorus of Jackson Browne overdubbed into harmony with himself:

> Don't bring your skates, don't bring your sled.
> Don't call your friends, 'cause they're all dead.
> There's nobody walking up ahead.
> There's nobody calling you home for dinner,
> And you can't make a snowman,
> No you can't make a snowman,
> No no no no no you can't make a snowman
> In a nuclear winter.

A dog challenges me on the sidewalk. I cross over, and he goes back in his yard to bark at the cardinals on a neighbor's feeder.

Every time I try to figure what must have happened, I feel as if I'm working on a calculus problem: the information is in there somewhere, but to me it's all just chaos and withheld information. I have no idea if Frank was telling the truth about anything. Maybe she's not in the hospital; maybe he has her under lock and key somewhere, like that sad family in the South Bronx who couldn't get any help from Mayor Dinkins for their drug addict daughter, and so kept her chained to the radiator.

Or maybe she is crazy. It's crazy to leave incriminating evidence around, if that's what she did. Maybe she left them out on purpose. Or maybe she's so afraid of her father that she told him whatever bullshit he wanted to hear.

And maybe I'll never know. Maybe this is one of those stories where my favorite girl in the whole world will be trailered off into a loveless marriage and I'll never see her again, and I'll never find out why she was so nice to me in the first place, until we meet again years from now, white-haired and wistful. The perfect Victorian epilogue: to find her forty years old in a three-Mazda family.

And even if I do see her again, I don't know if I'll ever understand her. She reminds me of a ghost or something, getting herself in trouble when she didn't need to, her purposes existing in some territory from which I am permanently excluded, the decisions of her body carried out far beyond the sight of us dull sublunary mortals in the process of losing our jobs.

I keep thinking and thinking about all sorts of things, but none of it does me any good. It just makes me sick to think that I should go for two years as an eligible single man and do nothing about it, and now the first time I have a little fun, the first thing that happens is that—in an expression somebody uses in one of the books I don't dare teach anymore—the stove explodes.

The strangest thing is that it's almost exciting. That's a terrible thing to say, but it's true. Everything is changed, like waking up in another country. Like waking up one morning and I'm in the middle of one of those nuclear war movies that Students for Justice and Peace used to come around and intimidate the graduate teaching assistants into showing to their classes. At first the kids in the class would be happy to have a day off from brainstorming, and clustering, and question-replicating, and sentence-combining—but then it turns out that they never show any explosions, just a bunch of poorly dressed people with cancer dragging their asses around the screen for the whole class period.

Chapter 11

The light on my answering machine is blinking when I get home, as I knew it would be. Dog-man jumps and woofs, the cat's litter box is days past the changing deadline.

"Packard, this is Sam Brunton," the voice on the tape says, in Brunton's expressive monotone, bullheaded but sensitive, like Jack Webb at an art museum. "We need to talk. Come in to my office immediately, as soon as you get this message. I'll be here."

I have put on my best blue suit. It says in *Dress for Success* that if you are dressed in an authoritative manner, people will be more likely to give you a break. Big chance of that, I guess. My head feels like a balloon full of blood, like something being pressed between two pillows. I can feel a dull throb from the swelling around the left side of my jaw.

☆ ☆ ☆

I've never heard Drury Hall so quiet, the stairwells empty, the bulletin boards stripped to blank squares of compressed cork. On the tiles of each floor landing, I can feel the cloudy, almost tacky coat of new wax under the soles of my shoes.

I rescued a bat from this stairwell once, on a lovely spring evening, a little brown gargoyle-faced apparition whom everybody else in the department was afraid to go near. I caught him in a box that I found in the computer lab, then set him free outside, and he flew away into the dusk, in that angular swooping way bats have, and everybody loved me. Missy, the most beautiful of the work-study students in the office, even started calling me Professor Batman.

Brunton's door is closed. His office is in the inner part of the English department office, along with those of the Director of Composition, the Director of Graduate Studies, and the Minority Studies Chair.

I knock. Brunton opens the door and stops me. I can see that Janet Vanderpool, the Dean of the College of Arts and Sciences, is there, as well as Sondra Burley, Dean of Gender Issues. Frank is nowhere to be seen.

"We'll be with you in a minute," Sam Brunton says. I sit down in the half-dark, in one of the chairs that the graduate students sit in when they are waiting to see Bob Hillburn about what classes to sign up for.

I've never seen it so dark in this office, with no light except for the light coming in the windows of the stairwell. I can feel my jaw throb and tingle when I rub it. But the bruise is barely noticeable, or at least it was when I looked into the mirror at home.

Whatever they're talking about in there, they are being scrupulous about keeping their voices down. I can't hear a word. Once the telephone rings inside. It is the only sound I can hear.

How strange it is not to hear the airy, hoovering groan of the big Mita copier, for which we have to sign our names on a sheet and fill in why we needed the copies; such a warm, alive office sound that runs and runs all day, like a breathing spouse when you wake up at night—something you don't notice until the day you come in to work and it's down; then for the rest of the day nothing sounds right, the phones ring too shrill from office to office, voices are strained with keeping quiet around the department secretary's desk.

One of the things I liked best about the whole job (and I notice I'm already talking about it in the past tense) was to watch Missy making copies for somebody. If she was copying from a book or something that didn't let her close the cover completely, a sliver of light, atomic green, would pass over the soft contours of her face, over her white blouse, the way the green laser light in the Petting Zoo plays over the bodies of my favorite tittie dancers.

☆ ☆ ☆

The corners of Sam Brunton's mouth droop slightly behind his straw-colored beard, a sad Emmett Kelly kind of face, as if everybody in the world has let him down. He is one of those fair-skinned guys with so little pigmentation that he seems bleached, even his eyebrows and eyelashes white, the irises of his eyes drained of pigment to a cold, silvery blue, like the eyes of a wolf.

He's famous in this department for being unflappable. Amy DeLuria, who has the office next to mine, told me that once when she was going through her divorce she was in Sam Brunton's office for something and she started to cry. To pass the time while Amy was struggling to stop crying, Brunton picked up a magazine from his desk and started reading it.

But then, I've also heard him say something nice. I heard him say once, on a September day a week before classes started, "This town isn't worth a damn without the students."

Deans Vanderpool and Burley smile, greet me warmly. The atmosphere is almost festive. They have even given me the most comfortable chair.

Everybody is dressed casually. The chairman has jeans on, so does the Dean of the College. Sondra Burley wears her usual one-piece coveralls. I feel like a man who has shown up at the wrong party. I wanted to look like a figure of authority, but I think I look more like one of those job candidates we get who has just been informed that this department hasn't hired a white male in five years.

"So," Sam Brunton says cheerfully, or as cheerfully as he ever says anything, "let's begin the meeting. Frank Iverson and I have decided that it would be best for everybody concerned if he stayed away from this particular meeting at this time. However, we do have a statement that he relayed to me a few minutes ago. I'd like to read it to you and hear your reactions. Does that seem to you to be a satisfactory course of action?"

Ordinarily I would say, "Sure, Sam," but now I just look at the carpet and say, "Yes sir." I remember again that I haven't had anything to eat since breakfast.

He picks up a set of continuous computer sheets with the rows of tractor holes still attached to the edges. Frank, who is the department's computer authority (he even has his Macintosh programmed to call the racquetball court reservation number at exactly six-fifteen the night before our games), has apparently sent this statement in from his modem at home. Sam reads:

> On December 24 of this year, at approximately ten A.M., one of my household associates delivered into my possession an envelope of photographic prints which on closer examination proved to consist of crude, but blatant, attempts at homemade hard-core . . .

(and here Sam pauses for effect, never altering his soft voice)

    pornography.

(With that word the room dips, like a plane in an air pocket, and everybody but me looks into everybody else's eyes.)

Recognizable in the primitive public dramatizations of what is usually considered to be private marital intimacy were two individuals known to myself, this despite the extremely poor photographic quality of each one of the discovered images.

(Frank is also a meticulous amateur photographer. He never shows any of his pictures around, but he is fanatical about his equipment, and will spend hours showing you his cameras if you are foolish enough to let him get started.)

I regretfully acknowledge at this time that one of those individuals is my own daughter, Ms. Sarah Marianne Iverson, a former student at Amherst University of Indiana, lately of Las Vegas, Nevada, presently residing at 4021 Madison Street, Amherst, Indiana. The individual in the pornographic photographs who was seen to be engaged in various marital embraces with Ms. Iverson was a Packard Schmidt, middle name unknown to the writer of this document, residing at 360 Verossika Lane, Amherst, Indiana, currently employed by Amherst University of Indiana in the capacity of Associate Professor of Composition and Technical Writing.

After questioning Ms. Iverson about this matter, she revealed to me the extent of her previously secret sexual liaison with Packard Schmidt.

(At this point I look up to see if Sam Brunton has noticed the dangling participle in that last sentence. "Questioning" refers to Frank, who is of course doing the questioning; yet the main clause of the sentence proceeds with Sally as the subject, as if she had been questioning herself—somewhat like the poor waiter in "Dripping with onions and gravy, the waiter brought our steaks to the table." But Brunson registers nothing, and I wouldn't expect Vanderpool or Burley to care about such things.)

I was at this time already aware that Packard Schmidt had been the instructor of a section of English 461 in which Ms. Iverson was a student. She revealed to me that the above-named individual had sought her out, making inquiries among her Las Vegas associates, under the pretext of returning a term paper which Ms. Iverson had submitted to him in completion of the requirements for the individual's section of English 461.

Finally, the individual succeeded in locating Ms. Iverson. Using the most subtle techniques of psychological intimidation, he led her to believe that her retroactive success or failure in his already-completed class was either wholly or partially dependent upon her willingness to engage in various sexual intimacies with him.

(At the worst possible time, my empty stomach growls.)

Under such duress, Ms. Iverson was regrettably unable to maintain the ordinarily modest standards of behavior characteristic of her upbringing. Thus, she engaged in the requested activities, even going so far as to pose for the individual's futile attempts to forge a profit-making operation from Ms. Iverson's undeniable physical attractiveness.

(Now it occurs to me that for the first time in my life, after watching Frank Iverson smash half a dozen good Head racquets in his rage, I have finally seen a man get so angry that he becomes intelligent. Beneath the obtuse drivel of this diatribe, with all its distortion, there is a mind at work that knows that on some crazy self-destructive level I like to think of myself as an honorable person, which is why I can't defend myself. So that despite the enormous omissions, including Sally's temporary livelihood and the part she has played in this "liaison," as he calls it, Frank probably has judged that I am not going to sit here in the presence of my enemies and tell them that I am innocent because my friend Sally had been working as a hooker.)

As a member of this community, and as an individual with some personal stake in the outcome of this offense, it is up to the administration of Amherst University of Indiana, as well as the Indiana State Police, to dispose of this matter in a way that will restore credit to our university, our community, and our justice system.

(Another dangler: Careening around the corner on two wheels, the library came into view. And the old Packster did not die, he just faded away.)

Let me conclude, however, with a short quotation from a well-respected reference book, to wit, *The American Heritage Dictionary*, Second College Edition, published 1985 by Houghton Mifflin. The passage reads as follows: "The crime of forcing another person to submit to sexual intercourse." In my mind there can be no doubt that Packard Schmidt's actions in regard to his former student Ms. Sarah Marianne Iverson constitute an act of if not physical then without a doubt psychological force. I urge all parties in positions of authority to deal appropriately with this action. Incidentally, for all those individuals who are curious as to the context of the short passage quoted above, let me explain that it is simply definition number one in the aforementioned dictionary's entry for the word "rape."

A long pause. Sam folds the three attached pages of the print-out. I wish that he would pull the tractor strips off. I can't stand to see those tractor strips left on a paper. Of all the things I've let slide in my classes, I will say that I've never let a student submit a paper with the tractor strips still attached.

"Well, Packard," Sam says, still as cool as a Zen monk, and speaking with a tone and diction hardly distinguishable from Frank's electronic message, "since this document concerns you directly, at least to a greater personal extent than it concerns the rest of us, I think it would be appropriate that we invite your reaction to these allegations before we go any further with our discussion."

There is something about this building that has always puzzled me. If you sit still long enough you can feel it shaking, as if it's having one of those tiny earthquakes that we get a few times a year. I can feel it now, in this little office, with no other room occupied, probably not on the whole campus, except maybe campus security, with some sad-faced unmarried secretary whom they forced to be there to answer the phone that never rings— and all the time, just barely perceptible, this wobble-wobble up on the third floor.

"It's a lie."

"A lie, you say. I think it's important that we be as exact as we can about that. What parts, what allegations, what descriptions do you think can be appropriately dismissed as, as you refer to them, lies?."

"The whole thing, Sam." He seems to bristle, to pull back into his tall swivel chair, as if I shouldn't be using his first name under such circumstances. "It stinks. And frankly . . . Professor Brunton, given the seriousness of these accusations, and I hope you don't interpret this as stonewalling or being uncooperative, but I'm not sure if I should be answering any questions without my lawyer."

Janet Vanderpool speaks up for the first time, smiling cheerfully out from her even row of protruding teeth: "I'm sure you can get the same lawyer you had when you were charged with sexual harassment."

Sam speaks up: "I wouldn't worry about that. I managed to reach the district attorney. She said that based on what Frank told her, as well as based on what he refused to tell her, she saw no basis for criminal charges. I don't know about the rest of you, but I would much prefer to have this remain as a university matter."

"That's fine with me," I say, perhaps a little too heartily.

"So I would like to invite you to speak freely about whatever has been bothering you," Sam continues. "Now, we all know you've been working hard. And I was genuinely sorry that I couldn't lighten your course load this semester, the way I promised. We want to resolve this matter in a way that helps you."

I know patronizing when I hear it, since I have to do it so much myself, especially with students whose typewriter ribbons break and cannot be replaced except from Chicago, and then not for a period of weeks. But I guess patronizing is better than straight persecuting.

It's strange. My job hangs by a thread, if I'm lucky, if they haven't made some drastic decision already, based on Frank's bullshit. But everything seems so light, up here on the third floor, like a game that I can hardly stay interested in on an empty stomach. I'll play the best I can, try the remorse angle, which is after all quite close to what I feel.

"I want to say that I made a mistake. I did something very stupid. But with all due respect, I think Professor Iverson might be overstating the ethical and legal problems here just a bit. I did something, as a free adult, in the company of an individual over twenty-one and not enrolled in this university, that I now know constituted an instance of very poor judgment. The young lady who was involved"—for some reason I can't stand the thought of saying Sally's name out loud in front of these people—"made a similarly bad judgment, as free adults sometimes do."

Sondra Burley speaks up for the first time, in a delicate little voice, her dark features precise, Ethiopian, her face calm as wax under her yarnlike little-girl braids coiled into a basket on the top of her head.

"What you're saying is—free, white, and twenty-one, is that it?"

"Well, free, sort of. And twenty-one. White's got nothing to do with it."

"Oh, I think it does. I think it has everything to do with it."

"Professor Burley, it's hardly my place to debate semantics with you. But I will say that I tend not to agree."

She smiles blandly. "Then I think you deserve a little time to think about that," and she leans back in her chair, as if in slow motion.

"I'm just going to sit back and watch," Dean Burley says, "sort of like the audience at one of those topless bars in Kentucky that you are so fond of, and I'll let you do your own thinking about your own attitude toward what you obviously regard as your own *entitlement,* while we go on with this *conflux."* She pronounces this last word with a delicate French intonation. Most people in this university try to pronounce all Spanish names in the manner of a native *salvadoreño,* but Burley extends this linguistic egalitarianism to include words from such places as Roma, and Polska, and even Nihon.

"I just want to say that it was a mistake. But I want to stress that she wasn't a student, that what happened had nothing to do with her grades, which were already recorded before any of this started, and that nobody got hurt."

"That's not completely accurate, Pack," Brunton says, using my common name for the first time. "Frank Iverson is in the emergency room right now with a broken finger."

The snow falls outside, blurring slightly the branches of the trees that stand close to the window.

Sam Brunton says, "You've been listening to all this, Janet, and I guess we could say that you're the ranking officer here"—chuckles all around—"but we haven't heard much of what you have to say."

Dean Vanderpool is probably the single best-known person on campus. She has given the keynote address for the midwestern regional convention of the Modern Language Association, and has even done a remote once, with Ted Koppel, on a slow news night I guess it was, to defend the university system against Kari Mirchandani, who had written a book criticizing it. Her bright smile, her pert gray hair, and her remarkably even buck teeth are a familiar sight on Indiana Public Television. Those teeth are so even, so white, and so substantial that one would think at first that they are dentures—and maybe they are, although I don't see why anybody would want bucktooth dentures.

"Well," she says, her face sweeping back and forth between Brunton and me like a radar scanner. "The first thing I want to say to Professor Schmidt is thank you for coming here on such short notice, so shortly after getting back from your gambling trip to Las Vegas." Every consonant is airy, fuzzed over a little, because of the teeth. But it feels good to see somebody smile at me and not just stare off into space; and it feels good to hear somebody call me by my professional title, instead of Packard, which sounds like a bad little boy being called home to his punishment.

"I realize that this is very hard for you," she goes on, "and I appreciate the forthcoming nature of your remarks. Teaching composition is hard work—*damned* hard work—and it's natural that it should be associated sometimes with problems that crop up in people's lives."

It's easy to see why she's the Dean of the College of Arts and Sciences. She's brilliant at working her way around people. Even though I know exactly what she's doing, and that I'm about to get screwed, I still like her. There is something wonderfully homey about this tall figure, as familiar as an old aunt, as she leans toward me, teeth pointing like a shelf.

"Be that as it may," she says, and pauses to let those words percolate, the way Secretary of State Baker in his famous press conference paused after the momentous word "regrettably."

"Be that as it may," she says again, "we've had an ugly incident that is going to be very hard for us to ignore. It would be nice to think we could smooth it over and go back to our . . . *happy-little-workbenches,*" and here she leans forward, grinning toothily.

"And there's another problem. I'm sorry to bring it up, but it's been hanging around like a rock in a bag of peanuts, as my grandmother used to say. You know you're going to bite down on it eventually." A strange simile for her to use. With those choppers she could bite down on anything: a number-two pencil, a rock, a lug wrench.

"As you probably know," Dean Vanderpool says, "that problem stems from the incident with . . . *The Joke.*" A pause. A grin. Her teeth gleam white as a boxer's mouthguard. Yet it seems we're almost in a good mood, just because of how good she is at working a crowd.

"Now at the time that . . . The Joke . . . occurred, and you were confronted for sexual harassment by your own students, I was understandably concerned. But in the end I let the matter pass, for two reasons. First, it would not have been appropriate to attempt to classify . . . The Joke . . . as a *detenurable offense.*" She has this mannerism, particularly effective on television, of pausing before a key phrase, and then lancing into it with her teeth at the cutting prow, neck thrust forward, like a goose chasing a bug in the water.

Every time she says "The Joke," I keep wanting to butt in and say it was a pretty mild joke. But I'm probably better off to keep still.

"Second," she says, "I didn't have any indication of . . . The Joke . . . being part of any larger pattern, at least not any kind of pattern that was discernible to me." Long pause while she scans the three faces in the room, back and forth, back and forth.

Suddenly she speaks again, as if the next sentence had popped into her head as a complete surprise.

"*And-likewise,*" she says, "when Professor Schmidt returned from his gambling junket and the present offense was brought to my attention, I *might* . . . have been inclined to regard it as an honest mistake on the part of a troubled individual. That is," and here her voice drops to a whisper, "if it were not for . . . the already established presence of . . . *The Joke.*" Every time she says "The Joke," her face moves forward a few inches, those impressive teeth gleaming out in front like a cowcatcher.

Edward Allen

"So, to be as brief as I can under the circumstances, I would say that The Joke by itself would not constitute a detenurable offense. And the present offense, were it not backed up, as it were, by the enduring presence of The Joke, would in all likelihood not prove to be detenurable.

"However, when you combine the present offense with the enduring . . . *echo* of The Joke, I think that what happens is somewhat akin to what happens (if I may be permitted to borrow a metaphor from our metallurgical colleagues) when you mix the two metals copper and zinc. What you end up with, of course, is bronze, an alloy far harder and far more useful than its two constituent elements. And at the risk of hammering this conceit to the point of . . . metal fatigue, let me just say that the two incidents under consideration here—the sex liaison *and* . . . The Joke— have together *alloyed* themselves into a pattern more damaging than those original component incidents that have brought us here to this . . . perhaps less than festive . . . holiday gathering.

"Now, as we all know, the process of separating a tenured faculty member from this university is not simple . . . is not speedy . . . is not the sort of administrative procedure to be handled carelessly, or petulantly, or for any of the many inappropriate or underhanded or frivolous reasons that could be advanced for such a motion. To switch the source of our metaphors from the world of smelting pots to the world of . . . lobster pots, I would like to caution you all that it's a long and difficult voyage we're all embarked on. However, its point of anchor-weighing is already receding on the horizon . . . aft. And our final landfall, in my official opinion, can and must occur only in a port whose chandler's registry no longer includes the name of Packard Schmidt."

Sam Brunton's cheeks sag behind his beard like the flews of a basset hound. "Sondra, how do you feel about what Janet has said?"

Dean Burley looks up, almost frightened, as if surprised by a teacher, and says in her flutish voice, "I think the whole situation is very unfortunate. But I agree with Dean Vanderpool. I feel sorry for Professor Schmidt"—and with this I almost flush to hear myself called by my professional title by someone who obviously hates my guts—"but I agree that his quixotic actions contain within themselves some element of the *ka-mi-ka-ze,*" and on this word she shifts abruptly into a Japanese accent, tripping lightly over the four staccato syllables.

"Do you have anything to say for yourself, Packard?"

"Yes I do, as a matter of fact. Two things. One: this isn't fair. Two: I'm not going to sit back and be thrown out of here for nothing. If tenure means anything, it means that I'm entitled to due process."

"Tenure is a method of protecting academic freedom," Dean Burley says, "not personal license."

"Packard, we'd like to help you through this," Dean Vanderpool says, beaming, kind as a lady who bakes cookies. "We don't want to make this any harder on you than it's been. And I think the best way I can keep things from getting harder is to delineate as closely as possible what I see as your options. Are you ready to hear those options?"

"I'm surprised to hear you suggest that you recognize more than one option," I say. For a second her cowcatcher withdraws a few inches.

"First of all, I need to tell you that I am exercising my option, under the 'unforeseen situation' clause in the Faculty Bylaws, to suspend without pay for one semester any faculty member, tenured or untenured, who in my opinion constitutes a gross threat to the well-being of the Amherst community. So whatever happens, you're not teaching in January. I understand that Professor Brunton has already tentatively reassigned your classes. Now I would like to invite you to consider how a detenuring trial, with all its attendant publicity, as well as the inevitable demonstrations by such groups as the Equal Justice League and Reclaim the Night, is going to affect your ability to find an alternative position.

Edward Allen

"And I also invite you to consider what the reaction on the part of a prospective employer will be when she sees your working transcript from here, complete with the notation that you were suspended from your position under suspicion of rape."

"You're using that word awfully loosely, don't you think?" I say, raising my voice very slightly for the first time.

"Packard, that word is going to come up, and I'm just trying to help you be prepared for it. Even though one might get away with it on the Supreme Court, I'd like to think this university has a good deal more integrity, as well as more meticulous personnel requirements, than that polluted institution."

"I'm glad we agree on something," I say, and her shelf of a smile comes back to me so warm it feels like somebody putting her arm around my shoulder.

"Be that as it may," she says, "the students are going to pick that word up, the *Daily Arrow* is going to pick that word up, maybe the *Star*. You might even get a chance to go on *Geraldo*, if you like being on television, keeping your back to the camera, of course. Packard, that word is going to keep coming up and coming up for the rest of your life. I just want you to be prepared for that."

"I'm not prepared, and I'm not going to *be* prepared. Pardon my language, but I think it sucks."

At first I think she's going to be angry at such a Bart Simpson-ish term, but then she says, "Well, of *course* it sucks," so warmly that she sounds as if she's about to give me a big hug. "That's why I'm trying to make it *easier* for you."

"And how do you propose to do that? Give me a gold watch?"

"We want to help you get started again, somewhere else. And the easiest way to do that is for you . . . to resign."

"Absolutely not."

"It would be strongly in your interest to do so, Packard. Not a word will get out of this room. Your transcript will remain exactly as it was, I promise you that.

"And I'll do one more thing to . . . sweeten the pot, which is an expression I think should be agreeable to a . . . compulsive gambler." And here her grinning shelf of teeth lances toward me again.

"I'm willing to subsidize your trips to the NCTE convention as well as the Four Cs, if that will help you find a job."

"I already have a job."

"You don't, Packard. The more you resist that fact, the more you're going to hurt yourself."

This is not just a nasty lady beating up some overweight professor, it's important that I stress that point. There is real warmth in her every word. And I almost feel happy that the meeting has gone as well as it has.

So I give up, as I knew I would. We've been in here for an hour. Outside, a tiny dust of snow blows around outside the third-floor windows. The knot in my stomach has loosened enough to remind me that I'm starving. I keep looking at the glass *Schneekugel* paperweight on Sam's desk, imagining that it is a dome-shaped meat loaf.

It almost feels like a Christmas party. Dean Vanderpool has taken the liberty of preparing in advance my letter of resignation, a handsomely laser-printed form which she produces from her blue vinyl Amherst portfolio.

"I hope you'll forgive the . . . boilerplate nature of this document," she says. "It doesn't do justice to your own individual style."

I sign.

The deans leave, shaking my hand. "You've done a very brave thing," Vanderpool says.

I have agreed to move out of my office immediately, but my stomach is so empty that I have to ask Sam if I can skip out and get some lunch and then come back.

"I can't do it, Pack," he says. "Any faculty member leaving

under emergency conditions is required to be in the presence of a security guard at every moment. That's why I'm here. I can't leave until he shows up. Do you like pizza?"

"It's all right."

"I'll send out for some."

"You don't have to do that."

The security guard gets here, a round-faced little man with a gray flattop. He didn't seem to come from any direction; he was just sort of gradually here. I tell Sam that I'll call myself and send out, but he won't let me.

"This is on me, Pack," he says, and shakes my hand and goes. I honestly don't know whether to laugh or cry or thank him or kick him down the stairs.

Chapter 12

wouldn't have ordered Domino's myself. I thought Sam had more class than that. The security guard, whose name is Tony, will not take a slice. He just stands there outside my office door, watching me eat. The pie came with two giant Cokes, in cartons with a scored hole you punch the straw through, but he is so poorly brought up that he won't even take one of those. Never turn down free sugar on Christmas Eve, my father used to say.

Everything in the office goes. It's a little room, but I've been there long enough to accumulate the sorts of things that fill the corners and the seams between cabinets without taking up space—until the moment they are moved, and then they mushroom out into enormous piles.

Everything goes. It's easy, because there are no choices, just

Edward Allen

fold the packing boxes that Tony found for me in the basement
out from their flat state and crisscross the flaps on the bottom,
and start throwing the books in, in whatever order they were in to
begin with up on my shelves, starting with the alphabetic fiction,
from Agee to Barth to Didion, just slammed into the box, Fitz-
gerald, my well-marked hardback desk copy of *The Great Gatsby,*
which I have not yet become afraid to teach; then some book I
didn't even know I had, by Dick Jekyll, called *Vealhouse Nocturne,*
one of those small-press books, fat chance I'll ever read that; box
full, open another, while Tony stands and stands, though I'm glad
he hasn't asked to help; from Lewis to Melville to Nabokov, from
Percy through Steinbeck to Updike, to Wolfe, to Wolfe, to Wolff,
to Woolf.

Then another box for the poetry that I never alphabetized, all
those thin little eighteen-dollar paperbacks from University of
Pittsburgh Press and Arkansas State Poetry Editions, and then all
those little basement presses named after birds and run by
bearded guys in heavy red hunting shirts: Chimney Swift Press,
Anhinga Press, Hummingbird Originals, and that remarkably con-
sistent combination of dull introspection and shrill ideology that
characterizes the Black Sparrow Press of California, a house for
poets so proud that they decline to publish with the evil New York
establishment that has declined to publish them.

The boxes fill with little books of little poems of which I cannot
remember a word, the imprisoned letters dumb, asleep, never to
be born, like William Stafford's fawn, which poem I do remember
and which does not exist between the covers of any of these
nervous little volumes—with pictures on the back in which the
author's eyes didn't come out just right. And then all the Stark
Poems About New England, a genre in itself, book after book,
thinner and thinner, some of them up around thirty dollars now.

The big load will be the textbooks, four whole shelves of Instructor's Guides and Directed Worksheets: *A Matrix for Clear*

Ideas, Visual Descriptions in Technical Writing, Exercises for Writers, Exercises for Teachers, Teaching Students How to Write, Writing Students How to Teach, on and on. None of them are any help, of course. *Patterns of Composition, Patterns of Reading, Patterns of Teaching, Patterns of Rhetoric, Patterns of Exposition, Patterns of Persuasion, Patterns of Editing, Patterns of Brainstorming,* until I can't see straight and I start asking myself: Christ, what are patterns for?

On and on they go, slamming into the box, into the box, as if somebody other than me with hands other than mine is lifting them off the shelf and stuffing them into boxes, some of which have bottoms too weak to trust.

Now the references, the good dictionary and the not-so-good atlas of the world, and the scattering of nonfiction, the *Barnet Directory of Textbook Publishers,* and the almanac, and the *Macintosh User's Guide,* which isn't mine, so I leave it on the computer desk next to the Imagewriter. Then a handful of Cliffs Notes, hidden in a red paper folder, and a self-help book called *Cut Your Bills in Half,* which I've never liked having around because every time I look at it from the wrong direction I think it says "Cut Your Balls in Half."

Now, on to the walls: my diplomas first, in their frames, these not flung around but laid carefully in one of the better boxes, the M.A. from the University of Maryland, and the larger Ph.D. from Syracuse, which was the source of the four most bleak and boring and poverty-stricken years of my life, brightened by the one good spot of meeting the woman who would be a temporarily beautiful and happy wife until her chin bristles drove me into the arms of tittie dancers.

Suddenly I remember that tonight, Christmas Eve, will be my last chance to see my tittie dancers, the only night I'll have free, before the stroke of midnight New Year's Eve, when State Attorney General Buzzy Bacon and his priests will wave their magic

Bibles and make all my beautiful girls go away.

Then this is the only night I have. And I've never needed it more. Christmas the bars will be closed; the day after, I'll be on my way to Philadelphia for MLA, not that I have any chance of getting a job at this late date, but I need to put in an appearance.

And by the time I get back, ready to begin editing my teaching vita down into a résumé for a textbook publisher's representative, or some such teenager's career at half my old salary, it will be too late. Those magic tittie-bar buildings with the pink fluorescent script glowing out into the Lexington darkness will already be half transformed into outlets for Family-Land Video, the chain that has made a name for itself as the All–*Honey I Shrunk the Kids* video store.

The padded chairs in which I have passed many a happy minute will already have been sold to the furniture liquidators, fumigated, retailed out for no money down to young women on welfare, to be subsequently repossessed, refumigated, refinanced, over and over, until one day the sometimes father of the woman's too many children takes too much cocaine and throws the chair out the project window. Union carpenters will already be nailing up the display racks for the empty video boxes, and the first truckloads of Rick Moranis will have been forklifted into the room over to the side of the main floor where we used to receive our private dances from the lovely lady of our choice.

It's a long job moving out, here in this office that I never knew I cared about, with that spooky-fingered tree right outside, and the strange sight of the Masters Library closed, all those round bubbly porthole windows dark. So many student papers boxed in the corner, which we are required to keep on file for three years, in their labeled cases from this year and last year and the year before. God, you could build a house out of all that paper, the draft printing on some of them dimmer than supermarket tapes, or big loopy balloons of lettering from a girl student, and the dark, knifelike slant of a guy who didn't want to be there.

And the topics: "Justicism of a City"—I spent half an hour in conference trying to explain to the kid why you can't use a word that doesn't exist, but he won the argument; "Night Verses Day, A Comparative Contrast"; "The Process of Applying for a Summer Job at the Four-H Summer Camp in Annandale, Ohio."

For the last two years all the composition teachers have gotten together and established a pool, with the prize going to that teacher who can come closest to guessing the total number of essays submitted to the English department under the title "Abortion: Auschwitz USA." It's a hard number to guess at too, because now even the students who sit on the pro-choice side of the classrooms have started submitting papers under that title, having found out that we will give them an automatic B-minus without reading it.

I feel as if I should hate all this stuff, but I don't. They're sincere. They're stupid, but they don't want to hurt anybody. Even the poor Auschwitz kids, with their parents' rage echoing in their heads: they just want things to be easy.

I keep thinking, keep coming back to it as if to one of those chewed sores I sometimes get on the inside of my cheek, that I should have fought the dean and stayed on through the petitions and the boycotts and the phone calls, brave as that guy at West Point who got unfairly "silenced" and stuck it out like an officer until graduation.

But I guess it wouldn't have worked. I like to have friends, even when my friends and I don't like each other very much. And when there's nobody to back me up when I'm wrong, which I usually am, and nobody to play racquetball with—then the world will no longer be the kind of place where I can sit up in my office for an hour with classical music on and look out at the warm library lights. If I tried to fight my way back into this building, I'd end up feeling about as welcome as a Jew in Montreal.

No need to clean, just pack away the pictures: Cath when she was still pretty, my giant land-use map of the state of Indiana, my portable Janet Jackson picture which I used to put in the desk when someone came in who might not approve.

The harder I work, packing the boxes with folders, and Macintosh disks I'll never use, and manila envelopes, and my special economy package of Liquid Paper, whose ozone-destroying molecules I will treasure for the rest of my life, because it might soon become illegal in this state as it has in California—the harder I work, the prettier this office seems, even the gray steely composition of the desktop, which I have doodled checkerboards on when I was talking on the phone with its twelve numbered buttons that I never programmed with anything.

It's illegal, but Tony unlocks the chain and lets me back the station wagon in from College Avenue and up the brick walkway, all the way to the front door. Now I'm starting to feel in a hurry. Lexington is two hours away. Drury Hall has that feeling in it already when a door closes and the light inside the door has more yellow in it than it had an hour ago, meaning that it's almost ready to get dark. I use the hand truck Tony lent me to bring the boxes down in the slow elevator that I never used when I worked here, when I used to work here, when this was my place and I didn't appreciate it enough, or something—or maybe I just didn't cover my own ass.

And up, with the empty hand truck and Tony smoking in the elevator, and down with three boxes, which I lift off and shove down the ribbed floor of the station wagon, toward the front seat, and then one more trip.

And that's the end of my office. No need to empty the trash. The tree quakes outside; the snow didn't amount to anything. I have to give him the key right now, and slam goes the door, and we go down in the elevator one last time.

☆ ☆ ☆

It makes me horny when the world goes to hell. You'd think that being scared and sick about something, with my stomach seeming to fall as if the muscles holding it up had ruptured, would make my interest in things topless and bottomless tend to shrivel, the way eighteen-year-old boys in the hospital for their motorcycle accidents are said to detumesce instantly under the nurse's spoon.

But for me, trouble makes everything go boom boom, as if I have stepped out of my hotel on the Las Vegas Strip and it's the middle of summer with the wind blowing and the fire is whooshing out of the Mirage volcano and painting everybody's face yellow, and I have a little handout magazine in my pocket that some scroungy old guy gave me—on the inside flap: "Wild Girls, Direct to your Room, Totally Nude."

That's what it was like during the Gulf War, on the same night Dan Rather was apologizing for not being able to control his emotions. Outside, the lights over Mr. Dollarsaver's parking lot were brighter than I'd ever seen them. I could hear how the war made all the traffic move faster, made everything at once more serious and more throw-it-all-in-the-fireplace-and-everybody-get-shitface-drunk. It made music louder at night; even the wimp-rock stations like Frankfort's WSFT started playing The Doors and Talking Heads.

In the daytime, when people were driving to work with their radios on and various-sized flags lashed to their antennas, the war concentrated the sun down to a blip of light such as you see on the ground when boys are torturing ants under a magnifying glass.

At night, when it was already morning over there, with the sun rising over whatever those blue dome things were in the background behind Arthur Kent, the music cranked loud around the exit ramps from the windows of Trans Ams and Camaros, and everybody was drunk. Outside the Baby Doll, at the corner where the mufflers roared past the Goodyear Service Center and the Buster Brown shoe store, a dark-haired girl flagged down the traffic.

When I walked past her, from the restaurant where I'd parked my car so my Amherst Indiana faculty parking sticker would not be seen among the dope deals and blow jobs of the Baby Doll parking lot, she smiled, showing a gold tooth. I walked back to the car as if to get something I'd forgotten, and she smiled again and said hello, and then when I passed her again on the way back into the bar, she said, "Hi, honey," and showed me her tongue, a long beautiful prostitute tongue, in the middle of winter, in the middle of a war.

☆ ☆ ☆

I've always found the noise of a cash machine exciting. I associate it with the smell of a girl's hair, when she dances with her ass rubbing my legs and leans back against me, looking over her shoulder. The moment the machine starts that airy official groan of acceptance, I start to feel the blood beat in the back of my head, and the area below my waist gets all cold and dizzy, as if I'm about to jump off a cliff. I've read that recovering drug addicts have a very hard time with these machines, because the associative link between that sound in their ears and the feel of the cocaine in their nose is so strong that it can send them on the spur of the moment back to their old dealer's beeper phone.

I'm a little overdressed for the Petting Zoo, I know, but that's not really a bad thing. When the girls see a man in a blue suit, they figure he's ready to spend some money. Maybe I won't have to make those obvious beckoning gestures to get the ones I like to come over to my table.

I would go directly from the bank to the bar, but all this weight in the back is making the car handle like a farm wagon, yawing back and forth on the road. So I head home to unload my office stuff. On Kentucky Avenue a "Turn Back to the Bible" billboard, with the chalk outline of a body on the sidewalk as illustration, fills the space between Mr. Dollarsaver and Hot Tickets Video, where all the R-rated films have recently joined the Xs and NC-17s in videotape hell.

MUSTANG SALLY ☆ ☆ ☆

The management of Hot Tickets was smart enough to know
that burning the tapes would be likely to cause an uproar among
those students not too busy demonstrating against the construction of Bloomington Particle Research Laboratories—so the
owners decided to shred the cassettes instead. The Indianapolis
television station showed the staff of Hot Tickets tossing the hundreds of tapes into one of those machines that chips up the small
branches from road-cleaning work and shoots them up a hollow
tube into the back of a truck.

All those boxes—it will take me half an hour to unload them;
and then it occurs to me, why don't I just dump it all in the garage
and take off? What is it, anyway? Just shit to be dumped, on a
night when totally nude nipples wait for me under the spastic
needles of laser light in a state the priests will not have caught up
with for another eight sexy days.

The driveway to my house slants down from the road. The
garage is really a separate building, at a level ten feet lower than
the main floor of the house, and joined to the house by a sort of
board running along where the rain gutter would be if there was
one.

What I'm going to do is back down, fast, and then slam on the
brakes, with the rear door open. Carefully, like Evel Knievel's son
Robby rehearsing a school-bus jump, I make a slow dry run, backward down the bricks, until I have judged exactly where I want to
put the brakes on. I can hear Dog-man inside, woofing, demand-
ing to be taken for a walk, which I'm not going to do until I get
back.

And now I try it for real, craned around backward and going as
fast as I dare; the screech of the tires on the concrete floor of the
garage fills the little building, but the stuff in the car doesn't budge.

I try again, faster, the car jouncing at the place where the
slanted driveway meets the level garage, slam on the brakes, and
jam it into first and squeal forward. But only one box tumbles out.

191 ☆

I'm getting mad, and tired, and one small pepperoni pizza from the people who call up poor Cath every day at work with their bomb threats isn't enough on a day like this to keep me thinking straight.

This time I don't care. I nose it all the way out into the middle of Verossika Lane, and then I'm hurtling backward, scared, with a metallic taste under my tongue.

I slam on the brakes. The tires shriek in the Christmas Eve gloom, the boxes tumble out onto the oil-blotched concrete, scattering books and comparisons-and-contrasts. The front end of the car skids around to the left and cuts the bottom two levels out from under one of those metal K-Mart shelf towers, which took me all day to put together. The open tailgate bangs hard into the back wall of the garage. The car jerks to a stop. The K-Mart étagère falls on top of the car with a crash, more heavy objects bang on the roof, and then my old toolbox with the wrenched lid slides off a broken shelf and smashes through the rear passenger window.

As I sit there, the windshield begins to go white, in V-shaped lobes from the top down. It goes white slowly, calmly, as if an unsymmetrical curtain is being lowered, or to be more precise, as if a can of white paint that I'd never gotten around to finishing the front porch with has opened on top of the car.

I have said "Oh shit" so many times today, in so many different intonations of disaster, that it really doesn't mean much anymore. So I don't say anything. I sit there, watching the fattening icicles of paint drip down the windshield. I turn on the radio. "The Little Drummer Boy."

Chapter 13

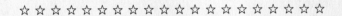

With mittens and a wool hat it's not too bad. The chilly exhaust swirls around inside the car, drawn in by the draft-vacuum of the wrenched tailgate that won't close. I have had to open the driver's side window so I don't get carbon monoxide poisoning.

At least I got the windshield clean. The turpentine had already spilled, so I had to use half a bottle of Bacardi 151, which was no tragedy, since I'd had the stuff in the house for two years and never drank it. The paint has drawn continent-shaped swatches of white over the Volvo's maroon surface, making it look now like one of those two-toned ponies that Indian warriors ride in the movies.

The streets are empty, the Italian catering houses on the outskirts of town dark except for the lights of their cone-shaped Christmas trees, whose pinpoints I can see reflecting along the contours of the engine cover in those places where the paint hasn't spilled.

It would be nice, driving out of town on a night like this, to hear some classical music, maybe some harpischordy Christmas stuff over the whoosh of the open windows, but tonight WPBK is running another one of those public interest discussion shows, this one called "The Magazine Rack."

As I head out into the darkness on Route 421, with the wind and the exhaust and the road noise howling around my hat and mittens, into the land where kids spray-paint walls and bridges with the names of the people they have a crush on, I am treated to a remarkably complete analysis of a publication called *Home Handicrafts,* beginning with a description of the cover, then a reading of the contents page, then going on with abstracts of each individual article.

☆ ☆ ☆

Just walking into the Petting Zoo you can tell it's one of the last days of the place. Somehow the music feels louder, deeper, if that is actually possible. I can feel, in the way my feet strike the floor beside the booth where you pay your cover charge, something no longer solid. This place, according to the *Courier-Journal,* is going down with a bang, bankruptcy papers already filed, unlike some of the other bars, such as the Cutie Pie, which is trying to survive by going along with the ordinance.

On my way over here I stopped at the Cutie Pie for one drink, out of curiosity. Its outside has been remodeled, looking now as clean as one of the family values video stores which would otherwise have taken its place. A translucent plastic awning, brightly lit from inside, showed a crude and lumpy cartoon of a supine woman in a red bikini, with a very small head.

Inside, it has diminished into someplace where the girls dance in a sort of brass cage with a ten-foot-wide empty space around it like a moat, to keep anybody from going near them. Each table has on it one of those little clear plastic display stands such as they have in Denny's to show you what the pie of the month is, each holding a paper containing a list of the offenses for which a patron will find himself ejected from the premises:

1. Foul language.
2. Rowdy conduct.
3. Attempting to buy more than three drinks.
4. Possession of drugs.
5. Solicitation to buy, consume, transport, sell, or possess drugs.
6. Solicitation to ride in a car with a drunk driver.
7. Solicitation for prostitution.
8. Sneaking own liquor into premises.
9. Touching dancers.
10. Propositioning dancers.
11. Suggestive remarks to dancers.
12. Touching the cocktail waitress.
13. Suggestive remarks to the cocktail waitress.
14. Propositioning the cocktail waitress.
15. Deceptive drink-buying practices.

With some of that latex-and-rum smell still stuck to my hands, and my breath heavy from a napkinless drive-through Quarter Pounder, I pay my ten dollars to the Petting Zoo bouncer and walk around the mirrored corner to the showroom floor. Inside, the long green strings and the long red strings of computerized laser needles jerk and wander among the thunderheads of cigarette smoke. The corners are lined with tubes of ultraviolet light. The square stage is furred with greenery; colored lights twinkle in the imitation ropes of pine. "Stairway to Heaven" is playing so loud that one of Jimmy Page's notes keeps finding a very unfortunate harmonic in my left ear.

Edward Allen

In this bar, "Stairway to Heaven" is requested and played on the average of once an hour, because it is so long. When you buy a table-dance, or a lap-dance, or a couch-dance from one of the girls, it lasts for only one song, so the longer the song, the more you get for your money. The second most popular song in the bar is Joe Walsh's nine-minute live version of "Life's Been Good." After a night in one of these bars a man will walk out with the verses to those songs repeating in his own head for hours.

On the square stage in the middle of the room, a plain-faced blond girl, with breasts so big that the nipples are stretched out and blurred at the tips like the ends of an overinflated balloon, swings around the upright brass pole with a violent spasmodic motion. The laser lights paint red and green squiggles on her body as she moves herself around the square tiles of the stage, which themselves have lights under them, shining up from below her body in blue and yellow and red.

Every minute or so the lights change; the lasers go out and a powerful strobe light kicks on above the stage, and the girl's motions are suddenly spastic, discontinuous, puppety, her arms going up and down in time-lapse jerks. The whole room flashes on and off five times a second, from the little round cocktail tables surrounding the stage to the two or three captain's chairs around each table, from the continuous banquette of couch running along the back wall to the little room off to the side where you go for what is called a "private dance."

Being Christmas Eve, it's pretty slow, but it's not dead. Enough guys have shown up so that the air is filled with the usual drifting continents of Marlboro smoke, which move under the strobes in a series of tiny jerks, generally in my direction. When you look down to the end of the room, the dancers taking a break at the bar are softened by a faraway smog effect.

I like it when none of the dancers come up to me until I've been here for a while. I can sit with a warm beer and let my eyes adjust, as much as they could ever adjust to these Jovian laser storms. I can look around and see if any of the girls I know from before are here, or if there's anybody else in particular from whom I want my private dance.

Through the smoke, through the rasp of guitar solo, through the red and green filaments of laser light that wave around in the darkness like glass rods, the tittie dancers move delicately, on high heels, from customer to customer.

The variety of their looks is surprising. Some are distinctly homely, or fat, or they wear heavy-framed glasses turned up at the corners. How the ugly ones can make a living here I don't know; perhaps the ugly girls can work cheap, to the benefit of those guys who are so liberated from the newly discovered vice of "lookism" that they can with impunity brag about all girls being the same with a sack over their head.

But then some of them are spectacular—in their lace bras and panties turned iridescent blue by the blur of ultraviolet—girls with hair so big and blond you can see them all the way across the bar through the muddle of smoke and light.

And I like it when I have some time to look and think and get used to how loud the music is, because then I get a chance to get excited on my own time. And until that happens I just tell anybody who comes by that I want to watch the show. Part of the problem tonight is that my hands still stink. That gyroscope-shaped soap dispenser in the bathroom is, as usual, empty of its pink liquid.

After a while a few of the black girls come around to my table, trying to impress me with how much perfume they have on. Once when I was still married I let one of these girls give me a dance, but all she did the whole time was rub this strong, marshmallowy scent all over my tie, a good twenty-dollar all-silk Aquascutum at that, which I ended up having to throw out the car window, on the bridge over the Ohio River, because Cath would have noticed.

Edward Allen

I wave them away. "I just want to watch the show," I say to each of them, which in a tittie bar is a polite way of saying "Go away." I am sorry to have given them such a rude brush-off, especially because I know it is unfair to Janet Jackson.

Many of the girls here, I notice, are giving out private party cards. With the bars closing down, their only hope is to build up an outside clientele.

"Stairway to Heaven" ends at last. The disk jockey shouts and harangues the sparse crowd with his usual half-comprehensible patter.

"All RIGHT, put your hands a ba-ba-ba-*sexy lady,* that was *TIF-FANY,* dancing on the center stage. And remember, you ca-ba-ba-ba-your favorite *sexy lady* over for a couch-dance-table-dance-lap-dance-slow-dance-private-dance just call'er right *OVAH!*

"And now," his voice drops to a normal and comprehensible tone, "we got something special for you, a real rarity on our Petting Zoo sound system. It's a special holiday record that *CINDY* is going to dance to for us on the center stage, and we want to dedicate this record to Mr. Attorney General Buzzy Bacon and his Purificational snake-handlers. So get those hands together for Lexington's own *Cindy!*"

Cindy climbs the stage from the corner, one of those girls with a perfect body but too much chin, coming down in a long shelf. As the song cranks up she launches into a very athletic dance routine, full of splits and high kicks and slides to the floor and brass-pole work. She wears a bikini with battery-powered Christmas lights set into the fabric, which blink and flash as she powers herself through her routine.

The record turns out to be something called "The Little Drum-mer Punk," from 1980 or thereabouts, by one of those short-lived bands from the "Shock-Punk" movement. I don't remember which group it was—either Chancellor of the Exchequer or The Steaming Pile.

MUSTANG SALLY ☆ ☆ ☆

It comes on with frantic, almost sloppy, drums, and a shrill hammering of distorted rhythm guitar chords, until the vocals start, in heavy cockney accents, more shouted than sung:

"Come on!" they pulled my arm—pah rum pa pum pum.
Some bitch had a baby in a barn—pah rum pa pum pum.
We put on our hats and coats—pah rum pa pum pum.
There he was, surrounded by goats—pah rum pa pum pum, rum
    pa pum pum, rum pa pum pum.
One of them took a shit—pah rum pa pum pum,
On my drum.

(And just to keep people from getting the idea that this group is completely crude and unsophisticated, this last line is followed by a sound effect: distinct from the drum-and-guitar-and foot-stomp-ing noise you can hear, if you listen closely, a cascade of little pellets being dropped onto a tightly drawn drumskin.)

The cows were dying of thirst—pah rum pa pum pum.
They ate the afterbirth—pah rum pa pum pum.
Then Joseph came home drunk—pah rum pa pum pum.
'e fucked her in the bunk—pah rum pa pum pum, rum pa pum
    pum, rum pa pum pum.
And then 'e put his foot—pah rum pa pum pum,
Through my drum.

Cindy grabs the brass pole with her crossed calves, and spins around and around, a brave move, with an upside-down smile and her hair centrifuged out into the air as she swings in a circle a few times before she runs out of momentum. The guitars get shriller and shriller, and then break off for a drum solo so violent that the drummer just seems to be kicking his drum kit around the studio, yet he keeps up enough of a rhythm that the rest of the band finds the right instant to join back in for the last verse.

The kid was thrashing around—pah rum pa pum pum.
'e knocked the manger down—pah rum pa pum pum.

'e had a bloody nose—pah rum pa pum pum.
'e shit his swaddling clothes—pah rum pa pum pum, rum pa pum
  pum, rum pa pum pum.
Then she spanked 'im—pah rum pa pum pum,
On the bum.

For the first time in five or six hours, I'm starting to feel normal. The next girl onstage is introduced as Kim, a very cute black-haired girl, with breasts like a fourteen-year old's. With a disorderly load of one-dollar bills in my shirt pocket, I step up to the brass rail around the stage and hold out the first bill. She lifts the elastic of her blue panties just above the crotch, to show me where to put it. When I do she says, "Thank you," in the most innocent southern belle voice I've ever heard.

To receive the next bill she twirls around and opens a little tent in the back for me to slip the bill in. The one after that she lets me put a little lower in the front, and then she comes close to say thank you, and abruptly gives me a whole mouthful of tongue.

"Will you come over to my table later?" I say, and she nods as I go back to my seat to watch her. They are back to regular music here: Van Halen's "Girls, Girls, Girls," a record they've played so much that you can hear where all the highs have faded out and the midrange notes gone muddy. At one point the whole song crashes into a blast of static from a disturbed needle. Kim just stands there in the strobes and the laser beams, her hands on her hips, glaring at the disk jockey, as the dry rasp of crowd noise continues.

Kim is definitely my favorite tonight. She's not much of a dancer, but I like the delicate way she just sort of parades around the stage, with streaks and whorls of red and blue laser light making crayon swatches all over her skin, and little tufts of dollar bills sticking out in every direction from the latex of her underpants.

I'm afraid I've been drinking my beers too fast, so this time when the waitress comes I order club soda with lime. When it comes it has a very peculiar taste, as if it had sat in a plastic jar for a month.

Kim is naked now, except for her white acrylic shoes. Guys are going up to the stage and leaning back and lying on their backs on the stage with five-dollar bills sticking out of their mouths, and when they lie back she sort of creeps over them in sixty-nine position and moves around there for a few seconds and then moves back with the bill held between her legs. I used to do that, but I guess you could say I don't like being onstage.

She has a special way of walking across the platform, her ass tipped up and her back arched, and her little breasts pushed forward, and her hands held out to the side, helpless, like little crippled bird's wings. She is so pretty that I can even say that this is almost no longer the worst day of my life.

☆ ☆ ☆

Things fall into place if you wait long enough, even with the music too loud and a battery of cigarettes churning out smoke like an old cartoon of Pittsburgh—and this is one of the places they fall into. Even the girl who comes around to my table with a cup of dollar bills, collecting for the music, kisses me on the lips.

And up in the lights, Kim scarcely dances, just parades, gently, slowly, as if she is afraid she will fall off her high heels. At one point in the song she lies down in the middle of the stage, half on her side, half on her stomach, with her legs scissored apart on the illuminated stage squares, the folds of her vulva clearly visible from behind, sort of pursed together like a little mouth. It is remarkable how pretty this is, a modest little pose, innocent, somehow not at all vulgar, not like some of the other dancers here who I have seen lie on their backs in the strobes with their legs apart and use rubber dildos on themselves.

When she's finished, gathering up her dollar bills and her underwear, clutching it all to her body as she steps down, a few hands clap, listlessly, while the DJ harangues the crowd: "Come on PUT your hands together for that *LOVE*-ly lady, that was *Kiiiiiiimmmm!*"

At the next song she comes over, with her clothes back on, stands next to my chair, moving almost imperceptibly to Bruce Springsteen's version of "Santa Claus Is Coming to Town," with all that jingly stuff in the beginning as the Boss jokes around with Clarence Clemons.

"Will you give me a tip?" she says, in a sort of little baby-talk voice, and I take a dollar bill and slowly carry it down inside the front of her pants until my hand just gets to the upper reaches of her hair and she pulls back and smiles.

"Hey, Kim," I say, close to her hair, voice raised above the Santa Claus chorus, "if I give you a five, how far down can I put it?"

"As far as you want," she says, her lips touching my ear. And she's telling the truth. I hold the bill between my thumb and forefinger while my other fingers lead the way, slowly down, until I am stroking the lubricated tissue. The music gets louder, Clarence Clemons screeches away on the alto sax, half out of control and at the same time completely under control, and Kim and I are looking into each other's eyes in that deep and vague and sort of half-swooning way that people smile at each other when they are touching each other's genitals.

She leads me back to the private-dance area, away from the loudest blast of the speakers, although I still have to raise my voice so that she can hear what I want to do. I've got a lot of money tonight—some of my remaining Vegas bankroll and some of the money I got from the bank machine.

I have gotten lucky with the music. Joe Walsh's nine minutes of "Life's Been Good" comes on. Kim is giving me the fifty-dollar personal nude dance. And it doesn't matter at all that she can't really dance. She has so much natural grace in the way she parades across the floor in front of me that she doesn't need to learn.

I'm leaning back in the white couch, my terrible-tasting-club-soda glass balanced precariously on the carpet next to my feet. She brings her body up close, her hair falling down on either side of her face until it cloisters my own face, so our two faces are together in the dark, in the tent of her black hair, and she brings her tongue to the front of her kisses.

Joe Walsh boasts, at the top of his chain-smoker's voice, about how much of a drug addict he is. Kim brings her tiny breasts to my face. The nice thing about small breasts, especially on a day when most of your friends hate your guts, is how defined, how crisply contoured, the nipples are at the moment when my mouth, blind as a baby, finds its way, through the smoke and the strobing darkness and the guitar solo, to one nipple and then to the other.

It's a fifty-dollar dance, which means that now she stands above me and scans for the matron, the fat lady whose job it is to supervise the waitresses and to make sure the dancers don't do anything illegal, although now it doesn't matter much anymore. The matron is far away, sitting at the end of the bar smoking a cigarette and laughing, with her arm around one of the black dancers. Kim kisses me again on her way down from standing to crouching to kneeling in front of me and looking the long way up into my eyes.

The only thing wrong is the light; it's gloomy back here, with only a dim spillover from the strobes and lasers and the throbbing red bubble-top light that goes on whenever the music gets particularly loud. I can't make out as well as I'd like how pretty she is, with her hair falling against the side of her full cheek as it moves up and down, as she keeps brushing the hair away from her face the way they used to do in porno movies, I suppose at the urging of an inaudible director, her eyes still almost invisibly twinkling with that unshockable smile.

The reason I'm disappointed with the light is that I've always believed that at least sixty percent of the pleasure associated with a fifty-dollar dance is visual, and that it is particularly dependent upon my being able to look down into my own lap into the oldest and most dreamed-about tableau in history, no pun intended, a picture I can smile at and the whole picture smiles back, with me included in it.

When the song ends she puts her clothes back on and sits down next to me on the continuous couch, her legs draped over mine, and her ashtray cradled over the crotch of her panties. The waitress comes around, and I buy a beer for myself and one of those too-sweet liqueur-and-fruit-juice shooters for her, this one called "Sex on the Beach."

"Cheers," I say, as we clink bottle against plastic cup.

"Merry Christmas," she says.

"What are you going to do when they close this place down?" I ask her.

"I don't know," she says, taking a sip from the syrupy red drink. "I wish I could be a dope dealer. They won't hassle you for that around this town. Not with Buzzy."

What she means is that Attorney General Bacon is a devout Purificationalist, and there have been several *Geraldo* segments about how the Purificational Church is the only church in which you can supervise other people's private lives without having to give up drugs yourself. Apparently, cocaine is very good for speaking in tongues.

"So what do you do?" she says.

"I've got the same problem as you. I just lost my job."

"Oh, I'm sorry," she says, cuddling against me and holding her cigarette out to the side. "That's a lousy thing to happen on Christmas."

"It was my fault, I guess."

"What happened?

"It's a long story."

"You'll find something," she says in that kid-gloved voice people use when they talk to someone who they know will not find something, and then she kisses me goodbye and goes back out on the floor to get more dances. You know you're in trouble when tittie dancers feel sorry for you.

☆ ☆ ☆

In the parking lot, over the boxed and wrapped thump and woof of the music inside the windowless building, a relative silence has fallen over this stretch of Richmond Road. Wal-Mart and Kroger stand dark across the four lanes of no traffic. It's midnight. Whatever that reality is that is Christmas, it lies over this road, over the Econo-Lodge with its twinkling bars of light running along the walkway in front of the second-floor rooms, over the lanternlike yellow interior of the never-closed Waffle House, over this parking lot full of me and my suddenly two-tone Volvo and all the kids in the neighborhoods around us not asleep, maybe some of them getting up already and tugging on their parents' bedspreads.

I want to say goodbye to this place, even though I know it's horrible—but their tits, their tits, that's all that's really important. When there are tits in the world, one may feel good; when there are no longer any tits in the world, one must feel bad; and the world, as it marches on in the angry gloss of its black shoes, will never see a place as pretty as this again.

With my car window open I can hear the bells of a church. A clutch of people stand in the floodlight in front of All Saints Episcopal Church, getting ready to go inside for the midnight service.

I am glad that this is not a snake-handling church, because on a night like tonight I might be tempted to take revenge, to steer into the middle of them and become another one of those very fashionable mass murderers who keep inspiring Congress to reject gun control. But this, after all, is an Episcopal church, and even I feel some nostalgia such as occurs in the made-for-TV movies about troubled families finding their Christmasy way back to happiness.

For a moment I almost pull into the parking lot. How comforting it would be to go inside, to listen to Handel on a modest pipe organ, to watch some candles being lit and later capped out with the bell-shaped snuffer, and to shake hands and exchange merry Christmases with people in suits who haven't become bastards.

But the problem with the Episcopal Church is that nowadays I would have to go through all that huggie-bear stuff with the Peace of the Lord, putting my hands over all these strangers, some of whom are older than I am. I would be a hypocrite if I said I had any legitimate reason to be against the touchie-feelie liturgy. But it seems to me that to slobber over strangers to whom I am not sexually attracted goes against everything I was brought up to believe.

Chapter 14

'm almost home, just passing one of those planned golf-course communities to the south of Amherst, with its brick wall running along the highway, protecting the cul-de-sacs and the community pro shop, and the pond in the middle, toward which most of the wide-windowed brick ranch houses turn their laundry rooms, when I see in my rearview mirror the lights of the Indiana State Police.

"Good morning, sir!" says the officer, a fat young guy, full of Christmas cheer. "How are you this morning?" His arms seem to be too short, and rotated to the inside, so that when I give him my license and registration and proof of insurance he takes them backhanded, with his right elbow up above his hand and his shoulder jammed up against his neck. It looks very strange, but there seems to be no real deformity.

"I stopped you because your car is pretty badly damaged. Just wanted to make sure there isn't any problem."

"There's no problem, officer. Just a little painting accident."

"You want to do me a favor, sir? Come over and talk to me by the patrol car."

In the rack lights he reads my license. Everything flashes—his face, his badge, the ground. Somehow the jerkiness of the light, like the lights in the Petting Zoo, makes it hard to be sure if I'm standing up straight or wobbling around.

"You work around here?"

I tell a lie, harmlessly I suppose, seeing that I'm only wrong by twelve hours. "I'm an associate professor of English at the university."

"Really. I guess I'd better watch my language."

"That's okay."

"My wife's a teacher. She always corrects me."

Now, with the Christmasy small talk over, he shifts cheerfully into what we both know is the thing he really wants to talk about.

"So . . ." he says, jollier than ever. "How much have you had to drink tonight?"

"Not very much. Maybe four beers. Over a four-hour period."

"That's a lot," he says, bobbing his head sadly. "You know that's enough to ruin some kid's Christmas if you run over their mommy and daddy, you know what I mean?"

"I guess I *don't* know what you mean, officer. I'm not drunk."

"Maybe not last year you weren't. But they've cracked down and changed all the measurements." He pauses, lets the short-toothed grin fade from his smiley little mouth, while the balloonish flesh under his chin twinkles red and blue in the roof lights. "So just to be on the safe side, I'm going to give you a little field sobriety test."

Probably not one car has come along this road in the past half hour, but now that I have begun to be directed through a series of contortions at the side of the road in the middle of the night, half a dozen cars go by, their lowered headlights soft behind the roof-rack glare.

I touch my nose. I count back from one hundred by sixes. I walk a straight line, one shoe planted directly in front of the other, in a way that I rarely walk in real life.

I think I passed that one. But the backward alphabet recital, while leaning forward on one foot like a ski jumper, gives me a harder time than I would have thought. All this time he's writing in his clipboard, the lights are flicking and flashing, and cars go by, staring at my face in the cop lights.

He stands there for a moment, staring at his clipboard, not saying anything.

"Here's the story, sir," he says. "You didn't do bad enough to be charged with DWI. But you didn't do well enough for me to let you go. I'm going to have to take you in to the barracks for a breath test."

At least he has been kind enough to handcuff me with my hands in front rather than behind me, as we drive north through Amherst. From High Street, I can see for a minute the light in one of the back windows of my house. I think of poor motherless Dog-man and the new rug if I don't get home in time tonight. We pass through town without stopping, under the glowing festoons bridging the street, past the Peace Tree, and farther on past the sorority bars, on our way to the Highway Patrol barracks in Batesville. My car has been left behind, to be towed, he tells me, into Midtown Marathon, the same place where I usually get gas.

"I think this is ridiculous, officer," I say, trying to maintain some professional dignity. "I wonder if you could suggest to your supervisors that if they want to arrest drunks, it might be a good idea for them to find some drunks."

"Believe me, I know where you're coming from, Mr. Schmidt. A year ago I would have let you go, no problem. But they had to go and lower the blood limit."

He's leaning his head back over the seat to talk to me, like an old-fashioned cab driver, back when they spoke English. With the kind of creeps he must usually get in this seat, I guess he's glad to have somebody he can talk to.

"And I know you're not drunk, Mr. Schmidt, but I think I should tell you that the lower blood limit does not look good for the results of your breath test. The law has a very specific permissible level, but we have a saying in the department: 'If it's detectable, it's bookable.' I didn't want to upset you, but I thought I should tell you that."

"For Christ's sake!"

"Believe me, I sympathize. I just wish you'd had a Camaro."

"What do you mean?"

"A Camaro, and a Trans Am," he says, "are what's known as a 'profile car.' It's been established that the driver of a Camaro is five times as likely to be drunk as the average driver."

He has his seat pulled way forward, and he holds the wheel with his elbows above the hands. "The problem is that if we stop too many Trans Ams, we can get sued by the Criminal Liberties Union, for 'profiling.' They say we're violating their so-called civil rights. So mostly we leave the profile cars alone."

"You mean some drunk in a Trans Am can drive right by you?"

"If he's doing something wrong we can stop him. But we have to think twice about a routine stop. So then we're stuck out here all night, pulling over old ladies in Ford Tempos—and professors in Volvos," and he looks back at me and grins. "And the pickings are mighty slim, let me tell you."

"Then I hope you're real pleased with yourself tonight, officer."

"Heyy!" he says. "Don't worry about it. It's not a felony. Is this your first offense?"

"It's *no* offense! You haven't convicted me of anything and you've already got me assigned to work in the damn laundry room!"

"Look, Mr. Schmidt. I'm just saying that stuff because I know how those breath tests work. But it's not that bad. Most jobs won't fire for DW. The jail part you can do on weekends, that's easy. And then if you go to AA once a week you can get your license back in a year."

"I'm not an alcoholic."

"That doesn't matter. It's very important to tell them you're an alcoholic. They'll go easier on you. They *hate* people who won't admit they're alcoholics. Heck, if it's a first offense, you can even get a permit to drive to work, after six months."

I've never seen someone so enthusiastic about my problems. He keeps talking to me all the way to the State Police Barracks, bending forward over his stubby arms, grinning with his small-toothed little mouth like the Gerber baby, and all the time selling me on this misdemeanor as if it's a Florida timeshare.

☆ ☆ ☆

"Just blow into the tube, sir," the woman at the police barracks says. There is a way cops use the word "sir," hammering on it over and over again, that takes away all the respect and authority the term implies—as if it is actually derived not from "sire" but from the dismissive Shakespearean "sirrah."

"Blow hard, sir," she says. "All your breath."

But I don't have to blow very hard for the machine to register above the minuscule amount permitted. Which means that I am now under arrest.

The same cop drives me all the way back to Amherst, to the county jail. Here they book me, and call me sir some more, and make me stand in front of a high counter answering questions about all the hundreds of possible diseases I have or do not have.

I ask if I can call my lawyer, and they tell me I might want to save my mandated phone call for tomorrow, since they can't set bail until the morning.

Gently they fingerprint me; another nursish matron holds my hand and calls me sir and tells me to relax my hand completely and let her do all the work, as if I am getting a massage.

Now I understand why the cartoon faces in the posters for Ace Bail Bonds always have such a surprised expression on their faces, as they are being led away in handcuffs, mouths pulled over to one side, like a stroke victim's, or as if someone had just hit them with a fish, as my mother used to say.

They're very polite, with their sirs, telling me to sign here and there, for an inventory of the contents of my wallet, and another form for how much money I had, the money being removed and placed in a personal envelope, giving me access, one of the jailers explains, to any items I need to buy from the commissary, and on a separate form for my "personal effects." I didn't know you could have personal effects until you were dead.

The walls are orange cinderblock, painted clean and thick up to chest high, then cream above, like in an elementary school. One of the guards leads me to a little studio and takes a mug shot, one face forward and one profile. I should have said I wanted to stand the other way because that was my good side, but I don't care anymore. I told them no on the heart-attack question, but right now I feel like a candidate, with a big block of ice in my chest, radiating its bitter cold out to my shoulders and my arms, the way they say happens when you are about to drop dead.

Everything this night takes place as if through the medium of clear gelatin. Like a sleepwalker I take my clothes off in the dressing room where I have been led, take a shower with no shampoo and a bar of yellow soap that smells like the deodorant trash-can liners I use in my kitchen.

After I come out of the shower, the guard tells me to stand with my legs apart and my hands against the wall, and then sprays me all over with an insecticide gun. It is one of those professional-looking things with a metal container and a long hose with a spray-pump handle at the end, by which the naked associate professor emeritus and contributor to *Midwest Composition Journal* is duly fumigated, in the crotch, between the cheeks of the ass, in the underarms, all over the small of the back, for the control of lice.

My prisoner's uniform is a bright orange suit of coveralls that zips down from the neck to the elastic waistband. The guard brings me a box of shoes, different sizes of wooden-soled clogs, and tells me to find a pair that fit.

Then up the elevator, slowly, between two cops, a man and a woman, and my official towel and washcloth and soap and Mennen roll-on deodorant and plastic water cup, like a kid packed off to summer camp, carrying my official sheets and pillowcase, up in this slow elevator to the third floor, still no bars anywhere, just walls and doors and unbreakable acrylic windows.

The woman turns a key in a console on the wall, a door opens with a bang, and he leads me into a sort of long windowed passageway between the door outside and the door to the cell area, which consists of a common room and a row of seven cell doors. She turns another key and the door behind us shuts and the one in front opens. One of the doors on the row of cells springs ajar and the light inside goes on.

In the bottom bunk a long-haired young man turns over and blinks in the light.

"Just make up your bed there," the officer says, pointing to the empty upper bunk. It has a two-inch-deep mattress with a thick green plastic skin of woven fibers. "I'll turn out the light in five minutes."

I've been shown to so many rooms in so many hotels for MLA, and the Four C's, and vacation, that I actually hear myself speaking to him as to a bellhop.

"Thank you," I say. As he walks out into the common area he turns around and looks at me as if I'm crazy.

There's no pillow. The mattress is hardly padded at all, more like a thick tarpaulin, like something from a kennel, so hard and tightly woven that dogs could not chew it up. I drape the sheets over, and the blanket, and then vault up into the bunk, having to put my foot on the metal desk right beside my roommate's face. He hasn't said a word. I'm just sitting up here, pulling off my union suit and stuffing it into the pillowcase, to use as a pillow, when he finally speaks.

"Hey," he declares.

"Yeah. What?"

"DWI?" he says.

"Yeah."

"I figured." Then I hear him rustle the sheets, turn over, and presumably go back to sleep, a luxury I have no illusions about being granted myself in these early hours of a holiday morning. I sit, on the sheets, on the dog-proof mattress, in the bright over-head light, which suddenly blinks out. I sit. I lie down. I sit up. I try not to make any noise.

☆ ☆ ☆

Christmas morning in jail with no sleep is about what I would have expected, had it ever crossed my mind to expect such a thing. At seven o'clock the doors of the cells are buzzed open, the lights go on, a young woman correction officer shouts, "Let's get *up!*" through the latched hole where two trustee prisoners from another floor are passing bowls of cereal with a remarkable amount of sugar on them onto the table.

"Listen up, guys," she says, pleasantly, as soon as most of the orange figures have drifted out from their doors into the common room. Everybody in here is about eighteen years old, most of them burglary cases, I think. "We're bringing Christmas dinner at twelve o'clock, and the visiting room is open all day."

Outside the window it's one of those sharp blue mornings we get once in a while—the sun hanging up there, seeming particularly small as it barely warms the dead patches of hay-colored ground where no snow has fallen this year. Up in the clear sky I can see, as I always do when I haven't had any sleep, those potato-shaped fatigue patterns rolling and falling through the blue atmosphere.

At one end of the commons room is a dial phone with a sign next to it saying it can make only collect and credit-card calls, all calls subject to a five-minute time limit. A chart shows the hours when the phones in the various sections of the jail are in operation. This phone doesn't open until noon. ALL CONVERSATIONS ARE MONITORED, the sign says at the bottom.

Nobody's particularly interested in talking to me. These young felons are bored by the endless parade of DWIs who pass briefly through the midst of their six-month terms.

The only people who have any reaction at all to seeing another face when they get up in the morning are the Monopoly players, who invited me into the game the moment I wandered out of my cell toward the sugar-and-cornflake bowls. Soon the first game of the day is spread, over the watery mottling of the post-breakfast spongework. They don't ask my name, and I don't ask theirs. Only one guy asks me anything, as he doles out the multicolored money.

"DW?" he says, using the customary abbreviation. I just nod. From then on we're fellow jailbirds with the same problem, a day to do nothing in, whether it's Christmas or your birthday or the day your dead grandmother comes to town, which is a phrase they use around here a lot that I don't understand the significance of.

The only problem with Monopoly here is that it's a boring game the way they play. They buy *everything*—every property they touch, employing no strategy, no fiscal policy, rarely saving enough to build, creeping around the board, overextended to an inmate, cursing the dice, *"Shit!"* when they land on a space that's already bought; and then as soon as someone does land on one or two people's spaces, the deeds start getting flipped over to their white mortgaged side.

I play along, not caring if I win or lose, waiting for the time I can go back to my cell, and sit back and fool my eyes into thinking they've been asleep; and even more important, the time when I can use the phone and call a lawyer. Finally I lose, and wander back to my cell. It sounds strange to say "cell." I'm going back to my *cell.*

Back in my cell, while my roommate, or rather cellmate, lies on his back and stares at the underside of the steel plate that forms the base of the upper bunk, I look out the window for what I judge to be about fifteen minutes, at the back of one of those student tenement buildings, wondering what window Sally gets to look out of in her hospital.

I have tried to close my eyes and transport myself away from here into a dream of tittie dancers; but there is something about the reality of jail that concentrates your thinking down to one person. Now I see Sally's face appearing on every tittie dancer's body.

I have discovered that we prisoners tend to focus all of our incarcerated thoughts upon one face. A democracy of sorts, I guess you could call it, in which the educated me is of a piece with all the other men through however many thousands of years of sporadically enforced regulations who have lain in jail, dreaming of whatever woman they are dreaming of, as her face hangs like a full moon and the outlines of her eyes get bigger, the way a girl's eyes do when the rest of your life is becoming smaller and smaller, and the contours of her nose become as three-dimensional as the lip around the edge of the tin cup, or in our case the plastic cup, from which the universal prisoner drinks his warm water out of the tap. I think, perhaps out of context, of an old poem by Norman Dubie—and without my library at hand I quote from an admittedly frazzled memory: "The approach of winter found us / At opposite ends of the city, / Each at a window, each lost in despatch."

☆ ☆ ☆

"Wanna play some Monopoly?" This is one of the burglars, or car thieves, back mumbling at my door, to tell me that another game is starting, his teeth covered with the excess of fine-cut tobacco, the rest of which is packed in the pouch of his lower lip. The guys here smoke cigarettes and chew tobacco at the same time. I play, hope to lose, buy as few properties as I can get away with, go mercifully bankrupt, and back to my window. The game feels as if it took about two minutes.

There doesn't seem to be much holiday activity, except for all the inmates being called out to the visiting room. "Hoke and Allison!" the young woman guard shouts. "Visiting room!"

My mother always told me that being in jail on Christmas is enormously helpful to someone who needs time to establish a clear picture of his financial future. (If I could get anybody to believe she ever said that, maybe I'd have been a good enough talker to talk myself out of the Breathalyzer.) But I have been thinking about mortgages and kennel bills and Volvo payments ever since I signed that cleanly laser-printed boilerplate of a resignation letter. Astonishing to think it was less than twenty-four hours ago.

What it boils down to is the same thing everything has been boiling down to for however long I am no longer willing to bang my head against a wall thinking about: with no money coming in, or even with a little bit of shit money coming in such as I could make, perhaps, in this economy if I had more friends and were to get very lucky, I am going to lose my house. An unmanly outcome, I think. But clean. I am going to lose my house in the clean and systematic way of the woman and her daughter who are seen in the Prudential commercial to be tearfully moving out of the house the mother could no longer afford after the death of the underinsured father.

Not that it's a great house. In fact it's almost certainly got shit all over the floor right now. But I had a wife there, and we were wonderfully compatible, if in nothing else then in our desire not to have some noisy little right wing political statement crawling around on the rug, and we had a dog and a cat, and I still do, and I wrote articles there in my whited sepulcher of an upstairs study that got published in the *Indiana College Composition Newsletter,* and I am so tired that when I stand on the orange-painted floor I feel as if I am in a tugboat going out to sea, and maybe I will never come back. Maybe I will fall off and drown, in all those fathoms. Those will be pearls that will have been my eyes, to put it in the conditional perfect future or something.

I do not want to lose that house, ragged and half painted as it is. I do not want to play Monopoly. I hate to see people's deeds get flipped over for the mortgage, before they get foreclosed, and the little hat retire from the board, or the little car, or the little iron, dispossessed. Yet here he is again at the door, pale, polite, waiting outside, like the ghost of a boy who has choked to death on the ground mulch of his Skol wintergreen.

"Wanna play some Monopoly?"

Under the fatigue I keep automatically calling the craps numbers each time somebody rolls. "Five, no field . . . Little Joe . . . Eight-eight-eight-eight-eight . . ." Early in the game I pick a "Go to Jail" card, to the hilarity of my opponents, who I secretly hope will ruin me quickly so I can go back to my *cell.* I'm glad to have the time to think. What I am thinking about, in that same thunderous jail-borne clarity with which a woman's face and only one woman's face will shine above the bars while a man warbles on his harmonica and everybody else tells him to shut up—what I am thinking about is that I need to get a job that will pay more than selling composition textbooks. And the only job I'd have a chance of getting, in this permanent recession, is one such as I just had.

There is, however, one force working in my favor if I can get back into the market, one current running against all those race quotas, and all those hiring freezes, and all those states driven bankrupt, and those little lines of fine print you see down at the bottom of the ads in the MLA Job List, about "Candidate must be compatible with a gender-focused, multicultural, third-world-intensive curriculum," in other words no Irish need apply. Nor fifth-generation Flemings who make the mistake of telling a Rabelasian anecdote to students whose sex lives are unutterably superior to that of their instructor. Nor French, nor Russians, nor Jews, especially not Jews, nor Italians, nor Poles, nor Swedes, nor Scots, nor guys whose glasses slip down their noses.

Still I'm not worried. Ben Wattenberg said, "Demography is Destiny." That "cohort" of GI Bill students who were all twenty years old together when they got out of the army have aged at the same rate, passing through the system, in his words, "like a pig through a python."

And now they're all sixty-five together, and offices are emptying out even faster than the states' emergency attrition budgets are shrinking.

Which means that a handful of those positions are still funded. So what happens is that after all the gender-focused, multicultural, third-world-intensive candidates have accepted (some with the old sixties revolutionary handshake) their endowed chairs at Harvard and Stanford and Swarthmore, and their department heads have begun memorizing how to pronounce their adopted Arabic-derived names without a flutter of awkwardness, setting themselves to the task with the calm resolve of a man starting a Russian novel—that still leaves a few leftover offices vacant, for the bad old guys.

The interviews for MLA are already set, of course, but there's always something popping up at the last minute. What I will do then, as soon as I get out of *jail* (it is very weird to have this element of being in jail clouding one's career plans), is to call everybody I know in the business and see if anybody got sick or committed suicide or got caught with a nonstudent of legal age, and see if I can get a last-minute interview for a spring position.

And then I'm sure I can rent the house out, to one of those loveless consortia of expense-sharing graduate students who leave snide notes to each other hanging from the faucet when the sink has been left dirty. A lot of ifs, of course, but it's a big business, in which I have many aquaintences, though few friends. I find myself in a good mood.

"You're out of jail, A. J. Foyt. Go on."

"What?" I look up. I have been spacing out over the Monopoly board, but now one of them has rolled doubles for me—a *hard eight,* and I have to go around the board some more, until I lose, I hope.

I should try to start thinking about it as being spelled *gaol,* even though it's pronounced the same. It looks more serious, more literary, although some people get confused. I had to sit and listen to a kid in one of my classes do an extra-credit presentation about Oscar Wilde's "The Ballad of Reading Gaol," but the kid lost a few points off his grade because all the way through he pronounced it "Reeding Gowl"—I don't even think he knew what the word meant. I didn't want to stop him in mid-presentation.

It's obviously an easy mistake to make. Even one of the kids at this Monopoly table always pronounces the Reading Railroad as if he's "Reading" a book. An activity which he's probably never done. So speaks the intellectual, in his orange union suit, in correctly pronounced gaol.

☆ ☆ ☆

Turkey dinner is delivered, on individual trays, through the little door that opens out onto the table, like the drawer in the drive-in window at the bank. It's quite good. I've had worse at my own house. Nobody says much, sitting around the table, but they're in a mood commensurate with the above-average quality of this meal.

When the guards and the trustees come back to pick up the trays, they begin passing through the same door dozens of small, colorfully wrapped packages, all of which turn out to be magazines: *Reader's Digest, Sports Illustrated, Newsweek, Hoosier Horizons, Custom Cycles, Popular Mechanics.*

"Hey, Mr. Schmidt," one of the Monopoly players says. (Some of them know my name by now.) "Here's a magazine you oughta like." He gives me a copy of *Car and Driver,* the cover modified in pen so that it says *Car and DRUNK Driver.* We all laugh.

☆ ☆ ☆

The phone opens up, though I have to wait in line. There are three lawyers in town, one of whom represented me in a thoroughly amicable series of divorce proceedings, which I still felt ended up unfairly, so I won't use her again. Another referred me, under the gathering clouds of The Joke, to an Indianapolis hotshot who did nothing.

That leaves a guy named Joe Frickerty, who sounds very confident and sympathetic when I finally call him away from his own Christmas dinner. He tells me everything's closed today and there's nobody available who can reduce the bond which will allow me to post bail.

"The best thing I can do is get you out first thing in the morning, Pack," he says, above a background of party voices. "Don't worry. We'll take care of you." On the television set, whose cable is broken so it gets only the one locally broadcast station, I can see the stop-action figure of Santa Claus gesturing and twinkling as Burl Ives sings, "Have a Holly Jolly Christmas / And in case you didn't hear / Oh by golly have a Holly Jolly Christmas, this year!"

How many men, I wonder, must have stood before this same phone, the concrete floor seeming to sink with bad news under their wooden clogs, on a day they thought they could get out but now they can't. I can't yell at the guy. All I can do is plead with him to do whatever he can, which he says he's doing, meaning I'll have to fix those sheets in my bunk so I can get some sleep tonight, in my *cell*.

I try my own number. I will not reveal what my number is, but I will say that it is one of those numbers in the 555 exchange. The answering machine picks up after two rings, meaning someone called, so I go through the sequence of silence and speech that I have to cue myself into remembering.

"Hey!" I bellow into the receiver after the second beep, to trigger the hard-of-hearing sensors, and everybody in the whole section looks up at me, puzzled, then silence, then three more beeps, and I shout again, and they look up again, turn to one another and shrug.

The tape rewinds. At first I don't recognize the voice.

"Hi, Pack. It's me. I don't know if you want to talk to me, but I hope you will." Sally's voice is quavery and expressionless. She sounds as if she's thought about what she wanted to say and half-memorized it. "I don't blame you if you don't want to talk to me. I heard about what happened at school. I'm really sorry. It's my fault. I wish I could make it up to you. I'm calling from the hospital. This place is really stupid. I think I'm the only person here who doesn't have holiday depression combined with bulimia. Well, maybe it's not fair for me to try to make a joke about this. Anyway, they have to let me out at seven tonight and I'm going to stay with my friend Katie in Madison. If you aren't too mad, you can call me here." And here she gives out another phone number with that same near-apocalyptic prefix.

For the benefit of those people who have not had the experience, I should say that it is very hard to stay angry for long at a woman who calls for you when you are in gaol. The voice is so perfect on the slightly wobbly tape of my machine that I can make myself believe I see, in my fluttering and exhausted sight, her face pronouncing the words, and a shine on her generous nose, and her best cocktail dress, with the diamond-shaped holes running down the sides, which I suppose I have a right to think about.

So perfect I must call again, shouting *"Hey"* as if to celebrate our loud secret, as felons gawk. Rudolph the Red-nosed Reindeer has already gone down in history; that useless remake of *Miracle on Thirty-fourth Street* just came on and they turned it off. The local radio station works from a very strict format: one Christmas song, one non-Christmas song, alternating continuously.

With my heart pounding like that of a teenage kid asking for his first date, I dial her number at the hospital. It sounds like a girl's dormitory as they call her to the phone, shouts and giggles in the background.

"Hello?" I've never heard her so shy.

"Hi, Sally?"

"Pack . . . you called back. Hey, that rhymes."

"So, how are you?"

"Oh, I'm okay, I guess. How are you?"

"Oh, I guess I'm all right," I say.

"It's good to hear from you," she says.

"Sally, this is a weird conversation. You know what it reminds me of? One of those old ALM language dialogues that I had in school. *Bonjour, Jeanne. Comment va-tu? Très bien, merci. Et toi?* De dah de dah de dah de dah. How are you? I'm fine."

"Are you mad at me?"

"I don't know. I'm not jumping for joy."

"I feel really bad about what they did to you," she says. "You were so nice to me, and then I had to slip up and it's not fair to you that this had to happen."

"Tell me something, Sally. What *did* happen?"

"I got *shafted*, that's what happened," she says, with a sudden brass of anger in her voice. "I hope you don't think I left those dirty pictures lying around."

"It crossed my mind."

"Well, I didn't. They were in a zipped pocket on the side of my suitcase. Maybe it's my fault, maybe I should have put them in my safe deposit box. But I had this psychiatric delusion that my private stuff was my private stuff. Silly me. Anyway, good old Mountains pokes around in my room and finds them and goes right to my father, and he gets a little upset, to tell the truth."

"What did you tell him?"

"Pack, I couldn't tell him anything. He's so mad I'm afraid he's going to have another heart attack if I even go back in that house. The only thing he knows is that you were in one of those pictures, and he's using his own paranoia to fill in the rest. Now he thinks you're my pimp."

"That's just the reference I need."

"Pack, I'm sorry. This whole thing sucks." She sounds as if she's about to cry. "I wish I'd stayed at work for Christmas. At least there you get paid when you get fucked."

"No swearing on this phone," a woman's voice breaks in.

"Pack, who was *that?*"

"I forgot to tell you where I'm calling from. I'm in jail."

"No way!"

I've waited through years of "Wayne's World" for the chance to say the next thing, so I might as well say it, because the next chance I get they'll probably be off the air.

"Way," I tell her.

"What happened?"

"DW," I say, using the abbreviation that I'm sure she's heard from her friends.

"I just feel so bad about this," she says. "It's really *weird* that we're both locked up at the same time."

"Romantic, isn't it?"

I tell her I'm supposed to get out in the morning, subject to what pretrial driving status I don't know. She says she'll meet me if she can borrow her friend's car.

And then comes that moment which has not happened to me

since two days ago when we said goodbye under the supervision of Mormon security guards. Suddenly it seems absolutely the right thing to say, no matter who in uniform is listening in. Out the window the open sky quakes with fatigue, flawless and sharp over the little basketball court under the windows of the common room, as the radio plays Elvis Presley's "Blue Christmas." Most of the guys have gone back to their cells to read magazines, I guess because that song is particularly hard to take if you're in jail.

"Sally, I love you."

"Oh, Pack, that's really sweet."

"I can't wait to see you."

"I can't wait to see you," she says. The five-minute timer is ticking its cut-off warning.

"I have to go. I'll see you."

"Goodbye, jailbird," she says.

"Goodbye, hospital-bird."

I tell her I love her again and we hang up. The floor moves under my feet again and my mouth is dry the way a man's mouth must always be at that moment when, surrounded by concrete, he tells his favorite girl that he loves her. It has not escaped my attention that she didn't say she loved me, but then I think that is explainable, based on the fact that she is incarcerated under so much milder circumstances.

It doesn't take much to make a man happy in this joint: a gift-wrapped magazine, boneless turkey with the candied yams quarantined on a separate plate so they don't get on the other stuff, and a woman out there, over twenty-one, let's be clear about that, for whom I would gladly get detenured out of ten more jobs, and thrown in ten gaols as easygoing as this one, as long as she could be there when they let me out.

I am happy. I believe that I am the happiest man in this building, and that includes staff. Under ordinary circumstances I would run up and down the stairs, get Dog-man barking, which is always fun, crank up Handel's *Messiah* so high the windows rattle, shout to myself as loud as I want, in that remarkable free condition of having the walls on all four sides of me border out against the open air.

I can't do that, of course. I can't do much of anything until tomorrow, when Frickerty will shake my hand and charge me a thousand dollars. I can't do any of those noisy at-home sorts of things, but I know I need to celebrate. Sally is out there, and we still seem to have something to talk about. Not that it makes much sense. I can *almost* understand why I'm still willing to talk to her—because I like her, and because all those hours of class when she wasn't there have at last been redeemed into minutes when she will be there. What she gets out of talking to me is a little more complicated, I think. That's the part I don't understand at all, especially when I consider that all she has to do is step into the right fern bar at any hour of the day, and a dozen empty-eyed studs with jobs better than my boss's boss's job will be falling all over each other's double-breasted jackets to take her by the hand and lead her away into California's huge rumble of Japanese machinery.

But it seems that she likes me, and I'm not going to question that too closely. I would rather be liked by somebody wonderful than loved by somebody mediocre. I want to call her back again, which I won't. The phone's busy anyway. I want to write her a long letter, which I'm too tired to do. I want to wave out the window to the secretive people in their corduroy coats going up and down the stairs in and out of the slum house whose rear faces us. But most of all, I want to play some Monopoly.

Chapter 15

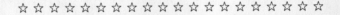

As I step out into the purposeful exhaust and cheap-shoe shuffle of the morning after a holiday, I can almost feel myself beginning to walk convict-style, my arms not swinging, cradled against me, like Oliver Hardy.

It is another beautiful day along the brick sidewalks, looking down the one-way traffic of Broad Street from the wide spot in front of the county jail, where the broken pay phones are lined up in their perforated boxes, severed cables hanging with their red and yellow wires out where the receiver has been pulled off—one of the basic items listed on the fraternities' midnight scavenger hunts, I understand.

Frickerty seems like a good lawyer. He got me a low bail, of which I paid the required ten percent with American Express.

Edward Allen

A red ZX stops fifty feet down the street from me, noses into the yellow loading zone in front of Jefferson Valley Furniture. Sally stands up from the passenger seat, shouts, *"Pack!* I'm here!"

In the midst of this sparse crowd, with the students gone, our gravitation toward each other is a sight to draw all eyes: a man in a blue suit and no tie and two days of beard beneath the vanity of his large mustache, and a girl half his age, all in half-bleached denim. It could be filmed as a commercial, for any one of the many things that make girls beautiful and men rich.

The preceding remark is not meant to suggest that I don't take the moment seriously. The sight of her getting out that door makes something open up in my throat, a kind of joy such as cannot easily be explained to the sorts of people who think of joy in terms of the Holy Spirit coming down and getting them appointed to the Department of Justice.

I cannot say for sure, but perhaps we even run toward one another in slow motion, her hair bouncing and falling in the thick air, my stomach bouncing and falling, our two mouths frozen open into a longing, half-pronounced syllable of the other's name.

We seem to move slower and slower through the final ten feet at the corner of the furniture store, through the usual exponential gelatinization of time and space that you see in such meetings, in which faces and clock towers and passing Subarus take on a Vaseline blur—but we must remember that not even Zeno's Third Paradox can prevent the two open mouths finally from being stifled upon each other at the terminus of a dead run, with coats flopping behind, yet the faces coming together slowly enough for the teeth not to clunk harmfully against each other. Her friend sits in the ZX and nervously slaps the steering wheel.

There is a way people smell when they have been in jail that is like nothing else in the world—soapy, smoky, with a touch of rusted water—but she doesn't pull back or say anything. Worsted against denim, stubble against a touch of foundation, hands

against hands, wordless—things aren't so great around here anymore; you can see it in the closed storefronts of our own street;
the last two senior proms at Amherst High have been canceled in
the wake of Satanism rumors; but I would like to say that there are
moments even the country I used to love cannot destroy.

Sally sits on my lap, in her friend's car, which has no backseat,
the automatic shoulder belt coming down, romantically, around
both of us. She picks at the hair on my wrist, the ancient primate
grooming behavior.

☆ ☆ ☆

"Do you know what you're going to do yet?" she says, at
the kitchen table over coffee, after her friend has left and I've
showered and cleaned up after poor Dog-man's numerous epi-
sodes of incontinence, these left with the scatterings of his emergency refectory among the eggshells and orange juice cartons
and all those cans and bottles and foam plastic things that I
should be recycling.

"I'm going to look for a job. I just hope somebody died somewhere." The peppery smell of dogshit still fills the house. I can't
bring myself to open the windows when it's cold outside.

"What about you?" I say. "Are you going to go back?"

"I don't know if I want to," she says. "Right now I'm too worried about Daddy. I've talked to him on the phone, but I can't do
anything to calm him down. Now he's all mad that I won't come
back home and listen to him go on about how much he hates you.
I don't know what he'd do if he knew I was over here with my
buxe."

"Buxe? Is that the same as a pimp?"

"No, it's just a guy. A boyfriend." She takes my hand and ruffles
the wrist hair again. "I didn't think you were before. I thought you
were just another fall-in-love. But then you got caught and now it
feels like you're my buxe."

"What's that, a UNLV expression?"

Edward Allen

"No, it's in *Gone with the Wind*. Scarlett and her friends are always talking about their buxes."

I don't want to imply that I have a thing about ignorant women—and I certainly don't think she's dumb—but every time Sally makes a mistake like that, I just want to take her in my arms and bring the both of us down slowly to a reclining position someplace where her father is not likely to come kicking the door open. I would like to hold her for hours and pray for our continued safety, pray to the same God as the God of the JC Penney catalog burners and the trance-protected snake-handlers and the Supreme Court, that we be allowed to make each other thankful for God's bounty more often than once every thirty-six hours.

"Sweetheart, I think that's prounounced *beau*."

☆ ☆ ☆

After Sally leaves I start calling acquaintances, until the shell of my ear aches with the receiver's pressure. In the academic business, the day after Christmas is a good time to call people, since almost everybody is at home getting ready for MLA, which starts tomorrow night.

I feel like one of those people in New York who hunt for apartments through the obituaries. My only chance, I know, is a death, a sickness, somebody getting caught telling a dirty joke, causing a spot to open up in the spring that the people shooting for fall positions can't accept. It has to be something last-minute too, because for a job advertised in advance, these departments are about as likely to hire a white male as they are a white whale.

Jerry Mirsky at the University of Maine has nothing. Beth Crawford at Amherst isn't home. Jonathan Stoddard at Williams doesn't sound at all happy to hear from me.

New York would be hopeless, I know, so I don't even bother calling my several contacts there. Michael Scheer at Pocono Community College doesn't know what to tell me, other than let's get together for a drink in Philly.

I'm working my way south and west, through the time zones,

230 ☆

through Virginia, where my good friend Roger Baumeister tells me the state's on a severe attrition schedule.

I would like to try my former officemate Bill Heath, now at the University of Durham, except that I don't want to work with the famous Norris Rappaport, who heads the department. In graduate school I took one of his poetry seminars. What I remember most is the time when a woman in that class did a presentation about Robert Frost's "The Gift Outright." The problem with the presentation was that she didn't say enough about all the minorities that Frost had excluded from the "we" in that poem.

Rappaport blew his top. I've never heard a white person use the word "racist" so many times in one sentence. He didn't even let up when she started to cry. I think that's wrong; it's okay to push the undergraduates around, but you're not supposed to make a graduate student cry.

I cover the south, including the budget-frozen listings of Florida, through Tennessee, where my friend Charlie Hyde at Cecil College is all good cheer and chin up, although nobody ever quits from his hotsy-totsy college, as he modestly takes pains to remind me.

My midwest contacts are pretty thin, strangely enough: only Ball State and Miami and St. Cloud State and Grinnell and the University of Kansas, and not a chance anywhere.

I'm more than halfway through my list that I have written on a yellow legal pad, through Oklahoma without even reaching anybody, through most of Texas, until I try my old graduate school friend Larry Eisensohn, who's held for years the unlikely position of head of the English department at the University of Texas at Abilene.

It turns out that two days before Christmas one of the janitors at UT Abilene found their technical writing specialist sitting at his desk with all the lights on and the computer booted and a bullet in his head.

What Larry says he's willing to do is use his emergency authority to put me on for the spring semester. In the meantime, he just lost two of the three speakers at the program he's chairing at MLA.

"It's a great program," he says, "if I can just get another speaker. It's called 'The Leukemic Muse of Literary Eroticism: Is Sex Dead or Just Immune-Suppressed?' What I need to ask you is—do you have *any* paper that you've done that you could read, or *any* idea you could bring to the session?"

I tell him I'll do it, that I'll come up with something. We shout sincerely happy and hearty words to each other. The whole conversation has taken less than two minutes.

☆ ☆ ☆

If I know anything about Larry Eisensohn, I know he likes to surprise people. Once, back in the sixties, I helped him conduct a poetry seminar in which he had established a live telephone hookup to the Temple University president's office, which was being occupied by the Revolutionary Student Underground. The students in the RSU began cutting up the president's books and shouting over the phone random words from the cut pages, which Larry then transcribed on the blackboard into a found poem that made more sense than any of us expected.

Obviously I couldn't get away with anything like that, nor would I want to, but I would like to come up with something a little more surprising than some pasted-together essay droning on and on. In fact, one of the things that I've always liked about Larry is that he *wants* to be surprised. I suspect that that's why he asked me to do this program with him, so that he wouldn't have to listen to another lifeless and well-intentioned academic paper.

It's a wild opportunity, when I think about it. Because if I could start off at Abilene with something dramatic, then I'd be a natural for the Permanently Funded position that will inevitably open up in the fall.

The question is—what can I do? What do I know that's interesting? What do I know that's both interesting and relevant to his topic about the leukemic muse? We composition specialists don't usually have to worry about such things.

Thinking and thinking, I pace in my socks across the splinterless acrylic-sealed floors, through the stink of Dog-man's bad night. I won't let that happen again. The next time I get thrown in jail I'll make plans in advance.

I start remembering something my father used to tell me: the best carpenter in the world has a friend in every lumberyard. Or something like that. Meaning, I think, that the most important intellectual resource I have is the knowledge possessed by my friends. Which leads me to remember the thing I have that most others don't: I'm probably the only academic at the entire MLA who is on speaking terms with working prostitutes.

So what if I really take a chance and see if I can get Sally's friends Kristy and Samantha to come to the program? Would that be surprising enough? Would we have anything to talk about? What if I got them copies of the other papers in Larry's program and then had them provide comments based on their own experience?

It's a strange thing to think about. But maybe the timing is right. Maybe I could get Kristy and Samantha to talk about the feminist aspects of prostitution, the idea of being in economic control of one's own body. I've read something about that somewhere recently, maybe in the *New York Times Book Review*. If we could look into that issue, it might do something to counter some of the ugly slogans you hear these days about all sexual desire being a form of animal abuse.

Ten more minutes of pacing and the idea still holds together, sort of. I know these girls won't be fluent in the same vocabulary, of course, but the time I met them they seemed smart enough that they should be able to come up with something to say. If I can get them to come, that is. If I can coach them, get them talking, maybe we could get lucky. Think of it: Professor Packard Schmidt and the search for a common ground between eros and ideology. That sounds like a paper in itself.

With anyone else, I would call up right now and plead my case and get clearance. But that's not the way to work with Larry. Larry Eisensohn takes a surprise as a compliment. So I might as well start on the right foot, and take a chance, and let him be a little surprised. And so as not to have him go into it completely cold, I'll explain my whole presentation when I see him in Philadelphia.

I call Sally at her friend's house, tell her what I have in mind, free plane fares and all. I tell her that I've already got a room for them to stay, being the generous fellow that I am.

Ten minutes later she calls back. Kristy and Sam both want to do it, but only if Sally comes along.

The receiver trembles in my hand. The papers on my phone desk are a mess. What follows is a flurry of airline calls, and frightening fares, written for industrial products salesmen, but I make the reservations anyway.

Five minutes later the airline calls back. My card was declined. I tell them that's impossible. They tell me it is possible. They also tell me that if I want to keep those reservations I'll have to pay cash at a travel agency or at the airport ticket counter. I call the 800 number for American Express, and they refer me to Trans National Credit Bureau in California.

"What's going on?" I say, after giving them numbers and numbers, even my license plate number and telephone number and birthdate.

"We've received adverse information about your future ability to handle credit," a cozy-voiced older woman tells me. "Have you been recently incarcerated?"

"That's kind of a personal question."

"Have you been dismissed from your job?"

"That's none of your business."

But of course it is their business, and I yell at a harmless old woman for a few minutes and then give up. People seem to be yelling at each other an awful lot these days. I would have liked to think I was above that kind of thing. They wouldn't tell me how they got all that adverse information so fast, but I have a good idea. The only account not frozen, it turns out, is my Marathon Plus gas card.

☆ ☆ ☆

Pack Schmidt is an asshole, but let it be known that once in a while he gets forgiven for that most common of shortcomings, that his vacation-bloated form still warrants a four-way hug in the Philadelphia International Airport, with Sally and her two friends, who seem a bit distant this morning, until I remember that they've been on a plane from Phoenix all night. Kristy seems shorter than I remember her, but she still has her blond hair gathered into the same broccoli bangs. Samantha acts almost formal, as she smiles at me with her full lips and says, "It's very good to see you again."

I met with Larry Eisensohn just after I got here earlier today. He gave me a copy of his paper for the meeting the day after tomorrow. I didn't say much about my own plans for the program, and he didn't press me on it.

Philadelphia International Airport seems less a terminal than an interconnected system of corridors connected to a train system. Being so close to the three airports of New York, it tends to be a quiet place on a winter morning, mostly just MLA people filtering in, from this flight and that flight, with their mild and impassive faces, many behind well-trimmed beards, most carrying the distinctive brown book that comprises the convention program.

Since I already have a room reserved for tonight at Bally's, I figure we'll go there first, and we'll have some time to look over the program. Then Kristy and Samantha can decide what they want to say—from their occupational perspective, to put it delicately. Plus, with my cards all canceled, I have a problem that hangs over everything this bright morning. I'm rather short of money. And since I've usually had much better luck in Atlantic City than in Vegas, this might be a good time to experiment.

We get on the overheated stop-and-go SEPTA train into the city, all lugging our over-the-shoulder bags, all of us in a jolly mood, as one has to be in a city one doesn't know well, with the rusty iron shapes going by outside, and a wide rise cobbled with tenements, then farther along into the middle of downtown, with its tall new buildings with gently sculpted points on top. I'm a little worried that one of the mild figures with the brown books will recognize me, and I will have a hard time explaining what I'm doing here with three beautiful girls. But then, life is tough.

At the Greyhound terminal we get our tickets and they load us immediately onto a Lucky Streak Express bus full of day-trippers. I'd forgotten that nobody on the East Coast ever rides a bus without reading a newspaper.

For miles the pages flap and flutter in the draft from somebody's partly open window, like a gallery of paper shooting targets.

Even under the quietude of newspapers, you can feel the tension building in everybody's throat. I know it well, the feeling of the action coming closer and the pocket tingling and some disequilibrium in the jaw when you look out over the pretty green craps layout. Craps is much bigger in Atlantic City than it is in Las Vegas; and you can feel the bus moving closer to it, through the flats and prefabricated warehouses and the remarkably tall churches of New Jersey marooned in the dead grass, now a few sprays of snow here and there in the stubbled horse fields.

One man takes pity on us, sees we are paperless and gives us the paper he just finished as he starts on the second. We ride,

Sally and me in one seat, Kristy and Sam in the seat behind, a tidy foursome of the editorial page and the sports page and the classi- fieds and the germinating paragraphs of the next war moving up through the back sections, closer and closer to its eventual home on the front page.

☆ ☆ ☆

Atlantic City faces the sea. You enter it from the rear, as if through the service entrance. Coming in by land, you pass through a stretch of tall brush for miles, on a divided highway whose wide median contains an employee parking lot, although it is still ten miles away from town, and we can see little green employee school buses picking up the dealers and cooks and janitors from where they have left their cars.

Farther in, you find yourself on elevated roadways over the mud and the cattails and the flat tidal pools, over the wash chan- nels with shanties on stilts built up over them, houses that seem to come from so far back in the fish-smell of the brackish history that it's hard to imagine the normal poor people living there today and watching their poor people's TV shows.

With our papers lowered, we cross the flat waste of estuaries, past Tinkertoy structures of wooden docks and old fishing boats with their masts and outriggers all clustered together over the colorless mishmash of railings and wires and ground with puddles of oil in it.

From up in the bus you can see every casino in the city, lined up tall along the Boardwalk. They stand like monoliths above the low clutter of drug houses, the cubelike shape of the the casino areas windowless below each hotel tower. Atlantic City has none of the little casinos you see around Las Vegas, no little street- corner slot joints, no video poker machines in restaurant waiting rooms. The law states that a casino must be connected to a hotel containing at least five hundred rooms.

Even in the day they seem to be lit up, giving off a still kind of

Edward Allen

light, not kinetic like Vegas, but radiating their motionless glow down into the slum portion of the bus route, where signs proclaiming a "Drug-Free School Zone" indicate a drug-infested school zone, in which the cops have given up but the community service organizations are hoping that the signs will retain some magic power.

It is a city in which the ordinary vehicular traffic has been taken over by buses, as if all the little cars have grown up to full size, their chassis swinging wide for a right turn off Pacific Avenue, lines of them waiting for a light. Our Lucky Streak Express pulls up behind several other buses at Bally's, shadowed by the blank rear of the casino with its mushroom-shaped ventilators.

Before we can get off we have to wait for the greeter, a young woman hired by the casino who hands us each a ten-dollar roll of quarters. A cold wind blows in off the ocean, across the Boardwalk, which forms a kind of wall to the east of us in this open space of trees and buses and girls with loudspeakers, bordered by Bally's to the south and the Claridge to the west and the Sands to the north.

☆ ☆ ☆

Up in the room I try to read Larry's MLA paper to Kristy and Samantha, so that we can get started on putting together some idea of what they want to say at the conference about how Larry's ideas relate to their own experience in the sex business:

THE DE-EROTICIZATION OF THE POSTMODERN
LOVE POEM:

(I read, aloud, as Kristy and Sam lounge on the king-size bed listening, still looking sleepy from their flight, their elbows propped on the glossy blue coverlet, heads cradled in their hands.)

HOW SEX, DRUGS, AND ROCK AND ROLL BECAME
PECKS, HUGS, AND THAT'S ABOUT ALL

At the conclusion of the late Spellman Booker's famous lyric "All Is Lost But the North Window," from his Hofstader Prize collection *Diving for Snakes,* he speaks with a sort of Lawrencian agitation of his former lovers, both male and female, all of whom have disappointed him, not so much because they have rejected him, but because they have insisted upon subjecting their perceptions of him to the false apotheosis that Booker throughout his work identifies with the life of fantasy, especially when that fantasy impinges upon the archeophrastic schemata of wish fulfillment.

Outside the window, the sea lies flat as a piece of upholstery covered with a protective sheet of plastic, a narrow glare visible out toward the artificial-looking horizon. I go on to the poem extract:

> Dirigent   creased   above sea level
> the gloom-fired collicles catch
> these days of gallium and sardines   days
> twisted into their old subjunctive
> tennising of   You call me up   no
> I call you up   no
> the phone just rings and it's a wrong
> number   Listen   The street sprouts
> motorcycles   Motorcycles sprout breasts
> Listen   in the chalk houses families
> are whispering to their alarm clocks   Breasts
> sprout milk   A continent of bone   Milk
> sprouts mold   I climb the stairs one half
> step at a time   Down the hall the doors
> slam slam slam   as if I dared
> walk backwards   home to the old
> extermination of wonder   Home
> to you and your impure
> thunder.

Edward Allen

"Hey, Pack?" Kristy says, raising her hand meekly. "I have a question. Can you explain something?"

"I'll try."

"What is this about?"

"Let me put it this way," I tell her. "What it's *about* is less important than how you react to it. This is what you call Subjective Response poetry. The *meaning* is subordinate to the experience."

"*I knew that,*" Samantha says, twisting a handful of brown hair in her fingers and grinning over at Kristy. "What are you, dumb?"

"I know it's a little ethereal, but I'll try to help you through it. What I was figuring we would do would be to let you hear the paper and then talk about how it relates to your experience in the hooker business."

"How can I do that?" Kristy says. "I never had any tricks who talked like the guy in that paper. If they did I'd be out of business, 'cause I wouldn't know what they wanted."

"I think what my . . . colleague is asking you," says Samantha, "is how are we supposed to make comments on gibberish?"

"Believe me, people do it all the time in my business," I say very quickly, and Sam picks up the cadence, looks over at me, and says, "Ba-domp, *bomp.*"

"Well, I think it's *crazy,*" Kristy says. "I could make up a better poem myself right now, and maybe they'll give me the Hogface Prize: *"cat dog house car mirror floor rug shoe foot window dish soap stupid crap poetry ceiling lamp."*

"Definitely an Aram Saroyan influence," I say, as Sam starts to get into it, and now they're both laughing, *white red blue purple airplane socks briefcase television switcher drawer clothes,* tossing words around the room, *dog cat bird bed was from the and ha ha.*

"You're not giving it a chance. It's not gibberish—it's just . . . abstruse," but something about the word "abstruse" always seems to make people laugh, I've noticed.

240 ☆

Now they have begun to abandon words altogether, moving into a mirth-peppered glossolalia, *abba-dabba-ooga-booga-hoojee-goojee-yabba-dabba-doo;* and what is strangest of all as I listen to them babbling and laughing and then beginning to get tired is something they would be genuinely shocked to hear, even through the armor of their escort service casualness: that if they took themselves more seriously and weren't so pretty they proba-bly *could* win the Hogface Prize.

"We have to do this program," I say. "I know some of this stuff sounds ridiculous, but if we don't have anything to say, I'm going to be the one that's in trouble."

"Don't worry, Pack, just play it by ear," Samantha says, wan-dering to the door of the bathroom where Sally's shower noise has abated, then back again toward the head of the discussion. "You can listen to the papers, and then you can ask us the ques-tions—translated into English, of course. And we'll talk about our sexy lives. Okay? We'll talk about all the blow jobs we've given to English professors. We'll say they're all the greatest lovers in the world."

"Sam, please. I know you think this is funny, but I have a lot riding on it. If you just fool around and make jokes it's going to sound as if I brought you here for nothing."

"You did bring us here for nothing. But that's okay. Don't worry. I promise we'll say all sorts of . . . hookeyophrastic things to make the intellectuals proud of you."

"I sure hope so," I say. She's probably right, too. People always seem to do better when they're on the spot, although I really would like to walk into that program with some idea of what was about to happen.

"Class dismissed," I announce, yet we find ourselves dismiss-ing in a direction opposite from the dispersal of a normal class, into a three-way combination of hugs and kisses in which nobody makes any nitpicking distinctions about who is whom.

☆ ☆ ☆

We try to have lunch in the Emperor's Garden on the third floor of the Paradise Regal, but the line in front of the restaurant stretches all the way along the hall to the terminus of the escalator, which keeps bringing more and more people up from the casino.

Between Christmas and New Year's this town gets so crowded that the streams of New York people and Philadelphia people begin to curdle and clot and develop stuck spots anywhere a passage narrows or a walkway turns a corner. Even on the wide space of the Boardwalk, among the countless thousands of heads bobbing and strolling and holding more or less to the right in a divided flow, you can see little clumps where the people can't move anymore; and then when it backs up you can hear people yelling and cursing, the way so many people do these days: "Move your fuckin' ass up there! Get going, buddy!"

The only thing we can find is a little cafeteria on the Boardwalk, downstairs, a surprisingly uncrowded room with the walls full of old Atlantic City photographs: the old Traymore Hotel and the Marlborough-Blenheim and the Shelburne and the Ambassador, all overlooking the beach in their ponderous gray, and the Steel Pier and the Jumping Horse, lifeguards posing beside their rescue skiffs in official full-body Atlantic City Rescue Department suits, and a shot of Pacific Avenue crowded with the square-humped old black cars that ran so well, in those grainy-photographed times when we didn't all hate each other's guts, cars that more than anything else make me wish I'd lived and died back in the days when everybody wore a hat.

After lunch we split up, Sally and I taking one of the digital plastic room keys, Kristy and Sam keeping the other. I can't ask for any more keys because the hotel thinks I'm in there by myself.

Sally and I walk through the crowd, over the herringbone planking of the Boardwalk, holding hands and not saying much, like a man who has a very close relationship with his daughter. The plumes of cigarette smoke and cigar smoke hang so thick over the procession that it looks like dust over a country road. Just to walk next to her and look into her blue eyes in the middle of the jostling crowd seems suddenly more intimate than if we were back in the room naked and fucking each other's brains out with the lights off.

In the widened half-circle of the Boardwalk in front of the Atlantic City Convention Center, a group of black women have set up amplifiers and are singing "Amazing Grace" in a polished close harmony. Sally veers in the other direction as soon as she hears the music.

"Don't make me listen to that shit," she says. "That's what they used to sing when they spit on us."

"Who?"

"The Community of Praise. On Mondays, when we went to the doctor to get our checkups, there'd be these nice-looking ladies standing in front of the limo, singing 'Amazing Grace' and spitting on us and calling us bitches and devils and going, 'I'll watch you burn in hell, you filthy slut!' Real nice stuff. The last week I was there, Herb got some American-flag ponchos, so maybe they wouldn't want to spit on the American flag, but they just came closer and spit right in our faces."

She looked as if she was going to cry when she was telling me this, but when we find our way back into the main flow of the Boardwalk, she smiles and holds herself against my shoulder.

The crowd moves, stops, gets stuck; voices from within it are raised like horns in a traffic jam. After a while the flow of the crowd pushes us over to a place where a slow-moving clump of bodies butts up against the railing. We stop for a minute and look in each other's eyes.

"Sally, I love you," I say.

"Oh, Pack, that's so nice," she says. "I'm really glad." In all the time we've been seeing each other she's never said anything about her own feelings. But at least she seems to like me, and for the time being that will have to do.

It makes me nervous to make such a mushy scene, such a sloppy May-October make-out in the midst of so many people; but then when I lift my head from her face and look out across the Boardwalk, through the golden blur of her hair, into the couples and their clenched hands—I can see that most of them are too angry about how crowded it is to even notice us, or to wonder whether we are man and prostitute, or teacher and wide-eyed student, or father and daughter gone terribly astray.

☆ ☆ ☆

It is almost time to go into the casino. When you are in a situation where the result of the game is actually going to make a difference in your life, things get serious, not like being a half-drunken tourist throwing a few stacks of red chips around Las Vegas. I've decided to try a strategy that I experimented with during the fall using the blackjack game on my office Macintosh. I call it a modified martingale, a strategy adapted from the discredited doubling-up system in which a gambler chases his lost money, and quits as soon as he either wins one dollar or loses $2,048.

In the system I've devised, you start with ten dollars, then whether you win or lose, increase it to fifteen, then twenty, and by fives up to fifty, by tens up to a hundred, and by twenty-fives the rest of the way up to five hundred, at which point you stop, unless you have already been wiped out, in which case you stop earlier.

I've run some trials of that system, even programming it to play a series of contests by itself. What I have learned is that approximately forty percent of the time you will be wiped out, thirty percent of the time you will win something under a thousand, and thirty percent of the time you will win more, up to a theoretical but never achieved win limit of $5,670.

But as logical as this system is, it's going to need some help. I have always believed that it is essential, before you step into any Atlantic City casino, to feed the birds.

By the time we have worked out way through the crowd to the edge of the Boardwalk, where a set of steps leads down to the beach, the gulls and terns and pigeons have already spotted a man holding his large order of Roy Rogers french fries in what they judge to be a generous manner.

I stand at the bottom of the steps and toss the french fries up in the air one by one. Hardly a one hits the ground. The gulls swoop in, spread-clawed, intense, as the high din of their voices spreads, and from all around this section of the beach they come flying.

Within a matter of seconds the number of birds is overwhelming, Hitchcockian, wheeling around our heads, shrieking, the herring gulls with a red spot at the tip of their open beaks buzzing our heads, their angry eyes staring into mine, pigeons fluttering and grabbing. Sally is frightened; she leans against me, keeping her hands up, protecting her hair. Actually I'm always a little scared myself when I do this. One of those germ-laden talons could catch my eye; and there's probably some exclusion for that in my soon-to-be-terminated group insurance.

"Ever seen that movie?" I say.

"Yeah," she shouts above the squawking. "This is worse."

I know it's horrible, and I know it's not fair to the people walking nearby who might get birdshit in their faces. It's probably even bad for the birds, to make them dependent on garbage, like Yogi and Boo-boo in Jellystone Park.

Still, it's fun to see so much teeming, angry life appear out of nowhere, from along the flat beach, from the rooftops of the frozen yogurt stands and the two-dollar fortune-tellers, a squalling, fanatically acquisitive life, an appalling concentration on those Roy Rogers french fries, the ravenous button eyes of those swooping and wheeling birds, with their dry claws grabbing my fingers, a few quick-winged pigeons making a try for the box. If I wanted anything in the world as much as those birds want those french fries, I do believe I would find a way to get it.

And still they keep coming, more and more, hungrier and hungrier, flapping in a straight line from under the darkness of the abandoned amusement pier, appearing out of the open sea, with its surf today no bigger than the wake of a drug boat.

☆ ☆ ☆

In Atlantic City the casino areas are clearly contained within their hotels, with no inviting banks of slot machines out next to the check-in desk. You walk down a few steps, past a security guard who is there to make sure no minors get in, past the sign, required by law, that says "Bet with Your Head, Not over It," and there you are, in the strong carpety smell, among the blocks of slot machines, thousands of them, and each one has a moderately overweight middle-aged woman in front of it. That is an important difference between here and Vegas. Here you would never see a man under sixty-five playing a slot machine. I've done it once and I walked away embarrassed.

The casino sound here is thicker than in Vegas, more oceanic, less magical, more like traffic noise, the thousands of voices murmuring over the crash and the clang and the electronic slots that play "We're in the Money" in that weird and timbreless tone of computer-generated music.

In the line for the bathroom all the men are angry about how crowded it is.

"Fuckin' gotta wait in line for this too, huh?" says a thick-jawed old man with a cigar, while others grunt and scowl in aggreement.

It is not quite time for the day-trippers to start assembling for their buses, yet the augmented note of people playing harder during their last hour of liberty can be heard all over the casino. The old ones have lined up by the hundreds at the promotions booth, with their canes and their walkers and their bus coupons entitling them to a free digital watch, handed out in bubble-wrap.

In Atlantic City when it gets crowded, the pit bosses go from game to game, raising all the table minimums. All along the row of crap tables, the minimums are up to ten dollars. Still the tables are so crowded that I could not pull my shoulders close enough together to squeeze in to a place along the rail.

Craps is much bigger in Atlantic City than it is in Las Vegas, with dozens and dozens of tables, reaching a hundred yards down one corridor, and then a hundred yards back around the other side, with guys pushing and shouting among the generalized agitation of the game. One loud shooter, whom we can hear a good way away through the crowd, yells the same thing every time he rolls the dice: "Talk to me *sweet-HEART!*" A well-dressed guy, probably suffering from a serious gambling problem. I've read that twenty percent of the businesses in Philadelphia are in trouble because of casino losses.

With Sally holding my arm, we dodge and apologize our way through the crowd, with "Talk to me *sweet-HEART!*" echoing behind us, moving toward the blackjack tables, which the pit bosses have raised from their usual level of five dollars up to twenty-five. Still the day-trippers cluster around the seats, some looking over other people's shoulders, in the din of the machines and the crap tables washing over the almost wordless card games.

It's bad when you play scared. I wanted to start with ten and run the modified martingale up to the point where we are either broke or over two thousand. This will be a little harder, starting at twenty-five. My head hums, walking, looking for a seat. We pass a space at a no-smoking table, and I almost sit down, but no-smoking tables frighten me. Finally we find a good smoky ashtray of a table with a free seat.

Sally stands behind me. We have pooled our bankrolls into two hundred dollars, which is a pitifully small stake at a table like this.

"Good luck, Pack," she says, close to my ear.

"Good luck, sir," the dealer says, under her tight frosted perm such as you see on middle-aged waitresses in cities less sophisticated than this one. She smiles in a way that mercifully ignores the small size of my buy-in.

This is it; the shoe is three-quarters of the way full; she won't be shuffling for a long time.

At least it will be fast. That's the way to play: real gambling, not this nitpicky chickenshit blackjack money management system stuff they sell on USA Network so late at night that the only time I get to see it is when I come home late from the place that Americans are not permitted to go anymore.

Fast in, fast out. The first hand goes for the minimum of twenty-five, from which I will progressively raise my bet, win or lose.

Dealer busts, I win. In and out. Hit and run.

Now at thirty dollars—I draw to twenty-one, and win.

At thirty-five—dealer draws to twenty-one, but we're still ahead. This is quick. Not the way most people play—the Grind, as the casinos call it, hour after hour, while the cards just keep slipping out of that enormous eight-deck shoe.

At forty dollars—I win.

At forty-five—bust.

At fifty, with a five-dollar dealer bet in front of my own bet—blackjack, and I smile at the dealer the way you're supposed to. She says, "Thank you, sir," as she drops the winnings into her tip box.

At sixty dollars—the dealer busts. My hands are shaking. Somehow when you play this fast, you feel as if you can rise above that inevitable house advantage, above the tyranny of the Law of Large Numbers.

Seventy dollars—I lose to dealer's twenty.

Eighty dollars—I double down with ten, swallow hard. And I win.

Ninety—lose. We're still way ahead. It feels weird to play with greens, weird to see them stacked up on the felt in front of me. I don't know how far ahead we are, but I'm getting tempted to cut and run.

One hundred—a bigger bet than I've ever made in my life. Two fives come up and I am almost too scared to double, hardly breathing as I place four more greens beside my original bet, Sally's hands kneading the implacable tissue in the back of my neck—and I win.

"Yes!" I say softly, and my whole body jerks like the body of a man who is having stomach cramps.

I've never seen so many greens. There are six other players at this table, and they're talking about this and that, mostly about how much they were ahead before they lost it all back, but I can hardly even see them; it's just a little twilight world of me, and the dealer with her tight coif, and the long box of the shoe at the dealer's left hand, and the green chips, and the cards.

I've only been here about five minutes. And whatever happens I'll only be here about five more, which is really our only chance—or else we'll end up like all the guys up in the hotel slamming their fists into the wall, or bragging to their friends how much they almost won before they blew it.

I figure we'll just go up until we're somewhere in the thousands, then run.

One twenty-five, with a ten-dollar dealer bet—we lose.

One fifty—I bust.

One seventy-five—I lose. That last one hurt. We're not broke, but suddenly we don't have enough to keep up with the progressive pattern.

I bet fifty—and the dealer turns over a blackjack.

Our last fifty—I bust. We are broke. I rise from the table, pushing the chair back, like a wounded animal.

It seems like miles to the front door, with Sally at my arm, silent, through the clumps and the blockades of the people with their smells, so many cigar smells and cologne smells and sweat smells and saliva smells, their voices shapeless, like dogs, in the mechanical chaos and frantic milling that so many other busted gamblers have fought their way through, a sound like something you might hear in the middle of New York City on a day when the new crime figures have been released.

We walk onto the beach, where the land is almost level, the water hundreds of yards away. The sand is so finely ground that you can walk on it in your shoes without sinking in the way you would farther north.

It is strange how few people come down here, when the Board-walk is so crowded you can hardly move. The breeze has shifted around so it carries the smell of the crowd out to the beach, their cigarettes and colognes; those dominant concoctions, agressive, grasping—odors that raise their voices in a crowd and tell you to move out of the way, strong as the tension outside the bathroom where men are angry about having to line up, in the unventilated intestinal stink that rolls out the door to be lost in the generalized weather of the casino.

I suppose the people walking up there are afraid that muggers may lurk among the pilings that hold up the Ocean One Shopping Pier. Perhaps they do, but if so, we are too smart for them. We walk, holding hands, in the other direction, into the sunset.

☆ ☆ ☆

Out to sea, a few tiny lights. On television, our old ene-mies the Cincinnati Bearcats, in the Banana Bowl against the University of Maine. The colors of the uniforms in these bowl games, and the blue of the turf against the deep yellow of hash-marks, is all so intense, like a Saturday-morning cartoon, that if somebody asked me who was winning I would have to wait for the score to come up on the screen again.

The door opens with its momentary servo groan. Kristy and Samantha come in and take off their coats. Earlier Sally told me not to worry about the money, that they were going to look for some dates, but now they don't look happy.

"What happened?" Sally says.

"Nothing happened, that's what happened." Samantha hangs her coat up on one of the permanently mounted and unstealable hangers in the closet, turns around in a maroon cocktail dress with a line of sparkles under her breasts. "We went to every casino bar. Nothing. I've had better nights in Laughlin, with the RV crowd."

"We must have run into a slot players' tournament or something," Kristy says.

And I can feel room sink, as so many rooms have sunk, when the people in them are sunk, that awful feeling, and one that I imagine is very familiar to the unseeing wallpaper of this room, to be financially embarrassed in a beautiful room, its airy-colored curtains gathered open in a festoon at the sides to show the darkness of the ocean, and French milled soap in the bathroom, whatever it is that they do to get that soap through a mill.

"That means that we've got a slight problem," I say. "We're broke."

"I wouldn't exactly say that," Samantha says. She reaches into her purse and begins to pull out handfuls of casino chips, mostly greens and blacks, a few reds . . . and even purples, which I don't recognize at first, until it occurs to me that the purples represent five hundred dollars.

"My God!" I say, my mouth falling open. "How did you win all that?"

"We didn't exactly win it," Kristy says, and when I look at her, she goes on, grinning. "We tried out a little system that we never had the nerve to do in Vegas. You know how crowded it is down there. You just sneak up and snatch it off somebody's table and get lost in the crowd."

☆ ☆ ☆

Not that America needed to be any angrier tonight than it was before, but I think I can say with confidence that a few gamblers, their blacks and purples snatched, are angrier than they have ever been in a lifetime of stomping away from cold tables.

I can imagine them in the manager's office, the hotness of their sweat reactivating their residual cologne, screaming for a refund, veins sticking out above their collarbones, threatening the casino, threatening the manager.

It is true that what has happened is unfair. Maybe these guys were ahead for the first time in their lives, maybe they really weren't going to lose it all back this time. But one of the blessings of the fact that life is unfair is that the anger stays downstairs, and up here it's just beautiful girls and a lopsided football game.

Meanwhile, the thieves, and their accessory to grand larceny, have sent for room service, though the thieves must hide in the bathroom when the guy brings four dinners for the healthy appetite of Mr. Schmidt. The waiter departs the hideout of the crooks carrying two reds, a tip not quite suspiciously large. The Banana Bowl over, I have found a rerun of "The Uncle Floyd Show," in which Loony Skip Rooney plays a job applicant being interviewed by Floyd's arm puppet Oogie, who keeps sticking pins in him when he's not looking.

☆ ☆ ☆

I have passed in idleness more than my required thirty-six hours; in fact it has been approximately forty-eight. Tonight I find myself with more friends than I know what to do with. What a confluence, what a kindness, of hands and hair, of softly articulated decisions about who will do what, shades of skin under the hotel bulbs, and faces the likes of which many a man happier than I will die never having looked on close up—all the room lights switched on and nobody peeking in the window except maybe the first mate of a Japanese freighter twenty miles at sea.

Chapter 16

MLA is a Christmas parade of muted browns and grays moving in a slant of escalators through space. The suits and the jackets and the high-quality woolen skirts move effortlessly through the air of the headquarters hotel, from conference level to lobby level, from mezzanine to exhibit hall. Old friends will meet each other going the opposite direction on the escalator, shaking hands quickly over the median, then waving, calling as they are inclined apart: "Good to see you, let's have a drink, what hotel are you in?"

The Modern Language Association is the parent organization for every college English department in the country. Its yearly convention draws so many thousands of registrants that the population spills over from the headquarters hotels into a dozen others, all of which are otherwise mostly empty in this week between Christmas and New Year's, allowing for particularly good convention room rates. The event is even too big to have a single central headquarters; the two main divisions must each have their own headquarters hotel—the English programs in the Wyndham Franklin, and the foreign language programs in the Four Seasons.

Everybody wants to stay at the headquarters hotel, especially in Philadelphia, where the hotels are spread apart all over downtown, but only the smart guys like me who sent their room requests back to the convention bureau the day they came in manage to get into the Wyndham.

I've always enjoyed being a conventioner, walking around the Christmasy streets of a new city, with my name tag, looking in restaurant windows. On the sidewalk of Race Street, I keep remembering last night in Bally's, thinking about how easy it is for four people to sleep in one king-sized bed if they are all friends, and how, as the pace of that night slowed toward sleep, the man and mistress of the room gravitated toward each other in the concavity of their weight on one side of the mattress, and the well-beloved serving girls, who had saved our movable household from bankruptcy, found their own domestic sag at the opposite end.

Now, in the Wyndham Franklin, with Sally and Kristy and Samantha upstairs catching up on soap operas, I have been drifting through the birchy, autumnal shades of professorial clothing—the herringbone gray jackets, the camel hair, the khaki trousers, the hats and overcoats, the woolly smell of people when they bring snow inside on their collars.

After several years of these gatherings, you find that it's always more or less the same group of people. Anybody who has taught freshman comp will understand the guiding principles by which those conventioners can be arranged into categories, like the constituent parts of one of those awful papers that used to end up waiting to be read, piled six inches high on my desk at home on a Sunday afternoon.

The calm and slow-walking white-haired full professors, often department chairs, are here to head the interviewing committees. Unless their school is rich enough to afford a drawing-room suite, they will meet candidates in the committee chairman's hotel room, with the candidate sitting on the bed, sometimes the maid asking to come in at the worst possible time, and all that awkwardness about coats.

Perhaps, in the manner of freshman categorization papers, one could say that the organizing principle for establishing these categories would be less their manner of dress than their way of walking. If you pay close enough attention to the walk, there will be little question about who has tenure, and no question about who does or doesn't have a job.

Closely associated in garb and gait with the venerable chairmen—yet a little darker in the hair and suit, a little sharper in the eye, and a little faster on the feet—the midlevel interviewers walk easily through the hotel corridors, their elbows patched, their hands in their pockets, until they meet somebody they need joyously to shake hands with.

For the women faculty members, the off-white blouse and the gray skirt is standard, with hair that hangs straight, and strenuously un-fussed-over. Occasional exceptions exist, of course, but then this is a freshman paper, not a national census. You can tell from the way they walk on their high heels whether they want to be here or not. They are not fat, yet most of them seem to have been widened uniformly, from shoes to forehead, as if in a stretched photograph.

Less direct in their steps, jerky, afraid, making false starts against the flow of the crowd, the sad-sack all-but-dissertation job seekers haunt the job opportunities bulletin board. You see them everywhere, bearded, gawky, their shirttails pulling out from the front of their only suit, its lapels too wide, sometimes double-breasted.

They cannot afford the hotel, even at the bargain-basement MLA rates. So they are staying with friends, as they will be staying with friends for the rest of their lives, sleeping on an air mattress with so little room on the floor that their foot keeps jamming up against the base of the police lock. Some have lined up an interview or two, with an old friend, or with a school that felt sorry for them, sorry for their cruel placement in the wrong gender, the wrong time, wrong place, wrong race.

Then the Affirmative Action wonders, whisking from interview to interview. These are mostly white women; the eligible minority candidates have secured their positions long before MLA, leaving the white males and the white females to exchange wordless glances back and forth in the elevators, each remembering, perhaps, that these were the kind of people they used to be friends with back in graduate school.

The gender-intensive job-seekers have lined up so many interviews that sometimes they must run through the halls in their heavy pumps, to Michigan at one-thirty, Columbia at two, then UCLA, then Wisconsin. They pull up in front of an elevator and brake to a stop, like city traffic, as their name tags shine against their off-white blouses.

Everybody is always sneaking a look at everybody else's name tag, to see what college they teach at; you watch people going by and try to read as many as possible, scarcely seeing the person's name. A conversation with a stranger is a matter of discreet glances down and up, along with to the side if somebody else goes by, someone who might be marked with the lettering of Yale, Harvard, Stanford, Princeton. Everybody else is Southwest Michigan State College, or Prairieview University Campus at

Lompton. To speak to a stranger at MLA is to know, I imagine, what girls with big breasts must feel like when men are talking to them and not paying attention.

It is quiet, but never silent; the hum of voices stays at a constant medium level. It is a convention without drunks, without guys slapping each other on the back, without high jinks or practical jokes. That is especially so this year. Much of the talk in the halls lately is of *retrenchment,* of schools whose federal funding has been cut even more drastically than that of the Centers for Disease Control. Although you can feel less jauntiness this year in the steps of the newly tenured, the halls are still alive with the cheerful scrambling of shoes and briefcases as the interview rooms receive another globally focused shoe-in candidate.

☆ ☆ ☆

When you are a crook, the world opens up. You don't have to wait in line for special provisional registration tags for your hotel guests, which they might not have let us have anyway. Easier just to go back to the Lost Name Tag desk three times and get the plastic holder and the MLA Philadelphia logo, with my name penned in, and then doctor up the card with a Bic pen, in imitation of the unchallenging calligraphy of my legitimate tag, with the names "Kristina Rousseau, Pecos State," "Samantha Bell, University of Northwestern Rhode Island," and for Sally, "Natalie Sparrowsworth, Illinois Normal and Mines."

Mostly the three of them have been staying in the room watching television and calling room service. I don't understand it: one of the great cities of America and they're doing nothing. They even went out and bought a Monopoly game. When they asked me if I wanted to play, I almost threw the thing out the window. Fortunately the windows here don't open.

But then, maybe they're right to be lazy. Hotels are best when you're doing nothing, when you can just look out the window into a city in the snow, at the dark shapes of buildings, all those windows with nobody in them. You can always recognize an office building, by those cold symmetrical bars of light stretching across the whole accounts receivable department. The lights of a hotel are softer, a shaded asymmetry of private rooms and half-drawn curtains.

☆ ☆ ☆

Sometimes it seems that everybody in the world but me has quit drinking. When I order a second Miller Light I feel like some kind of degenerate. Larry sips his Evian quietly, without thirst. Not only has he given up alcohol, but his whole agitated manner seems calmed, regularized, which is exactly what the institution of tenure is supposed to keep from happening.

"But what are their *qualifications,* Pack?" he says for the fourth or fifth time.

"Larry, don't worry," I tell him. "This is completely germane to the program. These women are in the perfect position to apply your theories to their practice. It'll be interesting."

"You mean these girls, with no experience and no credentials, are supposed to stand up in front of this crowd and evaluate papers that they've never studied before?"

"I've been going over the whole thing with them. Believe me, they're very articulate."

"Do you mean articulate, or articulated?" he says, running his hand through his gray hair as he stares down at the pages of his manuscript on the lobby bar table. "I don't know, Pack. Don't you have any of your old papers from the *College English Journal* that you could read?"

"It would be boring, Larry. And it wouldn't have anything to do with the topic."

"I'm really concerned about this," he says. "Whenever the topic is anything to do with sex, we get a very ideological crowd. They're not going to have much tolerance for those girls."

"I swear this is going to work," I tell him. "It's a common

ground. That's what I'm looking for. A common ground between eros and ideology—that's *my* theme, and these girls are the perfect catalyst for that search. If you'll forgive the mixed metaphor."

"Pack, I hope you don't think I'm being too cautious. But I've been to these meetings. You're not going to see a lot of open-mindedness."

"We're prepared," I say, lying.

By the time I leave I don't know if I've brought him around at all, but at least he hasn't demanded that I read an old composition theory paper.

It scares me, though, to think about bringing them in there unprepared, so for the next two hours I rent myself a terminal in the convention's temporary computer center and work up a paraphrase of Larry's paper, complete with an explication of the extracted poems, all of it presented in a form so rudimentary that I almost understand it myself.

☆ ☆ ☆

One floor below the lobby, on the Conference Level, the hundreds of separate lecture programs and panel discussions and open-floor conferences are scheduled throughout the day, from eight in the morning to nine at night. The partitioned rooms stand in a long line, the conference titles set into a glass display outside each mahogany door.

In this district of the headquarters hotel, little has changed since the days when Paul Goodman was the keynote speaker. You'd hardly know the Cold War was over, to see all the people who are still fighting it on the side that lost. The Schuylkill Room hosts a program called "Re-matrixing the Disappeared: The Semiosis of Franz Fanon in the New Argentine Criticism." In the Penn's Landing Room: "Joycean Concordances in Shining Path Communiqués."

Here and there, a tip of the hat to outside events. I see that one of the conferences in my program book is titled "After August in

Red Square: W(h)ither the Academic Left?"

Down here, the look is different, the atmosphere harder, more of those bristly red beards, guys in patched corduroys, and the monochrome gray of women's faces as they hurry to the next panel discussion. Inside the Poor Richard Room: "Five Hundred Years of Your God-Damned Glory: Is Columbus (Be)coming B(l)ack?" The Adjunct Lectureship Caucus is running a program in the Patrick Henry Room, with a discussion called "Grades as a Tool for Enforcing Cultural Diversity in Student Writing: Or Hey Hey Ho Ho, the Generic Masculine Has Got to Go." In the Brandywine Conference Room: "Yemen, Semen, and Phallustine: Gender Issues in the Literature of the Uprising."

I have come down here because I'm trying to find the Continental Congress Room, which is where we're scheduled tomorrow. I know it's on this level, probably near the Bill of Rights Room, which hosts "Foucault and Remedial Composition: How the Comma Splice Dejuxtapositionalizes Representationality," or the John Hancock Room, now featuring "Degenitized Selvings: Female Gard(e)ners on the Primrose P(l)ath."

I always feel better if I can see where I'm going to be speaking. And there it is, just another big door in the wall, and a room half full toward the front between the walls of red partition on either side, giving the place the appearance of a section of one of those twelve-screen theaters.

Given the schedules that people try to keep, it is not considered rude around here to walk into a conference late, or to leave early. People drift in and out; below the drone of speakers is heard a constant rustle of coats and papers, and if it's crowded, the sound of somebody politely moving up from the floor into a chair just vacated.

The program on right now is "Toward a Curriculum of Diversity: No Tears for the Dead White Males." Figuring that I need to get an idea about what the people who get the jobs are talking about these days, I take a seat inside, trying not to make myself look too threatening or too threatened. Fortunately I don't have my suit on.

The speaker looks about sixteen years old, a dark-haired woman with a precise little face. In my program book I can see that she is either Candace Wanamaker of Northwest Minnesota Community College or Bethany Schprekel of my old University of Maryland. The paper she is reading is called either "Reobjectivizing Herstory in the Post-Contemporary Rape Canon" or "Reading With the Lights Out: Pan-Gendral Reification in Ntozake Shange's Revenge Cantos."

Candace or Bethany has an odd habit of oratorical emphasis. Instead of raising her voice, or gesturing, or pausing, she emphasizes her important points by making a little dip in the direction of the audience while continuing in the same gradually falling tone of voice.

At the lectern she dips and dips like a Hasidic Jew at prayer. Every sentence begins on a high note, then trails off a few clauses later into a mumble, although to judge from the frequency of dips, her strongest points tend to bunch themselves toward the secret end of her sentences.

"THE RESULT OF THIS CRYPTO-INTENTIONAL (though some would call it merely self-referential) defielding is that the al- ready weakening thread of something-something is further hyperductilized into more of a something-something, something-something, bluh bluh bluh. *AT THE SAME TIME, THE HORIZONTALIZATION THAT AGAIN AND AGAIN she tries at the same time to amplify and suppress* is thus rereferenced from the surrounding assumptions, in a pattern similar to the way in which Carolyn Forché's *Philippine Sequence* mercilessly contrasts the something-something against what she something-something of the something-something-something."

I feel as if I've known this girl all my life, the good kid in the class, the one even the smart ones didn't like. In my own career, she is the one whose paper I never had to read because I knew it would be an A. This is the kid who cultivated the habit of speaking in such a tiny voice from all those years of sitting close to the teacher. It looks as if she has taken it all the way now, and at last she remains the good one, and I'm still the bad one, scarcely paying attention, looking through my notebook, trying to figure out a way of making my own slapdash program more interesting, or at least more audible, than this one.

I wander around, with nothing to do but get nervous. The International Boontling Society is represented as usual, with a program in the Valley Forge Room: "Yappers in the Beard's Florsh: The Joe-Billyish Bustwax of Backaway Harping." Farther down the long hall, in the Lenai-Lenape Conference Room, a poetry reading by Asian Lesbians and Gays. I walk in in the middle of a poem by a very pretty young woman, her face running to fat, who reads in a soft voice:

> ". . . and Hing Wu spoke like a warm
> graveyard, warm graveyard, bring me
> down in your poor penny-wealthy
> memory. His coin from the March,
> his yellow eyes like a dog, his
> yellow cigarette smile, said
> 'Cough with me and the sky will be
> silent.' My hand found a leaf,
> a green leaf, that did not speak
> to me, did not even collapse
> in my hand, alive with dust."

I don't know if this poem was any good because I didn't hear the beginning, but everybody here seems to like it, including this very enthusiastic old fellow with yellow hair brushed back over his ears and one of those old-fashioned hearing aids that fill the shell of his ear like Silly Putty. They're not supposed to applaud after every poem, but in the moments between poems several people in the audience make this peculiar poetry-reading sound that I've heard for years, a sort of strangled grunt of appreciation, a soft croak of wordless Frankensteinesque pleasure.

✩ ✩ ✩

The elevators run in packs. This is something I've noticed ever since I've been coming to MLA. In the center of the hotel you turn off from the hall into a landing that has five elevator doors on each side, and there are so many people being lifted up to their interviews, lifted down to dinner and a program they want to catch, that every car stops on every floor. And somehow, perhaps by a mathematical formula in which usefully random events like the arrival of an elevator decay into an orderly group march, they all bunch together. By the time they get anywhere the landing is packed, the first few cars to get there are stuffed close to their 3,600-pound limit, and the stragglers continue nearly empty.

I've persuaded Kristy and Sam to wear their coats on the way to our program, because I'm afraid that the rows of grommets along the sides of their cocktail dresses might provoke a feminist incident. It's snowing outside now; you can smell it on those few people who are not afraid of having their fur hats spit on. And you can feel it, a sort of quiet agitation indoors with no windows, a feeling that goes back to the earliest schools we remember, and the joyous yellow-lighted rumble of being sent home early.

To minimize possible antagonism, Larry has insisted that Kristy and Samantha describe themselves as former hookers who have realized how terrible it was. I've also asked Sally to stay back in the room, in case somebody from Amherst sees her in the conference. Kristy and Sam move close behind me out of the elevator crowd, down the escalator with all the other people coming the other way whom I hope I don't know.

When we get to the room, the previous conference is just

Edward Allen

breaking up, with a lingering chatter of issues still needing to be discussed. The poster being taken down reads: "Canon-Fire in the Bay of P(r)igs: One, Two, Three, Many Stanfords."

What I can't get over is that a pitcher of water has been placed before each of us, next to our individual tabletop microphones, as we sit up here and joke and look at our watches and count the audience as they drift in through the side door. I've never been important enough to have my own water pitcher before.

For a conference about sex, this meeting has attracted more people dressed in black than I am ordinarily comfortable with. We're also getting the very thin, and the symmetrically swollen, and some people with skin so coarse they seem to have been scrubbed with steel wool. Larry was right about getting a good crowd; already all the seats are taken, a few listeners are humped uncomfortably on the floor at the edge of the center aisle, and the back wall is becoming tall with standees.

We come to order. Larry steps up to introduce the program and to read his paper, which combines long and difficult stretches of argument with poem extracts from Spellman Booker and Wilhelm Throckmorton and Rachel Phillips Gallivander. The poems, mellifluous and lyrical, but hardly clearer than the prose, become a sort of Mendelssohnian interlude between the dry speeches, an interlude in which I can discreetly look up at the ceiling, squint my eyes, let the many lights of the central chandelier stretch into long upside-down icicles.

Larry's not the clearest writer in the world, but I can see why he's such a great teacher. His voice is soft, every word is felt, and believed, and he puts out his hand and seems to touch you with it. Ideology aside, imagine the persuasive manner of Ronald Reagan transplanted into a professor who knows what he is talking about. With every word Larry leans forward into the crowd, almost embracing them, his loose hair falling over his forehead, his black eyes expectant, sensitive, saying, "Please. Here it is. This is what I know. It's yours."

264 ☆

Loud applause for Larry. He introduces me, and Kristy, and Samantha. I take over, without notes, starting with a few general comments about how persuasive Larry's ideas are.

"We've arranged something a little different tonight, folks," I continue. "Just so we in this profession don't get too complacent with the old format of academics making pronouncements about subjects which after all affect people other than ourselves—which is not to undercut Professor Eisensohn's remarks—I've asked a pair of young women whose experience touches on subjects, or at least on a vocation, quite outside that of most university people, yet very pertinent, I would think, to the topics this session is addressing." Thank God I made it to the end of that thought. You hang around MLA long enough and listen to enough subordinate clauses branching off within other subordinate clauses, and you'll need an oxygen tank before you find your way to the end of a complete sentence.

"Ms. Samantha Bell and Ms. Kristina Rousseau should have some insights about the points Professor Eisensohn raised in his paper, because they have recently worked for an adult escort service in Las Vegas. I thought they might have a different take on how people's perception of eroticism has changed."

"In other words, we're hookers," Samantha blurts out into the mike.

"We *were*," Kristy says. "We're not anymore. Right?"

"There you have it, folks. A nonacademic viewpoint."

So far, so good. At least I have them paying attention—the People in Black, the widebodies, the beards, the whitehairs, all sitting up in their chairs.

To start off I ask Samantha what she thought about all the references in the paper to language as an erotic currency, but she just smiles at me.

"Some of that stuff went over my head, I'm afraid," she says.

"Can you tell me if any of it relates to your experience? Do you find people depending more on verbal foreplay?"

"Some do, some don't," she says. "Some guys just like to listen to our answering machine."

A minute into the act and I'm beginning to realize that Larry was right to be worried about this program. We don't have much to say.

"What about you, Ms. Rousseau?" I say. "Does anything you've heard in Professor Eisensohn's paper relate to anything that you've experienced in your profession—your former profession? Or let me expand the question. Does anything you've heard *contrast* with your work experience?"

"It all does," she says, mumbling into the microphone.

"It does what?"

"It contrasts," Kristy says, sheepishly, as if she would like to beg me to stop asking questions.

"Could you elaborate on how it contrasts?"

"Well," she says, "in the business, when people say things, I can usually understand them. But tonight, when people say things, I can never understand them."

Scattered laughter around the room, but choked off quickly, as if people know they shouldn't be laughing, a sentiment more directly articulated by a woman's voice toward the back of the room which shouts out, *"That's not funny!"*

No official ice water can quench my cottonmouth now. And it started out so well. I thought my opening comments were very thoughtful. And I was sure that being up here on the dais would give Kristy and Sam some incentive to wax articulate.

I seem to be surrounded by a low drone, like an organ pedal, whether from my own blood rushing in my head or from the rumble of all the people's feet outside hurrying to the next program I don't know. I've passed a note to Samantha—"I could use a little *help*"—and she smiled and passed it back with a large green question mark drawn onto it.

"How do you react to that, Ms. Bell?" I say, not even sure by now what I'm asking her to react to. Larry is looking away. That old lump of embarrassed silence hangs over the room the same as it has loomed over all the tongue-tied classes with whom I could never strike up even the most rudimentary dialogue.

"Pack, what do you want me to *say?*" Kristy says.

"I have no idea. Maybe we could open the floor up for questions from the audience." Not a hand goes up.

"I assure you all that Ms. Bell and Ms. Rousseau could bring a very original viewpoint to this discussion, except that I think they are unused to the format of an academic conference. Right?" I say to my left.

"That's right, Pack," Kristy says in that soft monotone. "We're scared of all these grumpy-looking people."

Loud laughter now, sustained for several seconds, then fading out like the orchestra around a solo violinist, around that one voice, persistent, from somewhere near the source of the Not Funny comment: "Can I say something? Can I say something? Can I say something?"

"I'm glad to have anybody say anything."

This is a tall young woman with the solid body of a former field-hockey player and straight blond hair in which the positively charged flyaway strands form a sort of nimbus around the gravity-controlled majority of her hair.

"I think this program is *terribly misguided,*" she says with a smile as lifeless as a pumpkin. Immediately the air in the room hardens, the gratuitous fidgeting of a failed lecture stops. "I am embarrassed to be witnessing this."

Again, the old teacher's standby: "Would you elaborate on that thought?"

"You've brought these unfortunate individuals in here and set them up in front of us like zoo animals, and you call it an educational experience. Well, I call it an insult. I would like to ask Professor Eisensohn what he had in mind by this disgusting dis-

Edward Allen

play. And do you have a pornographic movie for us when it's over?"

"I'll answer the last question first," Larry says. "It's *Long Dong Silver*. With White House approval, of course." I'd forgotten how much I admired Larry, the way he can let the air out of a tense moment.

"I think I can answer the rest of the question," I say as the laughter fades, "if Professor Eisensohn doesn't mind. First, I'll take the responsibility for asking Ms. Bell and Ms. Rousseau here. If I've done something wrong by that—"

"You *have* done something wrong," the woman interrupts, grinning. "You've taken a conference in which scholarship and intelligence are the cards of entry, and you've introduced individuals who have made their way by the random and valueless criterion of physical attractiveness. I consider that an attack on the legitimate accomplishments of women."

A few other voices now, over the general muttering disequilibrium: "That's true." "It's stupid!" "He's made it into a *joke.*"

"Please, please." Larry is tapping the metal end of his ball-point pen on his water pitcher. "Nobody's trying to insult anybody. Now could we have a little order in this meeting?"

"Could we have a little *apology* for this meeting?"

"Okay," I say. "I apologize for not programming our remarks to a strict format and for treating this meeting as a true social and intellectual experiment. I guess I must be in the wrong place for that. But I will *not* apologize for bringing Ms. Bell and Ms. Rousseau here. I welcome them. They're my friends, and I don't want to see them insulted."

"Professor Schmidt." This is another woman, with short dark hair, in a kind of loose beige leisure suit. "We've all been dancing around the real issue here, which is the issue of people being unfairly rewarded for physical attractiveness, so let's bring it out in the open. This is precisely the kind of self-oppression that

Naomi talks about in her book. I find it an insult to come in here
after publishing twenty papers and see a program dedicated to a
couple of high-school dropouts—"

"I'm not a high-school dropout," Kristy says into the mike. "I'm
a college dropout." Loud laughter again, but the short-haired
woman holds out.

"Number one, I don't think it's funny to listen to this individual
make jokes against her own intelligence. And number two, I don't
think it's right for this conference to apotheosize the ideal that
women should aspire to model themselves after a couple of uneducated . . . *bimbos* . . ."

And now a gale of voices whirls up, some shouting that the
word *bimbo* is the sexual equivalent of *nigger,* some saying "Let
her speak!" and others shouting, "Shut up!" or talking among
themselves or joining the others in a group *"Shhhhhhhhh!"*

". . . a couple of uneducated young women who have nothing
going for them but the accident of looks, and now they have to be
the center of attention up there in their pretty faces and their
makeup and their hair spray and whatever other commercial
products they might be advertising with other parts of their bodies."

"Is this better?" Kristy says, pulling the corners of her mouth
and eyes into that mongoloid Quasimodo face the way kids do.

"Believe it or not, ladies," I say to my co-panelists, "you've both
been given a compliment. She said you're pretty and that makes
her angry."

More confused voices. "She has a point!" "You can't make
everything into a joke."

"Hey, Pack," Samantha says, her mouth close to the microphone. "Can we leave?"

"Yes!" some voices answer. "Please do!" And all the time Larry
is tapping the pen rapidly back and forth between the microphone
and the water pitcher.

"Please! If you *please!"* Larry says, stifling the tremble in his voice. "Let's bring this meeting back to some sort of *order!* Now, Professor Schmidt has obviously touched some sensitive nerves here. I want to say that I support him in raising difficult questions." A short flurry of agreement, or at least that's what it sounds like.

"Now I like a lively debate," he says. "But I won't abide shouting and I won't abide bullies." Applause. "Now. Can we go on?"

After a pause, I start again: "I think we were talking about an attitude that has come to be known as lookism. Let me see if I can state this in a neutral way and ask the opinion of our guests. Ms. Bell or Ms. Rousseau, do you feel that being in a profession so dependent on looks has put you at a disadvantage in other pursuits?"

Samantha seems exasperated. "Pack, *I don't know.* You just do what you do and you try to make it work. This is our job . . . or it was. Until we quit the other day. If you're working and you're an ugly pig, you're not going to get many dates. It's not some evil system that makes it like that, it's the guys. I'm sorry, but it's true. Guys like pretty girls."

Only here would this near-tautology produce such a rustle of ill temper and another ding-ding-ding of Larry's water pitcher.

"But don't you see how that victimizes *you?"* somebody calls out. The swarm of voices moves through the the crowd like wind through dry vegetation, as if the wind were moving, in Wallace Stevens's words, like a physically challenged person among the leaves.

"Of course it's not fair that some people are born pretty and some people are born ugly." Sam says. "But I don't know what I'm supposed to do—march in the street?"

A young man's voice: "That would be better than being a sex slave!"

Larry glares back at the man: "In our profession we raise our hands if we want to speak."

"And anyway," Samantha goes on, "it all evens out. The pretty girls go on to get rich husbands—I hope—and the ugly ones go on to get Ph.Ds."

Again the angry voices. "That's the most offensive comment I've ever heard!" "Go back to your cathouse!" "Your makeup's peeling!" Sam tilts her notebook toward me: in large letters, "THIS SUCKS!"

"Before I acknowledge the next question from the floor," Larry is saying in his soft voice, "I'd like to say that I think this program can go down in MLA history as one of the most interesting . . . *if* we can all keep our composure. Now, with that in mind, I wonder if we can endeavor to reach some sort of a consensus to do just that, to refrain from shouting from the floor, and to ventilate our possible resentments in a way that's more in keeping with the spirit of academic discourse. Can we agree on that?" A general mumble rises, somewhat akin to the vocalizations associated with a good poetry reading.

"Thank you," he says. "More questions?"

In the front row, a young man in black: "I have a little question for Ms. Rousseau. I notice that you found it useful a moment ago to temporarily abandon language and to in effect make a remark by means of a comical facial expression. Since you're here to . . . enlighten us on the post-erotic poems of Rachel Phillips Gallivander—which I know you have read or you wouldn't be here—could you please share with us your interpretation of her repeated references to the interplay between extensional verbalization and metagraphic body language."

Kristy looks over at me in despair, then speaks close to the microphone. "Is this an essay question or multiple choice?"

Within the laughter that again fills the room, more voices are raised: "Not funny," "This is a waste of time," "This is embarrassing."

More ding-ding-ding on Larry's pitcher. There's nothing I can think of to say that would show what a dishonest and hostile question that was, and what its obvious purpose was, which Kristy thankfully has bounced back in the guy's face. The best I can think of is to ask him what he thinks.

"What I think is that this *display* is showing itself more and more to be seriously lacking a point. And I use the word *display* with a full understanding of its implications. I'm starting to get the feeling that you don't have much to say."

"You're right about that. I don't have anything to say. It's an experiment. Or it was."

Silence for a moment. We only have ten more minutes in the program.

"Well," says Larry, trying to gather the crowd in as the generalized anger builds. "Where would we like to go from here?"

"I'd like to ask some questions, if I may." A soft voice from the rear, with much resonance. As I stare at the large form, at the salt-and-pepper beard rising from among the pale colors of sport jackets, it takes me several seconds to fully realize that it's Frank Iverson.

I can feel blood rush to my head as he slowly stands up. From where I sit he seems to stand without bending, without pushing, more like some large machine part that has been extruded vertically from the flat jumble of the crowd. How he came in without my seeing him I don't know.

I can see immediately that he is drunk. He sways, in that moderate way of a man who has lapsed back into drink but has not lost the original focus of the anger that set him back into drinking.

"I'd like to ask Professor Schmidt some questions about human decency." His voice is calm, musical, almost caressing. "Human decency: that's what I'm interested in, on this lovely winter evening. I'd like to know how this assembly feels about a man who uses his authority as a professor to extort *sexual favors* from the daughter of his best friend."

No rumbling now, no hecklers. The crowd hangs silently on

Frank's words. I know it's not appropriate to be thinking about this right now, but I've always wondered about the term "sexual favors." You only hear that when somebody gets caught for something. You never hear some guy asking his girlfriend, "Honey, could I have some sexual favors?"

"Frank, we have nothing to talk about. Go home."

A voice from the middle: "No! Let him speak!" Larry taps the water pitcher.

"Am I correct in assuming," Frank continues in his resonant hush, "that you refuse to answer a simple, decent question put to you before an audience of your peers?"

"Frank, you've already gotten your revenge. Don't you think it would be better if you just got out of here?"

"What are you going to do, big shot? Beat me up? Is that your answer to things? The way you probably beat your wife?"

"I've stopped beating my wife."

"Do you refuse to answer?"

"I'm sorry about everything, Frank. Now go home and sober up."

"I want to tell you what this man did to my family." His voice is getting louder, of course, which stands to reason, because the only purpose in his earlier softness was to make more dramatic the planned crescendo. "I sent him to find my missing daughter."

"You didn't send me anywhere."

From the crowd: "Let him finish!" "What are you hiding?"

"And instead of helping her, which any man with a little common decency would have done, instead of trying to talk some sense into her, he did the *opposite*. He used his influence to buy a session with her as a common prostitute."

"Go home, Frank."

From the crowd: "You go home." "Let him speak!"

Larry hammers with his pen. "People, *please!* Hasn't this gone far enough?" The shouting goes on.

"I just want you all to know," he says, swaying slightly, "that this moderator of yours destroyed a man's family, he extorted sexual favors from a student, and he purposely collaborated with the *white slave trade.*"

"White slave trade is a *racist* term!" a white man shouts from the standing-room section.

"Don't you tell me what's racist!" says a young black woman near the front. "I'm sick of this racist canard that all you academic racists know what's racist and what's not racist."

"I'm not a racist," the man in the back says. "But I apologize."

"This bastard *forced* my daughter to stay in the white slave trade—"

"You shut up with that *racism!*" the black woman says. Larry quits hammering, sinks his head into his hands.

"He forced her into prostitution. He forced her to pose for *pornographic Polaroid pictures.*" The alcohol and the building rage and the unfortunate alliteration of that last phrase have combined to twist Frank's mouth into a Daffy Duck sputter—which is the sort of thing I really shouldn't let myself notice while I am being accused of a felony. "He took her own camera and he took pictures of my own daughter *fellatiating him.*"

Out in the crowd, within the general agitation, I can see a few men bending back in their chairs, surreptitiously holding imaginary cameras to test the position to which Frank has referred. Larry is stuffing his papers and his poetry books into his briefcase.

Frank's voice gets louder and louder. "I *tremble* for the future of education in this country when I think that a criminal like this should be here at MLA cruising for more students to sexually blackmail. And I *shudder* for the integrity of this organization when I think that a program like this could be conducted by a *child pornographer!*"

A commotion around the door: *"Daddy, I'm not a child!"* It's

Sally, pushing through the crowd. I don't know what brought her down here, maybe accident, maybe some family telepathy. Frank doesn't even change his tone of voice.

"Sally, honey," he says. "Tell them what this piece of *filth* did to you."

"Daddy, you've got to *stop this!*"

"When are you going to stop protecting the piece of shit who *raped* you?"

"Nobody raped me, Daddy."

"Bullshit!" someone in the crowd shouts. "Of course he did!" People are standing up and yelling. One voice shouts, "Pornography is rape!" Another: "Prostitution is rape!" "It's *all* rape!"

Kristy and Sam are out of their chairs, standing next to me, holding my arm. "Pack, I think we'd better get out of here," Kristy says. "I've never seen people like this."

Frank lurches out to the aisle, where the people who were sitting on the floor have stood up. "Come on, Sally. I'm taking you home."

"Daddy, I want you to *stop this!*"

"You're not going off with that *racist*—I mean *rapist!* I swear I'll see you *dead* before I let you do that!"

"Are you threatening her?" says a woman near Frank.

"Shut up, bitch."

"I asked you if you were threatening that woman."

"And I told you to shut up, *bitch.*"

The strange thing about anger is that no matter where you stand you're going to get drawn into it. I can feel it falling all over me like magic dust; and suddenly I feel strong enough to toss every one of these uglies through the movable Sheetrock partitions.

"Did you say you were threatening your daughter's life?" says the woman near Frank. The whole room is standing up now.

Another thing I've often noticed is that the various elements of an angry crowd become interchangeable. One person shouts one thing, another shouts something else, but it seems hard to find where in the crowd any one voice comes from.

"You shut the fuck up or I'll shut you up!"

"Are you threatening me?" the woman says. There is movement among the closely spaced seats with coats draped over them, bodies pushed close together. Larry has closed his briefcase, stands up, turns to me.

"Pack, this job's not going to work out," he says.

"I know." I shake hands with him and he hurries toward the crush at the door. Several other people are clutching up their papers and coats and rushing toward the exit.

By now it's a real scuffle over there—somebody shoved somebody, somebody else got pushed down over the chairs.

"Would somebody please call security?" I yell over my microphone. Next to me, the short-haired woman in the beige leisure suit has grabbed what used to be Larry's microphone.

"*Can I have your attention,*" she says. By this time Frank is throwing punches, and the whole clutch of chairs and people lurches back and forth like the nucleus of a bar fight. *"I am making a citizen's arrest of Schmidt here, for the crime of rape. I need some help in restraining him and placing him under arrest. Can I have some volunteers?"*

I must not be thinking clearly, but the moment she says this, I just react.

"Volunteer *this!*" I say, and empty the water pitcher into her face. She sputters and draws in breath. Almost immediately a water glass smashes against the side of my face just below my left eye. I feel the sudden tingling cold throb, too confused with surprise at this point to register it as pain.

As if on cue, several people rush the dais. I grab my hardshell briefcase in the instant before it falls to the floor. A table is pushed over, the crowd surges forward. Kristy and Samantha are trapped between the overturned table and the rear partition. They scream, but I can't help them. Some guy hits me low, like a football tackle. My knee hurts. Sally's out there in the middle of the fight, but I can't see her.

This is a literary gathering, it must be remembered, and all the time while men and women are being pushed onto the floor and glasses and cups and plastic bottles of Evian water are flying around and people are spitting and grunting and tearing the buttons of each other's shirts open—all this time there continues a verbal exchange as well, in which one must either be identified as a racist or a patriarchal hegemonist or a rapist or a sexist or a nosy bitch or a bad-breath bastard or a phallocentric asshole or a shithead or a liar or a whore.

The words fly, the fists fly, but not very hard, more like a baseball fight than a hockey fight. It's too cramped for anybody to have much room to throw a punch. Mostly it's just the force of bodies, pushing, slamming, shoving us back against the partition. I can feel blood running down the side of my face.

I can see Sally by the side wall, about twenty feet from what used to be the dais. She's trying to pull a man and a woman away from her father. They aren't really punching him, just crowding him against the partition and trying to grab his hands.

"Leave him alone!" she screeches above the crowd noise. "He doesn't mean anything!"

"Sally, come on!" I yell over to her. "We're gonna get out of here!"

"Sally, *no!*" Frank shouts, trying to shake the man and the woman off him. "You can't go! I'll take you home!"

And for a moment I can see her stop. A water pitcher smashes on the wall behind me. Sally keeps looking over at Frank, who struggles toward her and then gets pushed back.

Of all the dramatic choices to be forced on a young woman in the middle of a fistfight, this is the most embarrassing I've ever seen. She should have better than this; she deserves to have a better class of slobs fighting over her.

"I'm sorry, Daddy," she says, and pushes through the crowd toward me.

A man has his arms around my briefcase, but I still have the handle, and I'm jerking him back and forth. Some trails of blood, probably my own, run down the textured brown fiberglass. Next to me, the woman with the flyaway nimbus has a firm grip on Kristy's rivulets of blond hair.

"Oww! Let go, you bitch, let me *go!*" Kristy says, crying. *"Please!"*

"What's the matter, *slut,* you need it to make money?" All around, people are butting and elbowing and shoving, a few voices shouting that this has got to stop; and all the time the words fly, everybody shouting now: *"Get off me, bitch!" "Fuck you, racist bastard!" "Whore!" "Get out of my way!" "Don't you touch me, faggot!" "Go home, you sexist piece of shit!"* I can smell a strong odor rising in the motion of bodies in the heat, the sudden simultaneous failure of everybody's underarm deodorant. Here and there I can hear people shouting, *"Hey, break it up!" "Come on, knock it off!" "This isn't right!"*

The flyaway lady is twisting Kristy's hair. Kristy screams and says, *"Pack, help me!"* but I can't get to her without losing my grip on my briefcase.

Sally jumps across the section of the dais that wasn't knocked over and tries to pull the woman off Kristy. Samantha is pressed against me, my blood smearing on the blue satin of her cocktail dress. "Pack, let's get out of here," she says. "These people are going to *kill* us!"

"I'm trying!" I say. From the door, shouts and lifeguard's whistles. *"Break it up! Break it up, NOW!"* one of the security guards calls through a bullhorn, but the bodies push harder toward the partition behind us, and with a surge they knock two of the partition sections free from the bottom trolley so that they swing out by their top hinges into the conference next door.

It's so crowded in here that even if you're right next to somebody it's hard to hit him. I jerk back and forth, lurch out with an elbow toward the guy who has hold of my briefcase. I catch him in the face, hard, and he goes down—or he would go down, but everybody else is holding him up.

I never thought of Sally as strong, but when I see her jump on top of the woman who is beating up Kristy, she seems like one of those people who lift burning cars off their babies. She grabs the flyaway-hair woman from behind, by the arm, pulls her around, hauls back, and slugs her in the face as hard as I've ever seen a girl hit anybody. If ever a punch, in a bar fight, or a comic book, or a Batman episode, actually made the sound *biff!* this is it. The woman sprawls back, and Kristy scrambles up from the floor, crying.

There's no way we're going to get out of here through the door. By now the loose partitions behind the former dais have been split apart vertically. There seems to be a gap we could get through, if we can get the other people away.

"Come on!" I say, pointing to the tall A-frame shape of the broken spot. "Sam! Kristy! Sally! We can get out this way!"

Sam squeezes through. I'm trying to hold the breach open, but there are a couple of people jammed up against it, with Frank near the front.

If I take a step toward them they'll grab me, so to keep them back I start to swing my briefcase by the handle, in a vertical circle, faster and faster, so hard and fast that nobody can grab it.

"Get back, you bastards!" I say, brandishing the case. *"Yah! Yah!* Get away! I swear to God I'll deconstruct your fucking *face!"*

One guy gets clipped in the nose and staggers back. I've cleared a space, sort of. *"Sally! Kristy! Come on!"* I say, with the briefcase going round and round like a rock sling. They run behind me, through the space I have cleared. Kristy pushes through. Sally stops in the gap.

"Leave my father alone, you bastards!" she shrieks, her voice breaking up in the upper registers as she disappears through the space. Just as I back up to follow her through, a young man in denim, almost my size, makes a rush at me—but he times it wrong. I catch him square in the face with the briefcase. That is a sound I will remember for a long time, the muffled cartilaginous crunch of his nose, and down he goes, cold, with sheets of blood all over the gold carpeting as I draw back through the gap, and then shove the loose partition back so it catches in the bottom groove.

☆ ☆ ☆

We have breached our way into a room much like the one we escaped from, only instead of everybody yelling at each other, this room is full of people with their mouths open, silent, staring at us. On the other side of the partition the voices are shouting, "Stop that man!" "Stop, thief!" "Stop, rapist!" We hustle down the side aisle, our lungs wheezing like hand saws. Now people are starting to say things—*"What's going on?"* "What's the meaning of this?"—as the partitions go *boom boom* in the rear where the people next door are beating against them, trying to break them open again.

"Excuse us, excuse us," I say between wheezes, hurrying along against the wall, the girls right behind me. "No problem. Sorry for the interruption. Excuse us." The door of this conference room is on the other side from the door of the room we were in, so it opens onto a different hallway, and suddenly we're out, with nobody chasing us yet.

Even in the middle of the fight it had already occurred to me that all our money is still up in my room, which means that we can't just run out the front door.

I'm trying to figure out how long it will take them to find out where my room is. Probably a minute or two, which is all we need to pack and get out. As far as checking out is concerned, I'll let the Wyndham work that out with American Express.

We reach the elevator lobby just as a fleet of them arrives and the first two doors chime open. In the silence of the elevator, the rest of the people stare at us. Blood runs down the side of my face, drips onto my shirt collar and onto the lapel of my best suit. Sally and Kristy are both crying. The front of Sam's dress is daubed with blood. All four of us are puffing with frantic loud breaths. A few drops of blood fall from the side of my briefcase onto the elevator floor. Nobody in the elevator says a word; they just stare at the blood and listen to our puffing breaths. Aside from the panting and the tears and the dripping blood, everything else in the elevator is quite normal. We all stand still and watch the digital numbers climb.

We pack in a rush, panting, without words, stuffing clothes and toiletries into our bags. My garment bag bulges like a sailor's duffel. We walk out the door just in time to see a crowd hurrying toward us down the long hall.

We run the other way, to the fire stairs, running three steps at a time down the identical well-lit flights, our bags flying up and down and bouncing against us.

The stairs end, and there's nowhere to go but into the kitchen. We move with long steps through the warm beefy steam, trying not to slip on those pink ceramic floor tiles. It's a huge kitchen with a low ceiling, and rows and rows of those rolling galvanized tray-stacking racks filled with metal platters of what look like trimmed filets mignons.

A voice far behind us: "Stop, rapist!" We start running again, taking long awkward steps on the slick floor, our stuffed bags swinging wildly and bumping now and then against the ovens and the rolling food racks. I'm weighed down worse than the girls, with my big three-suiter and my blood-spattered briefcase. This is the only time in my career that I've ever had a blood-spattered briefcase.

Samantha runs a few yards ahead as we move down a long aisle toward some kind of door; I don't know where we're going, but it has an EXIT sign overhead. We run, or sort of skate long-leggedly, through a cluster of giant soup tureens, raised on legs like the landing gear of flying saucers in a Huckleberry Hound cartoon.

Just as we come to the intersection of another aisle, in a neighborhood of cutting boards and what look like giant salad choppers, Sam grabs onto an upright post and yells, "Stop! Pack! Look out!"

"What?" I say, already catching up with her on the slick floor.

"Fruit cart!"

Just then a rolling tray of lemons and limes moves slowly in front of us, pushed by a young black man in immaculate kitchen whites.

We hit, or rather I hit, and Sally and Kristy skid behind me, and the whole thing goes over, sending the yellow and green fruit bouncing, tumbling, spreading out and rolling as far as we can see behind the portable refrigerators and vegetable racks and the long table full of institutional microwaves.

"Oh no, *mannn!*" the black guy says, but we're up again and running.

"Stop those people!" rings out somewhere behind us. With every step something stabs into my knee and makes me run in a melodramatic parody of a limp, but I keep going, through the door we've been trying to get to, and out between rows of staring diners in what turns out to be the Skyline Room, then onto the escalator, bleeding and puffing, out through the main lobby, and out the front door. A man in doorkeeper's livery opens the door. As we hurry out into the blowing snow, he calls after us, "Good night. Thank you for staying with us."

☆ ☆ ☆

A city in the snow: I've always loved that, at night in the back of a taxi with my three favorite girls in the world. For the first few minutes we hardly speak, just sit there breathing in and out, especially me with that frantic wheeze that the older you get the longer it takes to slow down—watching the bright shapes of restaurants and Christmas windows going by.

In the back seat, everything but the breathing has slowed down—the decision about who needs to go where having already been made during the first minute, while they were still crying. Now, because the cab we are in is not licensed to go outside the Philadelphia/Camden metropolitan area, our driver has radioed for another cab from the same company to meet up with this one.

A few minutes later, in the process of saying goodbye between taxis, the biggest four-way hug of my life occurs, a hug so warm it would make an Episcopal priest blush, a snowblown embrace so complete and all-protecting that it seems almost elitist of us not to invite the two cab drivers in. We sway slightly, in a clear spot at the side of the street, as the snow comes down around us, around the warm idle of the two red-and-white United taxis, and makes fluttery binocular shapes in their expanding headlights.

Then we all get back into our separate cabs and we drive off, going in the same direction. The car that Kristy and Samantha are riding in doesn't have to turn off to the airport for several more blocks. As we move along side by side in two lanes of an empty street, it seems like the appropriate time to throw my briefcase out the window. It skitters and spins, then bangs open against something I can't see, and all my white papers go swirling around under a streetlight.

Kristy and Sam still haven't turned off for the airport. Sally and I lean toward the window and slowly wave into the darkness of the other vehicle. She keeps turning her head to follow the shapes of houses, some with a line of blue lights across the porch, or warm candy colors arched around a door. A few times she looks back into my eyes and we smile at each other as well as we can in the cab's dim light. I've never understood what's supposed to happen when people look into each other's eyes. I know it's important in porno movies—that the chemistry of eyes should be a sort of hypertext for the physical joining of the sex organs. But in real life things are less focused; the only thing I see when I look into Sally's eyes is how pretty she is, which I already knew.

We wave out the window. It would be all right with me if we drove around all night waving at people. With all the things we are going to have to talk about, with all the decisions we will have to make, about such things as "getting back on our feet"—an expression which I have always found supremely repellent—I would be happy to put it off until such time as the side of my face does not hurt so much.

Meanwhile, we keep moving along together in our parallel lanes, the two taxis pulling up windy sweeps of snow in the draft behind them. Then the passenger lamp goes on in the other cab, and for the last several hundred yards before they turn off, we can see Samantha and Kristy waving back at us, their faces soft under the dome light.

Available in Norton Paperback Fiction

Edward Allen, *Mustang Sally*
Aharon Appelfeld, *Katerina*
Rick Bass, *The Watch*
Richard Bausch, *The Fireman's Wife and Other Stories*
Stephen Beachy, *The Whistling Song*
Simone de Beauvoir, *All Men Are Mortal*
     The Mandarins
     She Came to Stay
Anthony Burgess, *A Clockwork Orange*
     The Long Day Wanes
Mary Caponegro, *The Star Café*
Fiona Cheong, *The Scent of the Gods*
Rick DeMarinis, *The Coming Triumph of the Free World*
José Donoso, *Taratuta and Still Life With Pipe*
Leslie Epstein, *King of the Jews*
     Pinto and Sons
Montserrat Fontes, *First Confession*
Jonathan Franzen, *Strong Motion*
Ron Hansen, *The Assassination of Jesse James by the*
     Coward Robert Ford
     Desperadoes
Janette Turner Hospital, *Dislocations*
Siri Hustvedt, *The Blindfold*
Ward Just, *In the City of Fear*
Ivan Klima, *My First Loves*
Thomas Mallon, *Aurora 7*
Bradford Morrow, *The Almanac Branch*
John Nichols, *A Ghost in the Music*
     The Sterile Cuckoo
     The Wizard of Loneliness